V A L E N C I A

Doug,
thanks for keeping it
interesting here in our
section of the world.
Your friend
James Nulick

~~James Nulick~~

Nine-Banded Books

Valencia

First printing October 2015

Published by Nine-Banded Books

Nine-Banded Books
PO Box 1862
Charleston, WV 25327
NineBandedBooks.com

ISBN-10 0990733521
ISBN-13 978-0-9907335-2-2

Editorial assistance
Anita Dalton

Cover design by Kevin I. Slaughter

For Angelo

These conversations side by side, at night, these shared and spoken secrets.

—Albert Camus, *Notebooks 1935–1942*

Jerome

Shortly after the September 11 attacks the drug manufacturer GlaxoSmithKline (GSK) increased its American television advertising for the antidepressant Paxil. In October 2001 GSK spent nearly twice as much as in October 2000.* Flash forward to winter 2002. A season of fear and bad blood. My first relationship was in the toilet. I vowed to stay inside the house. I would assess things as they were, without blinders. I grew lonely after eight months. The flesh holds sway over the body when one is in their early thirties. I went to a dark bar to be among my kind, a shrill and glittery lot. I despised them. The old ones were trolls. The young ones gathered together and clucked like spurned women. I didn't fit the mold. I liked rock and roll. I wore drab clothes. I didn't own a single Barbra Streisand record. I stood on the sidelines with a beer in my hand. I shooed away the antiques and watched the young ones create drama. I hated my kind and dreamed of being young, straight and single.

. . .

R— was my first serious relationship. He was a short muscular Latino. He was built like a linebacker. Things started out well, but some people just aren't meant to be together. We both had our faults. Square pegs and round

---

* Wikipedia, notes on paroxetine

holes, as it were. It took me six years to figure it out. He toyed with meth. He spent late nights with the wrong crowd. He became addicted. He became angry. He hit me. I had always believed a person could never hurt or harm someone they claimed to love. The day he hit me is the day our love died.

. . .

I stayed away from bars for eight months. I didn't want to see faces that would remind me of R—, that would ask me how R— was doing, what had happened between us, etc. I didn't want to answer such questions. They were questions without answers, and they solved nothing.

. . .

In high school people called me faggot. I couldn't blame them. I didn't like faggots either. I was sixteen when my father took me aside and asked if I was queer. I lied and said no. It was a tough question for a sixteen-year-old. There was a hint of disgust in his tone. I'd dated a few girls in high school but it always felt like a lie. The eternal impostor, I often did things simply to throw people off. I'd wear an Iron Maiden shirt on Monday and a Duran Duran shirt on Tuesday. I didn't want people figuring me out. I didn't like explaining myself. I had friends, but my friends tended to ignore the insults whispered behind my back. I pretended not to hear them just like they did. When my father asked if I was queer I resented the question for what it meant as much as I resented him for trying to figure me out. I didn't ask others what they were. I may have formed opinions but I never spoke them aloud. With queers I didn't have to presume. I knew what they were and they knew what I was.

. . .

After R— I wanted to be away from the bickering and the drama of queer bars. The loneliness was suffocating. The need to be around others like me became so powerful I found myself staring at the clock on Saturday evenings. I turned on the television. I played the stereo. I drank until the room swam. I stretched out on the couch until Sunday morning came along. I did this for eight months.

. . .

Loneliness kills. The flesh is dumb. I opened the door and walked into the night. I'd been away from the bar scene for eight months. It was still the same old drama, the same tired old queens zipping around young meth-head party boys like hungry mosquitoes. I was about to leave when a face in the crowd approached. It was Jerome. I'd met him through R—. He was a friend from his hometown. They were mutual transplants who occasionally got together to wreak havoc. I didn't think I'd see you here. It's been a long time, I said. I've been a little gun-shy after R—. I understand. He had a beer in his hand, which I found comforting. Had it been a daiquiri or some such nonsense I would've said hello and moved on. We had a few more beers. We decided to duck out before last call. Follow me home, he said. It sounded like a command. His taillights glared like angry jewels against my cracked windshield.

. . .

His apartment was sparsely furnished. A small dining table, two chairs. A one by twelve laid over two cinder blocks served as a coffee table. A print of a black jaguar hung over a black velveteen sofa. A small television sat on a milk crate. It was an off-brand I'd never heard of. Home sweet home, he said. He laughed.

. . .

Jerome was a petite black man. He stood five-foot-six and weighed 120 pounds. He was four years younger than me, which still qualified him as *old* in the queer world. If he was old at twenty-eight, I was ancient, a mantique. I was heavier than I am now. This counted as two strikes. I was almost out. Was Jerome lonely? Desperate? Did he want what was off-limits eight months earlier? I stood in his kitchen as he pulled a drawer open. A glass pipe, a Ziploc baggie and a lighter were nestled together in a cigar box. Jerome gingerly held the pipe in his hand. A wad of copper wool was bunched at one end. He opened the Ziploc, pinched a few rocks into the end of the glass tube and put the pipe to his lips. I'd had such a pipe in my mouth once before. I vowed I would never do it again. The memories of my brother's apartment came rushing back. I looked into Jerome's sink, trying to find an answer. Wanna hit this, he said. The pipe was warm as a lover's fingers on a winter night. I took the pipe from Jerome. I held a lighter in my other hand. The wool lulled me with its song as the smoke curled its fingers around my brain. Jerome groped my crotch. It was hopeless. There was no going back now.

. . .

We smoked crack in Jerome's kitchen until it was gone. I was hyperaware of the time. The clock on the kitchen wall hummed and flatlined somewhere around three a.m. Its black hands mocked me. Where did I have to go? Who did I have to go home to? R— moved back to Albuquerque after we broke up. There are reasons why it is called a break-up. All the reasons are true.

. . .

Our relationship ended violently. R— hit me in a meth-induced rage. His closed fists opened my lip. I punched back. I was no match for his squat muscularity, his football player's body. Police were called, photographs were taken. I obtained an order of protection. Our stuff, what little we had, was categorized and divided. A cousin came and retrieved his things. I moved out of the apartment. I went to the hospital. My skull was x-rayed. To check for orbital trauma, my doctor said. The imaging center gave me the films in a large envelope. Take these to your doctor, the attending said. The appointment with my doctor was on a Friday. I looked at the films beforehand. I saw death in black and white, my legal name in the upper right hand corner. No visible damage, my doctor said. May I keep them? Of course, he said. It's your skull.

. . .

A saint forgives, a fool forgets. I am neither. I have forgiven but I have not forgotten. When I was twenty-one I smoked crack with my brother. I managed to escape with my life. Eleven years later, barely into my thirties, I smoked crack with Jerome. I was not so lucky the second time. The gods looked down upon me and branded my body with the Mark of The Beast.

. . .

We made our way to the bedroom, stripped off our clothes and disappeared into a crack-induced haze. I emerged six hours later, slipping quietly into the courtyard of the Valencia Gardens apartments. My head ached, my jaw felt numb. My teeth were seated in my gums but I couldn't feel them. Was I supposed to?

. . .

Two days later I developed a rash on the right side of my groin. The rash resembled heat bumps. It was about the size of a silver dollar, nestled in the fold near my testicles. Did this kid have crabs? Herpes? I hadn't had either, so I wasn't sure what to look for. I'd always kept my body puritanically clean. On the third day I came down with a fever so severe I could barely walk. I called my father. He came to my apartment. He drove me home and placed me in the guest bedroom I'd once shared with paper sister 1965. It felt like home. Noise hurt, light was excruciating. I couldn't hold water down. I drank orange Pedialyte, the most disgusting substance on Earth. Paper sister 1965 brought multi-flavored Popsicles. I wanted to enjoy them for her sake but could not. Toward the evening of the third day I was vomiting so violently my stomach had nothing left to offer but green bile. My father called 911. I didn't want to cause a fuss. Men were suddenly in the bedroom asking questions I didn't know how to answer. I was moved onto a gurney. I was transferred into the back of an ambulance. I arrived at the doors of the hospital I was born in. Hakuna matata, all that circle of life shit. Would I die in the same hospital? The doctors looked at my chart, laughed at me. *This kid doesn't get out much.*

. . .

I had a temperature of 102. This wasn't good. I was subjected to allergy tests. A lumbar puncture was administered to test for spinal meningitis. A nurse held my right hand. Another nurse held my left. Shortly after the puncture I vomited into a beige kidney-shaped pan. There were too many nurses and too many doctors to count. Are you experiencing any pain? Yes, I said. I was given morphine. A narcotic halo softly caressed the top of my scalp. The hospital light dimmed to a pinpoint. All was well.

. . .

When I awoke a strange man was hovering over me. It was my attending ER doctor. He held an aluminum clipboard in one hand. He was greying, handsome, mid-forties. Was this heaven? If so, heaven smelled of piss and rubbing alcohol. I have a few questions to ask, he said. Try to answer them as best you can.

. . .

Have you recently engaged in any dangerous activity? Not that I'm aware of. Have you recently ingested, smoked or injected any illegal substances? How to answer? Yes. What was it? I smoked cocaine with a friend about three days ago. Have you recently engaged in any unprotected sex? I scanned the room quickly. It was only me and the doctor. A curtain separated me from the poor sap in the next bed. Yes. How long ago? About three days ago. Was this the same person you smoked cocaine with? Yes. The doctor wrote something on his clipboard, flipped a page over and wrote something else. Would my insurance be notified? The doctor placed a hand on my arm. This looks strongly like seroconversion. I'll have to run a few more tests. Zero conversion? What was he saying? In the thirty-two years I'd been alive I'd amounted to nothing?

I don't understand, I said. Seroconversion, he repeated. I believe you're HIV-positive. A nurse came into the room. She stayed with me. She asked if I was in pain. I said yes. I was given more morphine. I drifted off. I did not dream.

. . .

I recommend your primary care physician refer you to a specialist from this point forward. I don't understand. I thought it took years to show signs of exposure to HIV? This can really happen in three days? Absolutely, he said. Different people respond to the disease differently. For some, symptoms of exposure may take two to four weeks. Others may take a month or more. In your case, you exhibited symptoms after three days. It's not unusual.

. . .

My primary care physician gave me the name of an HIV specialist. I didn't want a new doctor. She said it was necessary. We said goodbye. My new doctor was a bit of a mother hen. He nagged me about my alcohol and drug abuse. He said unprotected sex was a big no-no. Was he my doctor or my coach? I was tested for HIV in his office. The test came back negative. This doesn't mean anything, he said. It could be a false negative. I was exposed to the virus in November 2002. My new doctor wanted to see me in three months. He would draw my blood and test it again. Come see me in February, he said. If anything unusual happens between now and then, give me a call.

. . .

I called R— a few weeks after I was exposed to HIV. We exchanged a few noncommittal sentences. I asked him how much he knew about Jerome. I think I might be HIV-positive, I said. Is Jerome sick? You slept with Jerome, he asked. Yes. I was drunk. It was stupid. Silence. Was he gloating? Jerome's been positive for five years, he said. How come you never told me? You never asked, he said. Why would I? I didn't think it was important. His voice was rising. He turned the phone away from his face. Mom, _____ is HIV-positive!

. . .

I was angry with Jerome. I thought of my father's .38 Special, the one he had given to me for protection. It sat in the top drawer of my nightstand. I wanted to kill him. I wanted to shoot him in the face. What did I care about a prison sentence, the death penalty? I was already dead. I was in a daze for weeks. I walked the walk of a dead man. Food was tasteless. Masturbation lost its hold over me. I was free at last. Should I bother paying my bills? The anger stayed with me for months. I called my father. What should I do? You've got to let that anger go, Son. It's not hurting anyone but you. I'd like to kill that motherfucker. I know. But you can't.

. . .

I saw the mother hen in early February. He drew my blood. He ran some tests. I'll call once the test results come back. It could take a few weeks.

. . .

It took eight days. You're HIV-positive, he said. I'm sorry. He said this over the phone. The words punched me in the gut. I'm not going to put you on any antiretroviral medication for now. Come see me again in May. We'll test your blood and look at your numbers. He explained what my numbers meant. Sometimes they would be in the low six hundreds. Sometimes they would be in the high four hundreds. The doctor visits were always the same. Blood draw. Testing. Waiting. Results. We would perform the dance four times a year. I got to know Dr. Mother Hen very well. The mood swings, the finger-shaking, the rare moments when a smile appeared from nowhere. He was in his late forties but already his head was a shock of white hair. My numbers dropped significantly in my fifth year. You need to begin antiretroviral therapy, he said. It will take some getting used to. Your body will rebel, but you'll be fine.

. . .

When Thomas Bernhard received a minor award for literature in 1968 he said Everything is ridiculous, when one thinks of Death. To the winds bearing down upon us death is meaningless, and the truth is ultimately unknowable. I felt an animal sadness. I would die as each of us do, knowing very little of myself. Loved ones would forget the shape of my name on their lips, the classic monosyllabic simplicity of it. I tried finding sugar in the salt. Very few men know how they will die. I would. It would begin with a simple cough, a sneeze. Someone would firmly plant their head cold into my lungs. There would be a trip to the hospital in a speeding ambulance. There would be tests and IVs, curtains drawn as nurses smiled down upon me benevolently. I would catch up on shows I hadn't seen since childhood. *The Price is Right. The Young and the Restless.* I would stop eating. Hospice would be discussed. Eventually I would slip into a coma. Death would come in the early morning hours as the world yawned. I would be unplugged, archived, and rolled downstairs with the others. I would hold congress with the dead. We would swap war stories. We would laugh at the living. Stupid fucks, we'd say.

. . .

I'm dying. Such a simple sentence, but it contains worlds. HIV-positive, late stage. Your CD4 count is below 200, my doctor said. This is a tipping point. A T-cell count below 200 is classified as AIDS. Very rarely does the body recover from such an event. French mathematician René Thom defined catastrophe theory as the value of the parameter in which the set of equilibria abruptly change.[†] Simply put, I'm shit outta luck.

. . .

My face is gaunt. I'm down to 142 pounds. I've had forty-two good years. I've scaled peach trees, their blossoms pink explosions in late spring. I've caught honeybees in Gerber jars. I stared at my captives for hours, fascinated by their simple beauty. I've raised pigeons in plywood cages. I learned their language and stood among them as they bobbed their heads indifferently. I had a new bike under the tree on my tenth Christmas. I've known the joy of climbing trees taller than a house, jumping from a roof and landing on my feet without a scratch. I kissed a girl for the first time when I was eight years old. I can still recall her face, her name. When I am dead all this will be gone.

. . .

When I was young my belly was hard and smooth as a dinner plate. It now beckons the knife. My legs have

† Wikipedia, notes on catastrophe theory

lost their shopping cart definition. My irises were once a crisp brown, the seeing but unseeing eyes of Kafka. Shadows move across them. My lazy eye has grown lazier. My energy level is down. This is a side-effect of the HIV. My doctor says I can take testosterone replacement therapy. I don't see the point. Sexual escapades are for young people. I now prefer silence, the stillness of a dark room. I see beauty in peach blossoms and overgrown backyards. An old wooden garage in an abandoned corner of the backyard provides consolation difficult to find elsewhere. Sitting in a dark bar in the afternoon makes me realize how much I miss my father. See the world while you're young, he said. Never pass on a piece of ass. Maybe he was onto something. I should've been a better listener.

. . .

My beloved's eyes are deep green. I will take the memory of them to the grave. My oldest possession is a green Goody comb. I've had it since I was a boy. I carried it in my back pocket. It eventually rubbed an impression through the back pocket of my jeans. It was a ghost comb. It lived on in the fabric, wash after wash.

. . .

I have lived a year longer than my beloved Kafka. I only wish for one last thing – a quick and painless death. It is the wish of every man who has come before me. It will be the wish of those who come after.

. . .

Our species is doomed. Who will light a candle for us when we are gone? The planet, free at last, will flourish once again. In a few hundred years all traces of humanity will be wiped from the Earth. Only our empty transmissions will remain, hurtling through space, reaching distant stars long after the artificial light of human intelligence has been extinguished. The boat is filling quickly, but things have a way of leveling out. Those who drowned did so because they needed to. Those who survive shall bear witness. Things come and go, people forget. Time passes over us like a cleansing wave. The beauty of time, if there is such a thing, is that it erases everything. Only when we are erased do we become fully complete. Annihilation is completion. Nothing that was alive ever truly dies. It changes shape, becomes something else. Traces of us remain in the fragments. This is called memory.

. . .

Some men live their lives in the light. They perform actions so that others might see them and, in turn, congratulate them. Some men feel they don't exist if they are not recognized by others. They haven't learned how to live with silence. My accomplishments are tucked away in a drawer I never open. When I hear men puffing up their insecurities, I turn away. When I see men compartmentalize nature's secrets, I pray for destruction. I am the Angel of Death. I look out my hotel window much like the figure in George Grosz' painting titled *I Am Glad I Came Back*. The light of the world shines upon the living dead. I prefer the darkness.

Let's get hammered

I was born a happy baby, but then I started breathing. My birth occurred during a forgettable winter, in the middle of January. I was an unwanted baby. My biological father was young. He didn't want children. I was an inconvenience, an extra mouth to feed. My mother's feelings regarding my imminent birth were not much of an improvement. She was a slim young Mexican woman in a grey wool coat. My soon-to-be-ness was troubling to her, not to mention the terrible weight gain. I was resented and I wasn't even out of the oven. Had I been a firstborn, I would've understood. The firstborn always ruins the mother's body.

. . .

Mother already had a baby to take care of. Sister was three years my senior. She was born in 1967, the same year as Kurt Cobain. Mother shared a story with me over lunch in Olvera Street. I was struggling. Your father wouldn't marry me, and now here you come. Beans and Kool-Aid, you would've been raised on beans and Kool-Aid. That's how broke we were, she said. It was early summer. The smell of tacos and gardenias hung in the air. Mother wore a pink floral dress, a Seventies number that may have been a bedsheet in another life. Mother wore things Goodwill would've thrown out with the trash. She leaned forward in a conspiratorial manner. I wanted to go out with a girlfriend one night, she said. I don't know where your father was, probably chasing some whore. Your sister was crying. She was always so fussy. I thought to hell with it, I'm going out. I was already dressed. I gave your sister half a Quaalude. I ground it up and put it in her bottle. Your sister was out when my girlfriend tapped on the window. Your father was always so childish. Who knows when he staggered in? Don't ever tell your sister, she'd be so upset with me. I was a terrible mother. I never wanted kids. I've always said that. You kids know that.

. . .

I snuck in later that night. Your sister was asleep. I tried being quiet. I didn't want to wake your father. There was no need. He wasn't home. I stripped off my clothes and crawled into bed. I waited. My hatred grew with every passing minute. I eventually fell asleep. I woke up when he dropped in bed next to me. He didn't care that I was asleep. He just fell in beside me, couldn't give a rats whether he woke me or your sister. I waited. I remembered the nights I spent looking for him in parking lots. Driving from bar to bar, searching for his stupid motorcycle. Once he was asleep I got out of bed, felt my way to the toolbox. He kept it in the closet. It was a big red metal thing. I took out a hammer. I remember standing over him. I couldn't do it. I opened the door and walked down the stairs. It was so cold outside. I started smashing his bike with the hammer. I hit it so hard lights came on in different apartments. Someone yelled at me. Your father came running down the stairs. By the time he reached his bike it was completely destroyed.

. . .

Did he take the hammer from you, I asked. Would you take a hammer from a crazy person? Besides, it was too late. His bike was totaled. We split up shortly after that. We saw each other off and on, but it wasn't the same. He's still the same. He's selfish and he'll die alone. Mother removed a wallet from her handbag. She opened it, shuffled through a few pictures. She showed me a photograph. Mother, visibly pregnant, stood next to my father in a brightly-lit living room. Christmas of 1969, she said. I was so young, she said. Life passes so quickly. You wake up one day and realize you're old.

. . .

The lighting in this place is terrible. My father once told me well-lit bars are best avoided. I remove a photograph from my wallet. It's been scissored down to credit card proportions. The photo is of Mother, looking very young and very naive. It's a weekday morning. The sunlight glinting off old cars in the background makes it look very much like a Tuesday. She stands in front of the entrance to her workplace, the little insurance office she worked at in her mid-twenties. She looks happy. She is content with herself, her tiny apartment, her record collection. The photo was taken before I was born, before I snuffed out her freedom, a tiny pink tyrant in cloth diapers. Who snapped this photo? Was it a co-worker? An office boy who ate lunch with her and had a secret crush on her? It couldn't have been my father. No, she's smiling. In the photo my mother wears a grey wool coat. Probably a cheap Sears number. She was very poor. The world was green and fresh and full of possibilities if one had a pretty face. No babies, no chores, just a coat and a job and a life without obligations.

. . .

Reverse maturation, telescoping oneself to a pinpoint until the story becomes a blank page. Death is a library with all the lights turned off. Each story sits on the shelf unread, the words dead and without meaning. A caretaker pushes a broom in the darkness, whistling a tune. He smells of cheap cologne. The tune is offensive, but what can you do? That's the beauty and the horror of the grave. The inactivity is wonderful, but we are left to the whims of the living.

. . .

Another one? Pedro asks. I consider the currency in my wallet. Sure, I say. I recall Vollmann's parable of the dead fly in the whiskey glass. How to live? How to die? In a drunken state, the fly says. Oh my lovely William the Blind, almost as lovely as my other half, white skin, red lips. But not quite. Sometimes truth trumps beauty, but it's very rare. We live in a world ruled by the retina. Beauty comes first.

Larry Flynt saved my life

When I was a young boy my father owned a wrecking yard. One of the services he provided was repossessing cars for banks. People would get behind on their car payments. It was the late 1970s. I was nine or ten. After we unhooked a freshly repossessed car off the tow truck it was inventory time. I would crawl through cars searching for change, my kneecaps poking through holes in my jeans. Quarters and dimes were the best. The occasional fifty cent piece was a miracle. Eight-track tapes, clothes in disarray, notebooks, sketchpads, grocery lists. Dollar bills wadded up in tight grey balls in ashtrays. Dear John letters, suicide notes, all kinds of weird shit. If the car's owner was male, my father would often find girly magazines in the car. They were usually stuffed under the front seat. Running inventory on cars was like being an archivist, if you happened to work for an archive that processed sad anonymous lives filled with longing and discontent. Sometimes, on the rarest of instances, the girly mag would be a queer mag. These were often stuffed in the back of the trunk, hidden under Chilton's manuals, corduroy jackets, crock pots and whatnot. I imagined the owner of the car to be a fellow traveler. What did he look like? Was he married, etc.? My father had an old city bus on the lot. The bus was used for storage. Pornographic magazines were stored in cardboard boxes in the back of the bus. When my father was off on errands I was left to answer the phone. It was an important job. I was always scared when I was left alone at the wrecking yard. Keep an eye on any customers that come in, my father said. What could I do? I was four foot one.

. . .

If it was a slow day I'd walk out to the old bus. As I climbed the steps my gut grew heavy with a wonderful sense of anticipation. I pushed forward, my legs moving without any directive from my brain. I'd make my way toward the back of the bus, near the engine compartment. I'd shuffle through all the girly magazines to find the occasional gem, the magazines filled with pictures of two young bucks making out. After I gathered up two or three of them I'd sit on my butt on the floor of the bus. Piles of clothes and stacked cardboard boxes hid me from the eyes of the world. I turned the pages slowly. Eventually the young men would strip and do what biology requires of us, their bodies gloriously aglow in lurid 1970s color. Though I was only ten years old, something deep in my animal brain told me these young men were up to no good, were doing things my father would generally disapprove of. I continued turning the pages. Warmth began at the crown of my head and moved slowly through my body until it gathered in the soles of my shoes. It reminded me of the heat one felt when sitting too close to a campfire. The things the young men were doing spoke to me, broke open things inside me I didn't understand.

. . .

Being the conscientious archivist that he was, my father had to keep all the property we found inside the repossessed cars for a period of thirty days. This was done in the event the car's owner paid the bank and reclaimed their vehicle. It was during these days I felt most alive, in the back of the bus, looking at old porno mags. The pages had a gloss that cannot be found in the digital pixelations of the internet. The pictures were clearer, the colors charged.

. . .

As a young boy I learned many things by looking at the world through the safety of my father's 1970s pornography collection. For instance, men really love blondes. A lot of sex occurs in an office setting. Men and women don't talk much, and when they do, nothing that's said is of any significance. Men love wearing uniforms. Women appear to love men who wear uniforms. The 1970s was full of bad hair. Men's penises didn't look plastic. People looked more realistic, and uglier. Women love wearing red nail polish. Flesh is malleable. Men looked like my next door neighbor, not like pinup models. Men had eyebrows. Staples were larger. The payoff is often not worth the effort, and life is full of disappointments.

. . .

I was a ten-year-old boy in 1980. Most of my friends were other ten-year-old boys from the neighborhood. Geography creates friendships. While they were busy reading Marvel comics I was in the back of the bus, a *Hustler* magazine draped across my lap, my straight razor bangs shielding my eyes as I furtively glanced up to confirm I was alone. I turned the pages and learned the way of all flesh, in glorious Technicolor.

. . .

Several years later, when I spent many a Saturday evening walking through the eternal night of meat markets with names like Berlin, Man Hole, and Mr. Fatfingers, I would pull up a prospective date's T-shirt, half-expecting to see staples running through the centerfold of his chest. I searched his eyes for a common language. We would go home, not talk much, and if we did, nothing that was said was of any significance.

. . .

A youngish black man steps into the bus and abruptly pulls me from my midday pornotopia. Hey man, there ain't no fucking Novas back there. Where you keep those fucking Chevy Novas hidden?

Hotels and barrooms

I'm registered at the Hotel Valencia. The hotel is on Calle Pascual y Genís. Valencia is a Mediterranean city located on the banks of the Turia. I have no roots here. I chose Valencia for reasons that don't make sense in daylight hours. A boy I went to junior high with had Valencia as his surname. I thought he was beautiful. I never told him. Though twelve, I understood the ramifications of sharing such a secret. I knew the outcome wouldn't be good. I chose to watch him from afar. He sat in the third row, second seat, near the teacher's desk. I watched him constantly. When he leaned forward in his chair his shirt separated from his pants and a crescent of cinnamon filled me with thoughts I did not understand. His face was soft and open, like a girl's. He had a boy's arms. His hair was rubber-banded into a loose braid that rested between his shoulder blades. On some days he wore his hair down. It was long and brown and flat, its loose wisps touching his face. He was only slightly aware of me. I was a smudge who sat in the back. In junior high I was no longer the class clown. My body had rebelled. I saw no reason to draw attention to the fact. I was silent and attentive. I watched my teacher with an open, rapt face. I watched her mouth. I focused on her teeth. If she asked a question, I regurgitated what she had just said. I was an A student. It was easy.

. . .

Girls often talked to me. I would listen. I was a good listener. I never felt uneasy around them. Their growing breasts were not a distraction. I was too focused on the Valencia boy to notice classroom relationships ending before they began. Do you like me? Check yes or no. If I intercepted any of these notes I always checked yes and passed them on. Perhaps I assisted others with a blossoming romance. The history of the world is a history of a thousand yeses. Why say no? I wanted my friends to receive notes that said yes. I wanted to push them toward larger actions. I was only a courier, a boy in brown cords and a Pendleton coat. My friends would hear no soon enough, from parents and from teachers, from the larger world outside the classroom windows, but not from me. A wire doesn't gauge, it merely passes the signal along, humming as it does so.

. . .

Our hotel is near the water, far from the scramble of beach tourists. We are booked for seven nights. Considering my modest financial means, it seems excessive. I booked two plane tickets, both round trip, which would give the appearance of the intent to return. He has no idea I intend to die in this place. I am sick. There is no cure. I'm toe-deep into my forties. I've seen enough. His mother lives ten hours from this beautiful, ancient city. They will visit, go shopping, have lunch, and carry on as if the years of separation were nothing more than a few days. Having three mothers, all semi-detached, I've never understood the easiness between mothers and sons. Boys should not know their mothers. I realize I'm in the minority. When friends or co-workers suffer the death of a mother, I can only guess at their emotions, as if I'm an observer from a distant planet. Surely not all sons are as removed from their mothers as I am? I stand outside the majority. The world insists we celebrate motherhood with cakes and cards. I prefer silence and Epsom salt.

. . .

The bar in the hotel is wonderful. The bartender, a young man named Pedro, is liberal with the alcohol. Good bartenders are angels sent from heaven. I learned Pedro's name the first night I visited the bar. One should always know the name of the person handling the spirits. In the States the control of alcohol is of a Puritanical stripe. In Spain, bottles are made to be emptied. An ethos my father would appreciate. There are a few tourists, but they are not loud. The television above the bar speaks to me in a language I do not understand. I am grateful. It's no Puss N' Boots but it will suffice. There is a young man in his twenties who is often perched in a dark corner of the bar. He is young and able-bodied. Does he not work? Spain has a high unemployment rate among the young. Perhaps he is a hustler. I nod hello. He nods back. I keep my distance. I have just enough money in my wallet for alcohol.

. . .

I brought very little. Enough clothes for a week's stay. A few books, all paperbacks. *The Book of Disquiet*, edited by Richard Zenith. The Kerrigan/Bonner edition of *Ficciones*. *Bartleby & Co.*, translated by Jonathan Dunne. The Vila-Matas is a buffer for security checkpoints. Kafka's *The Complete Stories*, centennial edition, edited by Nahum Glatzer. Kafka looks like an office clerk on the cover, dressed in a suit and tie. He has an inscrutable face, as one would expect him to.

. . .

I have sedatives, prescribed to me for my condition. When taken in large numbers with alcohol, coma and death may occur. Is this a warning or a promise? There is a small box of photographs, mostly childhood pictures. The photographs are rubber-banded together and stored in a cigar box. I keep the box in my hotel nightstand. The photographs now smell of the Dominican Republic. I don't mind. I'll never witness a sunset in Tokyo. I'll never step through the doors of the Taipei 101. I'll never visit Kafka's grave in the New Jewish Cemetery in Prague, or walk the streets of Madrid. I'll die before my three mothers. I'll skip bail on the Grand Climacteric. I will never again look into my other half's eyes. Death will erase me, and I will be free of this disease. I refuse to die in a hospital bed, my stink ruining the sheets.

. . .

A passage from Pessoa…

. . .

Everything I sought in life I abandoned for the sake of the search. I'm like one who absent-mindedly looks for he doesn't know what, having forgotten it in his dreaming as the search got under way…

. . .

I spent six thousand dollars to come to Valencia. My life savings. Was it a waste? My other half will see his mother.

I will visit architecture older than the oldest churches in America. It's only ones and zeros, irrational numbers embossed in plastic.

. . .

The nights here are careless and unnumbered. I prefer the night. I recall a few nights from early childhood. Climbing trees in the dark before my mother called me into the house for dinner. Riding my bike to a friend's house a few doors down, my wheels marring blue and yellow chalk marks on the sidewalk. I once observed a pygmy owl swoop down from a palm tree in silence, its wings beating as if behind glass. A mouse stirred in the grass below a carob tree, scurrying away from death. I have not forgotten how beautiful the desert can be, how desolate in spirit. Palm fronds blowing in the street in late July. A black sky suddenly cracking open to pour water on sunbaked caliche as creosote registers the shock by filling the air with its scent. Such scenes empty the mind. The earth, even in the heat of July, is alive. The memories of boyhood haunt me. The nights here are colored a much duller hue. Is it because I am older? People come and go in the lobby. Silverware gaily clicks against china. Now that death is so close all is possible, and everything is forgiven.

. . .

If I say 'I looked out the window of the house to the backyard – I looked out upon my beehives gathered in darkness,' you should know such a statement is nothing more than a fairy tale. I own no land here. I am a stranger to the language and customs of this country. I mingle with no one except Pedro. Citizens laugh and talk in a language I do not understand. Televisions offer images I see but do not comprehend. I own nothing but the clothes in the hotel closet, a few paperback books, and a cigar box of photographs stowed in a nightstand. My hotel is located in a Mediterranean city on the banks of the Turia. I have no roots here. I am nameless and faceless and in a week's time I will be dead.

The papier-mâché vagina

I hold a photograph in my hand. In the photo, a devilish blonde woman holds me like a possessed sister. She is not my sister. She wears a tight black evening dress. I wear a blue flannel shirt and Levi's. I look unreasonably happy. We are both twenty-two years old. Had I been wired correctly, this is the woman I would've married. My girlfriend didn't mind that we were friends. The three of us had even gone to dinner together. All was right with the world.

. . .

When I was thirty-seven I attended my fifteen-year college reunion. I hadn't been in Cedar Rapids, a city I hated for three years and grew to love my senior year, for a long time. It hadn't changed. It was perpetually 1972 in Cedar Rapids. As a twenty-year-old I hated the unchanging aspect of the city. As a man in my late thirties, the notion of a city unchanged by time was a welcome diversion from the city I lived in, which was constantly under construction.

. . .

I still had all my hair but my body had gone soft. There were very few people I wanted to see again. I didn't wish to compare soft midsections. I didn't want to talk about the old days. I was on the roster of official reunion events. I was scheduled to read a chapter from my novel. I was given a time limit of thirty minutes. I would be in the city for a total of three nights, from Thursday through Sunday. The college paid for my hotel room. I was appreciative.

. . .

I felt nauseous at the prospect of reading for an audience of one hundred and fifty people. It was a terrible book. It was published when I was thirty-six, but I had written most of it in my late twenties. It contained too much sex and violence. Its long clumsy sentences were embarrassing. I wince at its pyrotechnics, its loudness. Writers shouldn't be allowed to publish their first novel until *after* they've turned forty. The college had paid for my hotel room. If they wanted a performing seal, I would be a performing seal, and I would do it at their expense.

. . .

There was only one person I wanted to connect with while I was in Cedar Rapids. She was a sculptor, an unruly blonde woman named Heather Murphy. We were friends throughout college. She was beautiful. She used this to her advantage. I do not blame her. She had a head of blonde ringlets that curled down her face. The face was calm and midwestern. Heather knew from an early age what men wanted. She swallowed desire and twisted it upon itself. Heather and I never slept together. She knew I was queer. I told her I was. I couldn't explain my girlfriend, the girl studying the collapse of the Soviet Union. I didn't have the words for what Laura and I were.

It didn't matter. Heather didn't need the words. Once, when we were both drunk, I fumbled with Heather's clothes in the dark. We laughed until the buttons of her blouse disappeared. After a few minutes I gave up. The failure of that night created an unspoken energy between us. She laughed. It was enough that you tried, she said.

. . .

Heather was a talented sculptress. One of her great stunts was creating an enormous vagina made of papier-mâché. The papier-mâché was stretched over a skeleton of chicken wire the size of a Volkswagen. The labia majora were painted bright red. The sculpture stood six feet high from base to top. With her professor's approval, Heather worked on the sculpture in the bowels of the fine arts center. She worked on it for several weeks. Her professor was a tiny queen with a big ego. He often wore tie-dyed shirts, an old leather jacket and black jeans. He was much too queer for me. He liked to shake things up, but only as far as his midwestern sensibility allowed. I'd help Heather with the sculpture on nights when I didn't have a paper due the following day. I applied paper as she instructed me to. We passed a bottle of rum between us. When do you know it's finished? I asked. I just know, she said. When the sculpture was finished Heather and I dragged it into a dark corner of the fine arts center. She draped a black drop cloth over it. What now? I asked. Just wait, she said. You'll see.

. . .

I was never the kid who attended proms or school dances. I didn't know how to dance, and the kids who went to such things were not my friends. I always managed to find myself on the edge of the field, near the dugouts with the stoners. We weren't prom people. Not much changed in college. I had a few close friends. I wore black, as I had all throughout high school. My drug of choice was rum and Coke and the occasional hallucinogen. I thought I was significant, somehow different. I was not.

. . .

I was rudely jarred from sleep one Saturday morning by shouting in the hallway. Was this another stupid campus activity I would have to avoid by staying in my dorm room or hiding in the library all day? It was homecoming weekend. Is this what rich white kids did with their time? There were hoots and catcalls. Someone shattered a beer bottle against the block wall of the hallway. My roommate, a wealthy kid from New Delhi, was nowhere in sight. My dorm room was on the eighth floor of The Tower. It was known by most kids as the dork's dorm. One had to have a 3.0 or higher to live in it. I stumbled out of bed and shuffled toward the window. I ran a finger under a leg hole and worked my briefs out of the crack of my ass. I refused to wear the full body armor of Catholicism my stepmother had forced upon me as a child. The body should be covered, she said. In college I slept in briefs and nothing else, the long arm of the Church withered and forgotten. My window had a view of the quad below. Fifty or so people were gathered in the center of the quad. My small digital clock impossibly read 7:30. I cracked the suicide-proof window open the full four inches it allowed. More screaming and shouting came from below. Was someone being attacked? Were the jocks beating up a fat kid? I rubbed the sleep from my eyes and looked again. I pushed on the window with all my weight. I weighed one hundred and twenty pounds. The window didn't budge. Heather Murphy's sculpture stood in the center of the quad. It looked like an animal blown apart on a highway, a deer hit by a trucker high on Benzedrine and truck stop coffee. The perpetrators were all young men. A few women milled on the outer periphery of the crowd. Were they embarrassed? Terrified of the violence that usually remained buried deep within the psyche of the average American male? I imagined all the angry football players who'd failed to hike Heather's dress up over her face punching the sculpture with an unrelenting violence strong enough to shred chicken wire. She did it; she finally got the public opening she'd always dreamed of. The quad was more appropriate than a stuffy downtown gallery, its clinical white walls reflecting the horror on the faces of middle-aged housewives as they milled about clucking shock and disapproval. This was woman, writ large.

. . .

After a preemptory self-inventory of yeses and nos, I googled Heather's name. She still lived in Cedar Rapids. I was familiar with the street she lived on. Why wasn't she married?

. . .

I am married. I kept my maiden name. Chuck is ok with it. She laughed into her phone. Do you mind if I bring someone? Your husband, I said. Oh no, Chuck's away on business. I'd like you to meet my son Griffin. Where would you like to meet? Do you have a car? I'm at the Five Seasons, I said. I don't have a rental car. I didn't want the hassle. Let's meet at Kurt's. Should I pick you up? I'll walk, I said. I miss the old buildings. You're reading Friday night, she said. Yes. I'll read for half an hour. I don't want to torture anybody. Too many innocent housewives, you know? Housewives can be very dangerous, my dear. Heather laughed into her phone again. Does Matt still manage Kurt's? I asked. Oh, no. He owns it now, Heather said. That's awesome, I said. I'll see you at Kurt's. How does four o'clock sound? That sounds fine, I said.

. . .

I had lived in Cedar Rapids from age eighteen to twenty-two. Either I'd grown or the city had telescoped in the wrong direction. It was dirty, small and tight-lipped. Old buildings had new signs affixed to them. Car horns blared rudely. Pedestrians walked on sidewalks that no longer held any meaning for me. I rubbed my hand against the smooth walls of what had once been Merchants National Bank. Things were very different fifteen years ago. Not even the banks were safe from collapse now. I walked along a grey sidewalk and in a few moments I was inside Kurt's. I'd spent a lot of time inside Kurt's during my senior year. I would often sit at the bar scribbling notes as I nursed a warm glass of rum and Coke. The television whispered football scores into my ear. Then, as now, I didn't understand the game. I didn't mind the noise, the cheers rat-tat-tatting around me. I found it comforting. Matt managed the bar when I was a young man. Now he owned it. I didn't expect to see him behind the bar. I imagined him busy tabulating receipts in a back office as a young woman poured drinks. There was no young woman, just Matt's pock-marked face in the darkness. I pulled out a barstool and sat down.

. . .

Jesus Christ. I thought you were dead! How are you, my friend? No worse for the fucking wear, Matt said. Rum and Coke? You have a good memory, I said. It's my job, man. You still live on the West Coast? I live in Río Seco. Jesus. What a shithole. Are you here for the class reunion? Yes. You see much of anyone these days? Hard to say. People come and go. The smart ones leave this shithole and never look back. You still write? Yes, when I can, I said. How about you? No. Took a long time to realize I didn't have any talent. Matt laughed. This one's on the house, my friend. You meeting someone here? Heather Murphy and her kid. God, what a beauty. I remember boys were always sniffing at her heels. That fucking vagina sculpture. I wonder if she ever lived that down. Who knows, I said. People still remind me about the typewriter thing. That was fifteen years ago. You know how people are, Matt said. They latch onto the silliest details. When's Heather supposed to be here? Four-ish. She's bringing her kid? Boy, right? Yes. His name's Griffin. Did she ever marry Joe? I don't think so. She said her husband's name is Chuck. I wouldn't mention it. Trust me, buddy, Matt said. One thing you learn in this business is to keep your fucking mouth shut. When she comes in, just move over to a table. I don't mind the kid being in here, but sitting at the bar could get tricky. Customers start coming in around five. It's fucking great to see you, man.

. . .

Matt gruffly hugged me across the bar. He'd been in a few of my writing classes. He'd written a short story about caretakers stealing from patients in a nursing home that I would've killed to write. I told him as much. You've got to work in one first, my friend. Trust me; you wouldn't want to do that. I'd enjoyed the story so much I published it in the college's literary journal. It's not often a writer will write a sentence that stays with you for fifteen years. Or a lifetime –

. . .

Sometimes when we wipe we get shit on the base of our thumbs.

. . .

The ever-elusive perfect sentence. I'd written a few. The reward was near zero, a puerile story in a grainy literary magazine. Matt and I understood each other. We were failures. It takes a lifetime to see a diamond for what it really is – an over-priced rock. The door opened and in walked Heather Murphy.

. . .

Heather was still thin. The years had been kind to her. Her hair was long. The platinum halo had been replaced by soft brown hair that fell past her shoulders. I guessed it was her natural color. Her son's hair was nearly the same hue. She wore a dress that hinted at nothing as angry as the vagina sculpture. She had softened with age. She appeared at ease with herself. I couldn't say the same. I motioned her over to a booth nestled in a dark corner of the bar. Her son followed closely behind her.

. . .

You look good, she said. You look good, too, my friend. I hugged her. I shook Griffin's hand. We sat down. Griffin was a thin boy with a shaggy Seventies haircut. He wore khakis and a navy blue cardigan. I assumed he was enrolled at a preparatory academy. I didn't ask. I didn't want to put him on the spot. He looked to be about sixteen. He was a handsome kid, good-looking in a classic midwestern way that spoke of careful parenting and blind dumb luck. We talked of adult things and kid things. We included him in the conversation. Heather and I spoke as if hours, not years, had passed between us.

. . .

Griffin returned from the men's room. I hate peeing in public, he said. It's weird. I hate it too, I said. I told Griffin my piss-fear story. Heather listened with a bemused look on her face.

. . .

Griffin is sixteen. I clip my sentences, readjust. I went to school with a kid named Danny Norton, I said. The kids said he had a big dick, but how can you prove that, you know? One day I'm pissing in the boys' restroom at school. I'm alone. I'm standing at one of those shoulder-height urinals that goes all the way to the floor. There's six or seven of them. In walks Danny Norton. I shrink up a little. There are six free urinals but Danny stands next to me. He unzips and starts pissing. I can't piss anymore. I cling closer to the urinal. I pretend I'm still pissing. I count seconds off in my head. I slowly glance at Danny's crotch. His penis is the size of a baseball bat. He looks at me. I flush the urinal and tuck my baby dick back into my pants.

. . .

Heather laughed. So was this Danny Norton popular with the girls, she asked. He was. He was six-three or something in high school. He was a good football player. Not that bright, though. I guess you wouldn't have to be if you were packing heat like that, Heather said. Mom, gross, Griffin said. Matt brought our drinks over.

. . .

I visit with Heather and Griffin for an hour or so. Don't speed through the parking lot. Don't count the minutes. There's no need to tick the days off the calendar. I watch Heather interact with her son. I pretend she's my wife. I pretend he's my son. There is an unspoken beauty between them. I will never have a son or a daughter. This brings great sadness. I catalog it and order one final round.

Brothers and sisters

My family history is a history of confusion. When I say Mother, I'm referring to my biological mother. When I say mother, lower case, I'm referring to either my step-mother or my adoptive mother. My father is the man who gave me his name. My biological father is a cipher. I never knew him. I was adopted when I was seven weeks old. My name is my name. It was tacked on as an after-thought. I don't mind. What would have become of me had I not been adopted? Paperwork indicated the possibility of me becoming a dark-haired orphan of the state. Mother got pregnant out of wedlock. When I was born she was twenty-six. Her boyfriend, my father, was nineteen. He wanted nothing to do with me. Mother had to decide what to do on her own. Being a good Catholic girl, she decided I would be placed for adoption. She didn't ask me, though I was right under her chin. I would have opted for bathwater and Epsom salts. Save us both the trouble.

. . .

My adoptive parents visited the showroom, paid the hospital fees. The young housewife and the machinist stared into a Plexiglas box. We like that one, they said. The young housewife was sterile. She had ovarian cysts. Papers were signed. I was adopted. My new parents took me home. I cost seven hundred and seventy dollars, a bargain. I had a new roof over my head. I had diapers on my ass. I was given their last name. I sat on the lawn. I played in the grass. I marveled at colors. I cataloged sounds. Things were looking up.

. . .

My father wasn't home much. He worked. After work, he visited bars. My father found dresses hard to resist. He removed as many as possible. Mother was lonely. She met a young Latino through a friend at work. The ball drops. 1974 becomes 1975. I'm four years old. My parents agree to divorce. They remarry new people. My father, the machinist, marries my stepmother, an unemployed cook. My mother, an office worker like my biological mother, marries my stepfather, the young Latino. There were many children scattered between various adults.

. . .

I never lived with Mother or my biological father. I never lived with my blood sister. Another blood sister was born in 1982, a daughter of my biological father, who is not related to Mother. The Quaalude story was told to me by Mother. You may have noticed I never make an appearance in the story. That would have been impossible. But it fills in the holes nicely.

. . .

I was told I was adopted when I was six or seven. Why, I asked. Your parents were young, my mother said. They didn't have any money. They had another baby to take care of. Things were difficult for them.

. . .

I met my biological parents in 1991. I was twenty-one. I learned I had two more sisters, one born in 1968 and one born in 1982. They were sired by my biological father. I'm close to the girl born in 1982, as close to her as I was with my brother Andrew and paper sister 1965. Andrew was born in 1971. He was born a year after me. For a few weeks in December and January we are the same age. Eventually he falls behind again. It happens every year.

. . .

I grew up with many different people. I rarely talk to any of them. We live in the age of keyboard and avatar. Familial unity, once no further than a phone call, is now a memory of the recent past. I fondly recall the year 1999. The reasons are simple. Late night visits to record shops and bookstores. Visiting old friends and taping *The Sifl & Olly Show* on VHS while we were drunk and stoned. I keep the letters my brother wrote from prison in a box. I keep old clothes that are not mine. They housed other bodies I once knew.

. . .

The relative I see most often these days is blood sister 1982. It is always a joy to see her, perhaps because she is so far removed from what was once my family. On some nights we'll meet at a dive bar that's within driving range. These bars are always dark and dirty and filled with neighborhood people who smell of failure and nine to five lives. I wear the same cloak. Blood sister 1982 is refreshing and cheerful, a beautiful young woman whose life is spread before her like a strand of new lights on a Christmas tree.

. . .

I miss my brother Andrew. I miss our childhood walks among creosote and Palo Verde. I miss our fort building. I miss the games we played with a tin of plastic army men, their arms and legs bitten through. Injuries sustained in battle. I miss the beehives of my youth. The magic scent of wood and wax filled the air of the beekeeping supply store. Supers freshly cut and stacked in a corner were ready to be assembled. I've lost the ability to work my bees without gloves. Old age brings doubt and fear. The bees can smell it.

. . .

My brother Andrew was a giving child and a loving brother. He now has a ruined life, a compartmentalized life. I have very few pictures of us together. There will be no more pictures. When the last person to remember me dies, I too will be gone. Death is a blessing, an eraser that clears the blackboard for new pupils and new lessons.

. . .

We are all adrift once the umbilical cord is cut. I'm not sure what to make of my various siblings, blood and paper. My name is a sequence of letters typed onto a court document. What good is a name? Roll call on a court roster, a placeholder on a grave stone. I do not deserve my father's name. What's the difference between a whore and a burial plot? They're both warm holes but a whore doesn't give a shit about your name.

Iowa Boy

I left home to receive a midwestern education. I returned four years later to find home was no longer home but only a dusty desert town that looked much smaller when seen through the eyes of a twenty-two-year-old who'd lived, for a short time, in New York City. From Río Seco to Iowa, Iowa to Chicago, Chicago to St. Louis, a brief stint in Los Angeles, and back home again. My back had more miles on it than an international stewardess hobbling toward a jetway. The whiplash settled in once I found myself sweeping a Circle K parking lot at three in the morning. Pushing a broom in a parking lot builds muscle. I learned this when I was eighteen. I corralled shopping carts for a local grocery chain. My legs grew hard as pistons. But four years is a long time. The eighteen-year-old heart desires what the twenty-two-year-old heart tosses away.

. . .

I didn't mind being a teacher. The children were enjoyable. I wasn't much older than they were. I was much too young to be a teacher. I had nothing to give them, no knowledge to impart. I was mostly an impostor, a boy posing as a man, a child who hadn't yet figured out what the world meant. Twenty years later, I know little more than I did then, and I still find myself questioning the world's motives.

. . .

I met William the Blind in a dark bar near 66th Street and York Avenue called Katie O'Gallaghers. His girlfriend Janice, who would become his wife, was training to become an oncologist. Her residency was at the Memorial Sloan Kettering Cancer Center. I'll be wearing a baseball cap, he said over the phone. After the leafy-green sunlight of East 68th Street the bar was a dark cave one didn't see in as much as one felt around in, arms stretched outward like tentacles. Sitting at a single table against a mahogany wall was a slight man wearing a baseball cap. He had a very thin moustache and fine blond hair. It was William the Blind. He stood up and held a hand out to me. He had a firm but kind grip. A grip one would use for the dispatching of giant beetles, a Sig-Sauer P226 in hand. It is not easy to meet someone one has loved from afar. Our expectations are so great, and bars tend to be dark at three in the afternoon.

. . .

For a man who had traveled the world and fought to understand the terrible injustices suffered by the people of Afghanistan, William the Blind was simply dressed. He wore a T-shirt and jeans. His baseball cap bore the name of a Midwestern garage. To someone unfamiliar with world literature, I was a child having a drink with a mechanic on his day off. But I knew better. A waitress came over. William ordered two pints of Guinness. She asked to see my ID. I showed her my driver's license. It was my first Guinness. I was unprepared for the dark shock of it. I told William how reading *The Rainbow Stories* at nineteen made me realize other people in the world had thoughts similar to my own. I thanked him for creating such a beautiful document. I tried to do it without sounding psychotic. William the Blind sat quietly and took it all in as one would listen to a child telling a predictable story.

. . .

William asked me why I wanted to become a writer. I answered him like an unpolished grocery boy. There are only three reasons one becomes a writer, William said. Fame, money, or preservation of the written word. What do you seek? I thought about which of these he most likely wanted to hear. Preservation of the written word, I replied. I hope you didn't say that because that's what you thought I wanted to hear. I didn't know how to respond. Was I a fake? An impostor? I drank my Guinness and kept my mouth shut as William told me stories of Afghanistan.

. . .

William's three reasons for becoming a writer are good ones, but to those I would add a fourth. Nothing as bombastic as changing the world, helping my fellow man, or I write because I have no choice but to write, etc. The fourth reason is simple. World travel. To see portions of the world normally closed to us. To map the globe as William the Blind did with *The Atlas*. To document the remnants of a physical world that is quickly disappearing as we move toward the digital. I would gladly sell all my books for a trip to a foreign land. Gone would be the modern first editions, the monographs, the signed hardcovers. All boxed and sold for the gift of travel. Knowledge can be found in books, but the knowledge is limited. Experiencing a foreign land is the only opportunity – outside sex and death – that allows us to discover our true selves, the body loosed from the parochial flesh.

The Pleiades

Childhood is the scent of peach blossoms in the backyard. It is a Saturday afternoon. I am eight years old. My straight-razor bangs hang in my face. They are blinders. They protect me from the outside world. My father's 1957 Chevy pickup sits in the backyard like a forgotten lover conquered long ago. All four tires are flat and heat-cracked from the sun. Black widows spin gossamer webs near the axles, their egg sacs fat white spheres that hang in the darkness. You are eleven. Three years older than me. You are a girl. Your hair is long and black and parted in the middle. Sometimes you wear it in a ponytail. You wear pants like a boy. Loose, suggestive. When you bend to pick up a brightly-colored stone your girlhood bleeds through. What changed me from girls to boys? Was it my neighbor, a boy eight or nine years older than me? The boy who showed me things an eight-year-old shouldn't see? He taught me how to move my legs. He taught me how to dance for him. How to get what I thought I wanted. Dance like you mean it, he said. In my backyard, hidden among the undergrowth, he touched me like he owned me. My chest tightened and my head throbbed, a baling-wire coronation. If mother had only looked out the window while doing the dishes, perhaps she could have saved me from a life of bed-hopping misery. As it was, the meatloaf needed tending to.

. . .

He was a teacher of sorts. He was also a thief. He stole many things from me. He told me the stars in the sky had burned out long ago, that what we were seeing was only the past. The past was traveling so slowly it was already dead by the time it reached us. Like receiving a phone call from a dead relative, he said. When the next star is born you will be dead, he said. I will be, too. I did not understand.

. . .

You are a girl. Your name is Nikki Hutchinson. You took me in your arms and held me. You kissed me on the lips. It was my first kiss. The stars burned above us. They were invisible. It was enough to know they were there. You kissed me in the sunlight. It was a Saturday afternoon. We walked among crushed thistle and orange blossoms. The scent of my mother's garden as green-skinned onions broke underneath our shoes. We made our way to the pigeon cage. The pigeons bobbed their heads in recognition. Let's feed them, you said. They're always hungry.

. . .

We sat in the cab of my father's old Chevy truck. You kissed me. We're moving, you said. Where to? I asked. California. The faint smell of gasoline hung in the air. Cotton sprouted from the ruined bench seat like hair on an old man's head. Your hair was long. It fell to the divots in your back. My hands fit in the indentations. Bees danced above peach blossoms that sprouted from the tree in small pink explosions. Its purple bark peeled away like crepe paper in our hands. Sometimes you wore your hair in a ponytail. Your corduroys were a rust-colored promise. I smoothed the wale stretched over a kneecap. Your legs were inside your pants. Your legs felt strong. You were a few inches taller than me. I ran my hands along your body. Your skin was charged. It popped and crackled under my fingers. I leaned in to kiss you. The shifter knob was an overbearing den mother poking me in the ribs. You moved away that summer. I never saw you again.

. . .

I pick up the phone to call you. I realize I never knew your number. You lived two doors down. We were always within walking distance of each other. We kept homing pigeons in a plywood cage in my backyard. Your pigeons were white, beautiful. Before you moved away you told me I could keep them. They were sad. They knew you were leaving. *Kuuudderrkoo, kuuudderrkoo,* they said. It was a language only we could understand.

. . .

You are married now. You live in a town I've never heard of. You are ten thousand miles away. I put the phone down. There is nothing left to say. People never call one another anymore. Everything is digital, ones and zeros. And the words I would say to you, like the stars above my head, burned out long ago.

The death of the pixelated image

I've been watching reality television on an ancient set that is so old there is no longer a name for it. I had issues with my cable a while back. The cable man, a twelve-year-old in a blue and grey uniform, came inside my apartment to determine the cause. He was flustered by the Smithsonian piece that stood before him.

. . .

I recently acquired a Samsung 46 inch flat screen television. It was a gift from Mother. Why? I asked. I hear *high def* is all the rage, she said. She brought it over in the back seat of her Honda. We carried it inside the apartment. I was shocked at how light it was. We unpacked it and pried the unit free of the Styrofoam clam shells taped on both ends. I plugged it in. The self-programming took less than five minutes. I've come to a startling conclusion – I don't like it. It's too real. It makes the actors on the screen too real. Instead of looking at a television screen I'm looking through a very clean window. Every flaw on an actor's face can now be seen with horrible precision. The clarity is startling. HD television removes the fantasy from reality. Actors, once the only perfect human beings on Earth, are now as real as you and me.

. . .

We can no longer distinguish the real from the unreal. The pixelated image has disappeared from our visual culture. The images we now see on television are more real than reality. The actor's physical flaws, once hidden deep within the primary colors of the pixelated image, are now larger than life. They exist in a clarity previously known only on daytime soap operas. Fantasy has been stripped away by the digital turpentine known as high definition. The images on the screen are hyperreal. It is reality that has become pixelated, unreal, cheap and obsolete. I walk through a market. I can no longer determine what is real and what is not. The colors of fruits and vegetables are brighter than a whore's dress. They beckon me to pick them up, fondle them. Peaches and cantaloupes are sexualized by garish colors that do not appear in nature. My eyes have been permanently scarred. I can no longer distinguish between the real and the unreal.

. . .

I thought I was special because I could see the scaffolding behind things. This is no longer the case. I am no longer shocked by reality because nothing is real. If I were to see Snoop Lion talking with James Joyce about Afrika Bambaataa's influence on hip hop music I wouldn't be the least bit shocked. I frequently have conversations with Franz Kafka as I drive through construction zones on surface streets. I remind him to please buckle up. A worker signals me to slow down. All clothing is a symbol, Kafka says. Barricades are remnants of our totalitarian past. I'm too focused to ask Kafka to explain. I don't want to rear-end the car in front of me.

. . .

At the office, I work under the drillbit hum of fluorescent lights. The need to puncture the membrane of the unreal is all-consuming. I remove an X-ACTO knife from a desk drawer and pull it across the life line of my palm. Blood comes to the surface. I feel pain. I hold a tissue paper against my palm to stop the bleeding. I walk downstairs to the break room. Nineteen steps. A television is mounted on the wall near the refrigerator. Even at work, it's impossible to escape reality. I mute the sound. I rip the tissue paper from my throbbing hand. The clarity is startling. But at least I have an excuse now. When I bludgeon my landlady to death I shall blame my television set.

The Honeycomb Kid

I have been an occasional beekeeper for the past thirty years. I hold a photograph in my hand. In the photo I am eleven years old. I look distracted, sad. I glance down toward the earth. To my left are six jars of honey. They sit on a table. The gold-filled Mason jars ooze out of the frame. They are quart-sized jars, the kind my stepmother used for canning. Propped against the jars is a cardboard sign that reads HONEY FOR SALE—FROM OUR OWN HIVES. Why so sad? Perhaps it was my father's orange juice and Popov breakfasts. They were usually good for ruining a school day. My hair hangs in my face like California rebar. My jeans are two sizes too small. Likely they are from the previous school year. In fifth grade a classmate once said be careful, his jeans are possessed. They never come off. A brilliant insult, he publicly acknowledged the poverty I lived in. My friends laughed. I would run a comb through my hair but my bangs always ended up hiding my face. Is this why I look sad in the photo? Is it a trick of the light? Was the sun in my eyes? To my right, a beehive stands three supers high. Bees hover near the entrance. They are forever suspended in time by the flash of a Vivitar. I would never be this brave again. The bees scare me now, yet I am still fascinated by them. Honeybees work together to create the only perfect society I am aware of. They are mostly female. Each member has her role. She performs her duties without question. She does this for the good of the whole.

. . .

I was a boy when I obtained my first beehive. It is thirty years later. I wish to live freely, untethered to a scrap of land. A few hives behind the house. The land here is so much older than my oldest memories. I am an American in a foreign land. I was tired of the United States. I came here. I did not come here to conquer. I am the conquered. I threw in the towel at age twelve. I asked God to please let Christina Linares fall in love with me. God refused. Christina sat on the grass with another boy. Perhaps my possessed jeans frightened her.

. . .

I am immersed in a language I do not understand. A layer of gauze separates me from the locals. I place the photo back in the cigar box and drop the lid closed. Personal histories are sometimes best left in the dark. And why stare at an old photo when Spain is so lovely? I take the elevator to the ground floor. I walk into the bar. I nod to Pedro. A football game is on the television. There is only me and Pedro and a young man sitting at a table in a dark corner of the bar. I order a rum and Coke. I've known Pedro less than a week. We are quickly becoming old friends.

. . .

I have no beehives yet I am a beekeeper. I am in Spain yet I am not Spanish. These ruminations are but a signifier, a mile marker. They are not intended for instruction.

Those looking for a didactic manual on the essences of beekeeping should study the classics of the field. *The Hive and the Honey Bee* is an excellent work, perhaps the bible of modern beekeeping. *The ABC & XYZ of Bee Culture* is essential reading for those who prefer gleaning knowledge in a more encyclopedic fashion. Think beekeeping meets Pynchon, without all the self-conscious asides. A countrified *Gravity's Rainbow*, if you will. Finally, those seeking instruction via the occasional sting of a black and yellow-bellied Golden Italian will find solace and beauty in the works of Dr. Richard Taylor. I first acquired *The Joys of Beekeeping* when I was thirteen years old. It is a lovely work with a philosophical disposition. My paperback copy was given to me by an old beekeeper named Bill Miller. He was a friend of my father. I met Mr. Miller toward the end of his life, when mine was only beginning. He gave me three or four books on beekeeping, his name written in a shaky scrawl on the flyleaf of each one.

. . .

When I met Mr. Miller I was a coltish boy of thirteen. Boys of thirteen are usually brimming with book knowledge but possess very little real world application. Mr. Miller took me aside and gave me a bit of advice. You don't keep bees, Son, they keep you. Keep your mouth shut and your veil tight. Don't be a disgrace. You never know when people are watching you. I'm not sure how I took this when I was thirteen. His words confused me. Looking back some thirty years later, they would seem to suggest I was now part of some mystical brotherhood, a sort of backwoods Freemason. Don't make a fool of yourself, and don't bring shame upon the craft.

. . .

Mr. Miller would be proud of me. I almost always keep my mouth shut. Perhaps keeping bees, or letting them keep me, is a personal disconnect, a way to avoid other people. But this is not entirely correct. I often drink with strangers. I sit among barstool friends in a dark room. I do not know their names. What good is a name? Roll call on a court roster, a placeholder on a grave stone. I have always been an outsider. What once troubled me has now become a comforting presence. I prefer sitting in a bar talking to no one, but if I must talk, strangers make the best conversationalists. I do not know their history and they don't know mine. Barstool friends are friends because I see their faces so often. The language barrier is not a complete circle. I get along well enough. I'm comfortable with the iconography. I too have been dipped in ancient waters, an old man's hand cradling the back of my skull. The old ways of the Catholic Church never change. We will ruin your children. We come between you and God. Without us you are nothing.

. . .

Christina Linares sat on the schoolyard grass with another boy. The cottonwood trees blanketed her face in darkness. It is impossible to read her expression. Read me, Christina. Open me up like honeycomb. Let my contents spill over your fingers. That other boy will only lie to you. I am predictable, solid, and shelf-worthy. I've worn the same pair of jeans for years now. I may granulate with time but a pot of boiling water will set me right again. I am your mirror, your honeycomb kid. Take me off the shelf, turn me upside down and use me as you see fit.

. . .

I'm registered at the Hotel Valencia. The hotel is on Calle Pascual y Genís. Valencia is a Mediterranean city located on the banks of the Turia. I have no roots here. I am nameless and faceless. I'm a city boy, you see. Never walk the smooth path, my father said. Paris was too predictable, New York too dirty. I chose this place because of the Valencia boy of my childhood. I always wanted what could never be mine. If Spain was good enough for George Sanders, it's good enough for me. I'm surrounded by the conveniences of modern life. I do not speak the language. I am a stranger here. My clothes are drab. My face is quickly forgotten. It's fine. I prefer the anonymity.

. . .

I read passages from Pessoa's novel *The Book of Disquiet* in the afternoon silence of the bar. A few locals eye me as a curiosity. I am quickly dismissed. It's for the best. Some readers may take offence. *The Book of Disquiet* is not a novel, they say. On the contrary, my friends – it is the novel of a lifetime, told in fragments, as only the summation of a life can accurately be told.

. . .

Borges wished to die in Room 16 of the Hôtel d'Alsace like his literary hero Oscar Wilde. He visited the hotel in 1969. There is a photograph of him standing in the lobby. He stands on a medallion. It points to the four corners of the globe. I wanted to die in a Mediterranean city on the banks of the Turia. My reasons were not lofty. The Valencia boy was my first love. I stared at him for hours in homeroom class. We were both twelve. We turned thirteen. He barely knew my name. I bought Valencia oranges when they were in season. I took a trip to Valencia, California to smell the earth. I believed standing on the soil in Valencia would bring me closer to him. When I died I wanted to die in Valencia. The heart is a twisted knot whose mysteries are seldom undone.

. . .

Spain is a beautiful country. I will die in this country. Its sidewalks know nothing of my plans. They were here long before me. They will remain long after I'm gone. Reverse maturation, telescoping oneself to a pinpoint until the story becomes a blank page. I shuffle through a cigar box of old photos. I find nothing to restore the actuality of an event. Did this really happen? It must have, for here it is trapped forever on Kodachrome. I pick up a book, walk outside and step into a backyard that spills into forever. Bees buzz around me. I walk gingerly toward one of the hives. I recently read a scientific article that claimed honeybees can recognize their keeper's face. Pattern recognition. Can honeybees see ghosts? I place a black King James Bible on the lid of one of the hives, the word of God filling the bees with fear, their wings bristling as Matthew reminds them of the cleansing of the Temple, the importance of keeping a clean house. I grow nervous standing near their feminine power and acid sting. I really shouldn't be. They fly through me as if I'm not there at all.

Gherkin

I turned twenty-two in 1992. I had a newly-minted bachelor's degree in a box somewhere in my closet. I was depressed and single. I soon found myself sweeping a Circle K parking lot at three a.m. I was in my early twenties. I didn't care. If God wanted me to work at Circle K, I would work at Circle K. I wasn't excited about my work, but I had a good time doing it. I worked at Circle K for three months. I worked graveyard shift. Ten p.m. to six a.m. I found the observations I made working graveyard provided a lot of writing material. I enjoyed watching all the weirdos come in. Drunks would stumble in and ask me to sell them alcohol after two a.m. Is tonight the night I get shot? Is some crack head going to put a bullet in my head for the thirty dollars in the register? It's a drop safe, my friend. I can't open it.

. . .

Working in a walk-in freezer seriously fucks up your hands. I was instructed by my supervisor to wear gloves, but wearing gloves led to dropping beer bottles, and dropping beer bottles was a big no-no. I didn't wear gloves while stocking the freezer at three a.m. I didn't drop any beer bottles, but the tips of my fingers were destroyed. They're still ruined, even now. Most of the time I feel them, but there are days when I cannot.

Occasionally they crack and bleed. The stigmata of a convenience store clerk. If I brought a suit against the Circle K Corporation for cracked and twitchy meth lab fingers, would I win? I should consult an attorney.

. . .

I worked at Circle K from August through November of 1992. I bailed shortly before Thanksgiving. I couldn't take it anymore. I found it impossible to sleep during the day. Sleep deprivation brought on hallucinations. A Native American walked through the door at three a.m. on a Saturday night. He told me he was taking a suitcase of Bud Light, and I was going to let him, otherwise he'd lock me up in the walk-in. Ok, I said. Don't follow me, pink, he said. I won't, I said. He was a dead ringer for Ben Nighthorse. I didn't see a sweet chopper in the parking lot, so I knew it wasn't him. On another evening, looking up from a *Time* magazine review of *Husbands and Wives*, I watched my little brother cross the parking lot with his friend Baby J. Baby J was wearing a silvery Adidas track suit. It resembled crinkled aluminum. I knew this was impossible. My brother lived sixty miles away, in another town. On yet another evening, as dirty rain blew through the parking lot tossing palm fronds to and fro like disobedient children, I observed a ghost filling the gas tank of a 1964 Chevelle SS. The ghost was watching me watching him. I say ghost because it was my friend Douglas Shepherd, who'd died a suicide in a car crash five years prior. The car was cherry, spotless and shining as always.

. . .

Reality was a constant, but it was a warped reality. There were specific things. The devastation of Hurricane

Andrew printed on the cover of *Time* magazine. R.E.M.'s *Automatic for the People*, released in early October. I bought the CD the day it was released. I thought it kicked ass. The jewel case was a weird yellow color. It was the color of bile after a rough night of binge drinking. Was Michael Stipe dispatching coded messages about his sickness? When my work was done I would read magazines and eat Dove bars. On really slow nights I would pop the red tip off a Reddi-Wip can, hold it upside down, put it in my mouth and push the dispenser with a walk-in damaged thumb. The trick was not to shake the can. The gas from the can pushed all the oxygen from my brain. My head lit up Day-Glo orange. The fluorescent world was a halo tightened around my skull. The high would only last thirty seconds. That meant several empty Reddi-Wip cans. I laughed as I skidded across perfectly waxed floors that had been polished to a mirror-shine. A bored housewife would come in the next afternoon to buy a can of Reddi-Wip for junior's birthday, wondering why all the kick was gone.

. . .

My supervisor told me if anything came up missing there was a camera in the store. I knew she was lying. I looked the store over as one would inspect a potential date before heading toward a dark corner of the bar. Nowadays things are different. Cameras are everywhere. But that wasn't the case in 1992. In those days, not all Circle Ks had a camera in the store. If you were male you worked graveyard alone. Company policy. It was a recipe for disaster.

. . .

Two neighborhood boys came in on weekends, usually around ten p.m. They were both sixteen. They were sophomores at Río Seco High School. I was twenty-two. I had to be careful. I couldn't sell them beer. They asked once. I said sorry. They never asked again. I called them the Ice Boys. They'd hop onto the counter, remove the cover from the carbonated beverage dispenser and fill it with ice. They were very polite. I gave them free soda and candy bars. They wore Wranglers and T-shirts. Their hair was cut short. Indentations in their skulls suggested baseball caps or cowboy hats. They were farm boys. They talked sideways. They had a certain charm. I could relate. This was Río Seco. The fastest things in town were the tumbleweeds blowing in on the heels of a dust storm. One boy smiled at me longer than I thought he should. I knew where he was headed. A life of misery. This was especially true in a small town like Río Seco. I entertained thoughts of pulling him into the walk-in and making out with him. Then I'd remember I was twenty-two and he was sixteen. After they left, their pockets bulging with candy bars, I'd hang the *Back in 5 mins* sign on the door and lock it. I'd slip into the bathroom to jerk off. I had to get the one boy out of my head so I could concentrate on my work.

. . .

Working graveyard had several requirements. I had to clean the store. I also had to sweep, mop, and wax the floors. Stock the walk-in. Push a broom through the parking lot. Empty the trash bins near the fuel pumps. Rotate the stock so the labels were facing forward. Lock up the alcohol after two a.m. to prevent beer runs. Drop a thirty foot long wooden measuring stick into the buried fuel tanks to check for levels and evaporation.

Record the results on a spreadsheet. Clean the beverage dispenser, soaking the twist-off tips in bleach. Clean the bleach from the caps with fresh water. It was my job to make sure everything was ready for the morning shift. It was a lot to do in an eight-hour shift. And let us not forget the cashbox zombies.

. . .

The jobs I held as a youth provided great insight for writing about the human condition. Circle K clerk, exterminator, shopping cart wrangler, salvage lot boy. People are people. There are good people. There are bad people. There is a profound misery among the working class. Alcohol drowns it. Meth speeds it up. Marijuana slows it down. The alarm clock rings every morning, its digital chirping a death knell.

. . .

I was twenty-two. I was a dumb hick kid from a small desert town. I worked the graveyard shift at Circle K shortly after I graduated from college. Kafka and Beckett did the best they could, but I had to learn a few things on my own. My jeans were two sizes too small. I had a six dollar haircut. The soles of my Chuck Taylors were worn smooth. My expectations went out the window. Fuck it, I thought. In the words of Convenience Store Clerk, who may or may not also be Boat Car Guy, both characters from the immensely entertaining Richard Linklater film *Waking Life* – If you're going to microwave that burrito, I want you to poke holes in the plastic wrapping because they explode. And I'm tired of cleaning up your little burrito doings. You dig me?

Corporate space

There is a woman in the cubicle two rows over from the row I'm entombed in. She is very large. She is in her early fifties. I walk by her cubicle. I smell piss. The smell is very faint, nothing more than a suggestion. Like me, she has nothing personal on her desk. No photos to delineate her place in the world, no tchotchkes placed ironically on the white space of her desk. There is only her and her computer and her desk. Wait, scratch that. Sometimes I notice a purse. It looks expensive. I walk by her cubicle to use the restroom. I walk by her cubicle when I head toward the break room. The restroom and the break room are downstairs. Nineteen steps. I never eat in the break room. I always bring my lunch upstairs and eat at my desk. Eating at my desk eliminates any unnecessary conversation. The woman in the cubicle a few rows over also eats at her desk. The Corporation tells us not to eat at our desks. People do it anyway. The woman is eating whenever I pass her cubicle. I try not to look at her. If she says hello, I say hello. I smile. I'm pleasant enough. She works in the infrastructural technology group. I work in the network operations group. I read blueprints and translate them into English. I have a master's degree in a subject that has nothing to do with my work. The Corporation paid for it. Another useless degree stored in a box in the closet.

. . .

My face is thin and forgettable. I have a lazy eye, a vestigial remnant from childhood. I have bad skin. It's scarred from teenage acne. I wear a cheap tie. I have a simple American name. She wears black pants and a black pullover. Sometimes she'll wear a grey pullover. Her face is white and doughy. Her hair is the color of cherry cola. It looks like an expensive dye job, nothing that would come from a box. Her hair is teased from her scalp like a porcupine's quills. Despite our proximity, we work in different departments. We have little in common. I smell urine and the faintest hint of shit emanating from her. She tries to look nice. I can tell she is uncomfortable in her clothes. Her stomach droops onto her lap. Her skin is not wrinkled. I believe she was thin at one time. I have no way of confirming this. She has a managerial air about her. She is not a manager. I sense a downgrade in her past. With my education I could be a manager but I've never been a manager and I don't want to be one. I would hate managing people. Being a teacher helped me come to this conclusion. I walk by her cubicle quickly. I keep my head down. I find her physically repugnant. I'm almost compelled to speak to her but I don't. I try to guess her weight. I peg her somewhere near three hundred and fifty pounds. I'm a terrible person. This is why I'm not a manager. I look through people as they talk to me. I have terrible thoughts. I imagine their heads severed from their bodies. They continue flapping their lips. I smile. They smile back. I look normal. It's not right. I have always been like this.

. . .

I passed her space one morning and saw a copy of Ballard's *The Atrocity Exhibition* next to her purse and a pair of Fendi sunglasses. I'm not sure which item I found more shocking. In that moment she became exponentially more interesting than any of my other co-workers. I tried hurrying to the restroom but she caught my glance. You're a Ballard fan, I said. Yes, she said. I've just started it. Have you read anything of his? I read *The Atrocity Exhibition*, I said. I also read *Crash*. Oh, that's a good one, she said. Yes. Ballard is mercifully short. I don't have the attention span for long books anymore, I said. I blame David Foster Wallace, I said. She laughed. That's understandable, she said. There was a stretched silence between us. Would you like to have a drink sometime, she asked. Her words were like WD-40 to an old door hinge.

. . .

We went to her favorite bar. It was downtown. It was dark and cool. The walls were covered in red velvet wallpaper. The bar itself was a slab of deep mahogany. Its highly-polished surface suggested thousands had come before me to worship in its presence. A flat screen hung above the bar. A baseball game was on. I'm in church, I thought. I pulled out a barstool and sat before the altar. The woman behind the bar recognized her. She asked how she was doing. I'm wonderful, my dear. Jim Beam and Diet, she said. The bartender asked what I wanted. Rum and Coke, I said. There were half a dozen people in the bar. In another hour more people would start milling in as office doors closed behind them for the day. We drank and avoided shop talk and departmental gossip. I was grateful. They have a great bar menu, she said. I asked the bartender for a menu. She handed me a small padded book. I looked it over. I placed the menu on the bar. Too rich for my blood, I said. Oh, go ahead, she said. Don't worry about it. Is it possible to order a steak this early? Yes, the bartender said. What would you like? Ribeye, she said. Medium rare, she said. And for you, the bartender asked. New York strip, I said. Rare, I said. The bartender returned a few moments later with sliced baguettes and cheese. She was a goddess in a black vest and cummerbund.

. . .

I never see you in the break room, she said. I avoid the break room, I said. All anyone does in there is talk about work. I'm already at work. I don't want to talk about it. I eat at my desk. Sometimes I go out. Sometimes I go out, too, she said. But usually I eat at my desk.

. . .

Over the next few weeks I explored other bars with her. Eventually she invited me to her condo to see her library. I'm queer, I said. I know, dear. You said you wanted to see my books, she said. I scanned her collection. An idea of her began to coalesce. I'd read some of the books on her shelves in college. Others were fairly recent. There were several by a Canadian author who dabbled in speculative fiction. I'd always meant to read her but never got around to it. There were very few translated titles. I made a note of it. A collection of bottles sat on one end of the kitchen counter. A bottle of rum was among them. She saw me eyeing the bottles. Would you like a drink? That would be great, I said.

. . .

Do you have plans for the Fourth of July, she asked. No, I said. Do you have a garage card, she asked. Yes, I said. Oh good, she said.

. . .

The Corporation paid well enough. I was able to eat and pay rent. I translated blueprints for a living. I wore a lanyard. I had a simple American name. It had nothing to do with my real life. When I was young I was a teacher. I taught fifth grade. I lived with the illusion I was helping people. The work I do now is meaningless. I help no one and there are no illusions. My real life happened at night while I was alone. I sat at a desk. I worked on a novel I should have never published. I scrapped it several times. It was poorly written. It was written under the influence of meth and cocaine and late nights battling with my ex. I don't offer that as an excuse, only a statement of facts. It's a terrible book and my name is on the cover. What would William the Blind say? We all have doorstops in our backlog, shit we'd like to forget, he said. That was William for you, always polite and ever the humanitarian.

. . .

We packed two lawn chairs and an Igloo Playmate into the trunk of her car. She had a lot of junk in her trunk. I moved it around. How long has this shit been in here? I asked. She laughed. Since my last move, she said. The cardboard boxes had black bottoms, their edges dulled from countless stop signs and traffic lights. I think I found Jimmy Hoffa, I said. Shut the fuck up and let's go before the crowd gets too thick, she said.

. . .

The parking garage was an ugly seven story Brutalist structure. It sat adjacent to The Corporation's high-rise. Swiping a card reader allowed access, depending on your security level. I was a Level II. I had twenty-four hour access. I often brought my nephew to the garage on weekends. We would drink on the top deck of the structure and watch cars as they made their way through the arteries of the city. The top deck was camera-free.

. . .

There was a public park several hundred yards from the parking garage. It was visible from the top deck. The city used the park for fireworks displays on the Fourth of July. I watched fireworks from the parking structure if I had the energy to drive through the city. Usually I stayed home. I don't like crowds.

. . .

We took the lawn chairs and the Igloo Playmate from the trunk. I opened the Igloo and scooped ice into two tumblers. I poured her a Jim Beam and Diet Coke. I filled mine with rum and a splash of Coke to give it color. I sat next to her. Cheers, I said. The July night formed a dark canopy above us. The fireworks were scheduled to begin in half an hour. How's your drink, I asked. It's wonderful, my dear.

. . .

I marveled at the beads of silver suspended in the sky. She let out a big wet fart. I burst out laughing. Sorry, she said. It happens sometimes. She laughed with me. We clicked our tumblers together. I could hear people gathering seven stories below. Fools, I thought. We had the entire parking deck to ourselves. Why did no one else think to do this? I was grateful for the darkness, her company and the icy drinks melting against our tongues. Should I read a few pages, she asked. Go ahead, I said.

. . .

We watched explosions in the sky over smuggled cocktails and pages from Ballard. The scent of contrails burned into our nostrils. I closed my eyes. The red flare of a Portuguese man o' war burned into the underside of my eyelids. A few months later a similar effect would occur while preparing for work one September morning. I watched the South Tower of the World Trade Center collapse on the morning news. Twenty-nine minutes later I watched the North Tower collapse. The world was finally ending, I thought. 2,753 souls lost in a satanic free-fall. It happened in the space of ninety minutes. I watched the binary towers collating all those ones and zeros, their surfaces forever pixelated into the collective memory as metal became one with flesh. A commercial airliner zipping across the sky would never look the same after the events of that day –

. . .

tall buildings shake
voices escape singing sad sad songs
tuned to chords strung down your cheeks
bitter melodies turning your orbit around

. . .

We eventually forget, my father said. I wanted to disagree with him. I wanted to remind him there are some things one never forgets. After a few weeks of charred footage on a continuous loop I realized he was right. I got up. I took a shower. I went to work. I came home. Six months after 9/11 I saw Wilco live. The small venue had a maximum capacity of 1200. It was an unusual concert. The band was plugging an album that hadn't been released yet. I went with an old girlfriend. She was married, she had a young son. I'd known her since high school. We both liked Wilco. I bought a T-shirt. I was too old to do such a thing. The shirt had a picture of a tractor on it. A satellite dish was attached to the cab of the tractor. I thought it was funny. I bought my friend Rachel a T-shirt. Her husband didn't mind that she went to the concert with me. She told him I was queer. He said ok, fine.

. . .

Jeff Tweedy was born in 1967. Like my blood sister, he is three years older than me. Seeing Wilco on the stage six months after 9/11 was miraculous. Everyone was grateful to be alive. People were dancing. A large white screen hung behind the drum riser. Halfway into "Jesus, Etc." the band reversed the damage done to the World Trade Center. On a reverse loop the Twin Towers rebuilt themselves from fire and glass. People soared from the ground and hovered on perches in thin windows. People in the audience were crying. There was a mixture of happiness and sadness. The words took on a different weight. I danced with Rachel six feet from the stage. I never dance. People were very forgiving. Ninety minutes later the concert was over. The doors opened. We scattered into the darkness. I pulled my new T-shirt on over my old one. It was mid-March. We lived in a small desert town. The night had a cold bite to it. That too was a miracle. The large woman from work did not know Rachel. I kept work associates separate from friends. They constituted two separate laundry piles. The clothing from each pile fit differently.

Molotov

I weighed one hundred and ten pounds. I was nineteen. I was having a bit of a rough time. I slept on various sofas. I owned none of them. My parents and I were at odds. This is completely understandable when one is nineteen. The reasons were simple enough. My stepmother and I had a disagreement. She thought I should pay closer attention to the dishes. Dishes don't need much attention, I said. I was kicked out of the house. My father took her side. So be it, I thought. Suddenly the world was an open door. I had many friends, but nothing seemed permanent. I would be leaving for college in the fall. I had an escape route. Fall was still three months away. There was so much time to get into trouble.

. . .

The summer of my nineteenth year was a dark and malevolent time, awash with the promise of mystery and violence. New friends came and went like ghosts. The old ones remained true. I was homeless. I borrowed the empty space on strange sofas. I watched television under the dust of heavy green curtains. I held a remote that was not mine. I drank Coke from glasses that were peanut butter jars in another life. I did not have a set schedule. Existing outside of regular time sharpens one's mind. You become hyperaware of the time. I drifted. I drank. I got stoned. Most of my friends did not own cars. I became a taxi. I was a thumbtack, forgotten until someone stepped on me with their bare feet. I didn't mind being a nonentity. I was responsible for nothing. I was beholden to no one. I passed through walls unnoticed, hovering over the pain of others.

. . .

I spent my days working minimum wage for my father at his wrecking yard. The yard spanned three acres of vintage metal, both foreign and domestic. The cars had managed to retain their value in a world that was quickly moving toward the disposable. My father and I kept a respectable distance. I performed the work that needed to be done. He paid me for it. My nebulous living situation was rarely touched upon. I found meaning in the silence. My father lived in our old house, the house I grew up in. I did not. My disagreement with my stepmother had consequences that moved beyond the simple realm of dishes. I was banned from the safety of familiar furniture, private space, and reliable appliances. Rather than wrestle with old difficulties, my father and I chose to ignore them. I found comfort in the silence. I no longer lived in his house. I no longer had to explain where I had been or what I was doing. If the sofa I slept on at night was less than stellar, what did it matter? If the remote I held in my hand was not mine, what did it matter? The results were the same. The days were hot and oppressive. I walked through walls with kerosene gauze over my eyes. Nights bloomed possibility, and were filled with the promise of violence.

. . .

I was homeless but I owned a car. My homelessness was well-traveled. One particular house that had a powerful center of gravity for me was populated by four or five kids. The kids were around my age. A boy who lived in the house was a friend of mine. I'd met LC through a mutual acquaintance. LC knew several people who dabbled in dark things. I thought the people were dangerous, but I felt safe when I was near LC. We recognized something in each other. Our friendship was a tight knot, the friendship that develops between addicts. LC and I were inseparable that summer. He was smarter than he let on. Of this I was certain. People came and went. Meals were eaten, drugs were taken. There was always a knock at the door. The hour didn't matter. The kitchen was grimy from constant use. Every now and again someone's girlfriend would push a few dishes around in the sink, but never with any real conviction. We harbored no illusions regarding cleanliness. Every person in the house existed as they were. The house possessed the pungency of closeness. Cabinet doors were either loosed from hinges or were missing entirely. Once the doors of propriety are removed, everyone has access to your innards. I didn't mind. A girl I didn't know was visiting a friend. They laughed and drank and talked of their boyfriends. I envied their beauty and their happiness. I sat next to them on the sofa. The girl opened her purse and produced a tiny Ziploc filled with a million crystals. They were broken to perfection, like shaved ice.

. . .

LC and I spent the evenings driving around aimlessly in my car. It was the most perfect thing I owned. It got me where I needed to go, and rarely broke down. In a pinch, the backseat served as a spare bedroom. I slept off the haze of Robitussin nights, only to wake the next morning bound for a new destination. I picked up friends and escaped the third world void of houses without addresses, bathrooms without doors. I kept a small aluminum baseball bat on the passenger side floor board for protection. When one is young, the tethers of the world are not so obvious. But habits have a way of developing at an early age, when the world is still new and full of wonder. With God and dextromethorphan on our side, the world was an open flower waiting to be plucked. I've never been as free as on those nights, with LC in the passenger seat as we drove toward an unnamed oblivion.

. . .

Back at the house, friends welcomed us with an acceptance that was hard to find elsewhere. Anyone feel like Roboing tonight? The question came from the darkness of a hallway that terminated at the thresholds of three small bedrooms. PermaFry sauntered into the kitchen. He was a friend of LC's. He didn't bother with quaint social customs like the practice of wearing clothing. He was eighteen, a year younger than me. I never knew his real name. I don't think anyone else knew it, either. Even LC, the glue that kept us all together under the same roof, confessed to never knowing his real name. I think it's something stupid, like Ralph or something, LC said. When LC suggested that he put on some clothes, PermaFry reacted as if he'd been asked to suffocate his own grandmother. Put some clothes on, man. No one wants to see your shit, LC said. On the contrary, I often stole quick glances of PermaFry when I thought no one was looking. He had a whipcord frame and a hornet's waist. The heavy barb of his manhood hung like a lazy, pendulous menace. PermaFry caught me looking at him a few times. This only boosted his cocksure swagger. If he was on to me, he wasn't telling. His girlfriend didn't mind his perpetual nakedness. He's a free spirit, she said.

. . .

Roboing cocoons the body in a warm freefall. Passageways open, stairwells are erased. Climbing into a car intensifies the uterine effect. All the colors of the universe rush at you in the ecstasy of creation. LC is behind the wheel tonight. I ride shotgun. LC has driven my car several times. Where you want to eat, he asks. From the backseat someone says Jimmy Jack's. I clutch the seat with both hands. I pray the orange phosphorescence subsides long enough so that I might gather my wits about me. I want the car ride to come to an end. I close my eyes. I follow the tracers through the dark. In a few moments we are at Jimmy Jack's, an ancient burger stand. The only people at the tables are a few teenagers. They're out of school, like us. I open my door. I float toward the take-out window. I have feet, but I can't feel them. I ask LC if we should bring something back for the baby. Yes, he says. One of the girlfriends has an infant daughter. The girl is teething. Milkshake? French fries? I'm at a loss. The Robitussin isn't helping. Basic tasks are monumental, even impossible. My eyes are an open door. I think of the baby. In the fall I will escape this desert nightmare for a tree-lined campus filled with scampering squirrels and the carefree sounds coming from dorm room windows. The baby doesn't have a choice. What would you like? I stare at the clerk behind the counter, unable to make a decision. LC pushes me toward the small grimy window. You're up, brother.

. . .

PermaFry filled an empty Popov bottle with gasoline and pushed a greasy shop towel into its mouth. I imagined him pushing his fingers into his girlfriend, his nails dirty and broken. He shook the bottle violently. He motioned for us to come outside. We stood on the concrete drive under the harsh light of a single yellow bulb. Someone killed the lights. I heard a satanic giggling coming from the darkness directly behind me. Someone struck a match. The street was dark. The streetlights had been shot out long ago. The City never troubled with replacing the missing lamps. In this neighborhood they would likely be shot out again. Perhaps the city fathers believed the neighborhood was best kept in darkness. PermaFry tipped the rag toward the lit match. A violent explosion illuminated our faces. PermaFry twisted his naked body in a jubilant rage. He ran barefoot onto the asphalt. He threw the Molotov cocktail toward an abandoned house that sat directly across the street. The will of human sinew connected with the dumb silence of roof joists. The Popov bottle exploded, a bright orange fireball bathing our neighborhood in an otherworldly glow. We ran into the darkness of the house. Twenty minutes passed before the fire engines rounded the corner with their rude sirens and brute force. The firefighters were cattle hanging from meat hooks. When they finally jumped off the truck the house was already gone, a blackened shell. We hunkered down in the darkness of the living room, our collective silence an unspoken agreement.

. . .

The summer eventually ended, as all summers do. I escaped to the great white void of Iowa. I found myself among new friends. They were a little less rough around the edges. They spoke in clear tones. They held their beer bottles just so. They comported themselves with an air of restrained wealth. I liked my new friends, but I was no longer part of an inner circle. These people bathed too much. Adjust, focus, rewire. The alcohol flowed freely. Drugs opened doors previously locked. New experiences were imprinted upon my brain. I memorized my place in relation to the sun. I moved easily among them, but I was not part of their world.

. . .

I never saw LC or PermaFry again. I've often wondered whatever became of LC. PermaFry was an easy guess, but LC's existence was based on trickier assumptions. Somewhere in his brain resided an intelligence that was turned down low. Bright lights tend to attract moths – best to dim the bulb so trouble doesn't find you. I've thought of looking him up on the web, typing his proper name into a search engine. I believe technology would fall short in this case. It's best to remember him as he was. Digital pixelations would only weaken the effect. I watched a program on the Trinity nuclear detonation site. It was on late at night. It was a Saturday night. I couldn't sleep. If it doesn't bring further understanding, why bother? In *Profiles of the Future*, Arthur C. Clarke said 'any sufficiently advanced technology is indistinguishable from magic.' Technology fails us, memory fades, and roof joists collapse under the weight of time and human will. I never told LC that I loved him. I never told him his friendship was important to me. I have failed him. I am ashamed.

The ladies of Irving Park Road

I hold a photograph in my hand. In the photo my friend Donald and I are sitting at a dinner table. On the table is a birthday cake, candles lit. It's Donald's twentieth birthday. He's looking at the photographer. His expression reads *what is this shit?* My fingers appear skeletal, almost monk-like. I look sickly and disturbed, mentally unbalanced. It looks like every other photo of me from this period. Donald and Katie were sophomores. I was a junior. We attended the same small college in Iowa. We were friends. I'm not sure what Donald and Katie saw in me. I was a black-haired moody loner. I was a stranger on foreign soil. I was glad to call them friends. None of us fit in very well with life at school; somehow we would not fit in together. College was a difficult time for me. I was two thousand miles from home. I was queer. I had trouble adjusting to small town life in Middle America. I was only myself with a few people. Donald and Katie were part of that small group. Donald knew I was queer. He didn't mind. We found a common ground in our voracious appetite for drugs. Hallucinogens were our drug of choice. Katie did not share our proclivities. She didn't even drink, as far as I knew. One of us had to play the straight man. She did it without complaint. She was an angel among demons.

. . .

We did things together on weekends. Walking, hiking, movies, late night trips to Dairy Queen. In a small town one must create one's own entertainment. I would walk downtown into the heart of Cedar Rapids. I wanted to be among buildings that were older than any structures where I came from. Loneliness would often point me in the direction of a dark bar. I didn't want to become an alcoholic while still in my early twenties. My feet had other plans. I thought it best to stay away from downtown. Too many old man bars beckoned. Sometimes I would find myself in a lonely graveyard, looking at headstones. All these people had once been alive, had once rushed to and fro, making appointments, cataloging furniture, achieving nothing. Were their lives so extraordinary they needed to be commemorated in marble?

. . .

I sat next to a gravestone underneath a sugar maple. The dead held congress beneath me. The grass was wet. I felt it through my jeans. I forgot the names as soon as I read them. You crumble beneath me yet you once lived and loved as if it would last forever. Does anyone remember your name? I grow tired of the dead. I get up, brush the grass off my butt and walk downtown. I want to be among the living, sitting on a barstool, mindlessly watching a game on television. The bar is dark and welcoming as I push the door open. The bartender is in his early thirties. His name is Matt. He greets me with a familiar hello. We attend a few of the same writing classes. I imagine working in a bar or a funeral home to be the best spot for gathering writing material. I say so. Matt says I can one-up you – nursing homes.

. . .

Donald asks if I've ever been rappelling. I tell him I haven't. We'll go to Devil's Lake, he says. You'll like it. You look like you could use some sun. You're right. I've been hiding in the library too long. We leave Cedar Rapids for Chicago in someone's car. Once we're dropped off in Chicago we gather supplies. Donald laughs at my ridiculous shoes. You'll need something stronger than those to rappel in. We have the same shoe size. I try on a pair of his old hiking boots. They fit fine. Donald borrows the family minivan. He gathers a few peripheral friends I'm only slightly aware of. Another group follows us in a separate car. I sit in the back seat of the Dodge Caravan. I observe everything from the vantage point of a cat prepared for escape. There is excited chatter coming from the cab. Donald leads the expedition. I'm glad someone who knows what they're doing is in charge. We have four solid hours of driving ahead of us. Outside my window the green heart of the Midwest rushes by. I catalog every farmhouse as we leave the city. I record things I've never seen before. The girls in the group talk about the boys. The boys pretend they aren't listening. I take it all in from the fulcrum I've carved in my corner of the minivan. I record the chatter in my brain. I mentally undress one of the hikers, a boy named Pete. He's a granola. He has long black hair and wears a short beard. He wears cargo shorts. I stop myself from wading through the dark hair on his legs with my eyes.

. . .

It is late May. I am twenty-one. I have traveled with Donald and Katie to Spring Green. We spend the day hiking and rappelling. I am in the best shape of my life.

My body is a taut plank. We go rock climbing at Devil's Lake with a few friends. I step through the harness as an amateur would step onto a wrestling mat, cocky and unaware of the possibility of defeat. I make my way toward the top of a crag. My friends slowly disappear below me. I am too young and too stupid to be afraid. What could nature possibly do to me? My legs work on command, in sync with my hips. My back is strong. My hands move with the rope as if by secret propulsion. In a few minutes I am at the top of the crag. I call to my friends, wish them luck. My crotch is on fire. The harness is a reminder. I am alive. My friends reach the top. We sit with our backs against the trees. We will never be this alive again. We eat a late breakfast at a café named Susie's. I pull air into my lungs. Sunlight shines through the window. You were pretty brave on that rock, Donald says. Maybe I have a death wish, I say. I am only half-joking.

. . .

Nights in Wisconsin can be beautiful. The three of us lay under the stars. Our other friends have dispersed. Donald and Katie lay together in one sleeping bag. I pondered the stars zipped in my own. The sky was a black velvet blanket. Pinholes of light pushed through. I had one year left of college. What would the future hold for me? Would I become a writer, a professor, an editor at a publishing company in New York? Each sounded wonderful. Anything to escape the small desert town I came from. The thought of pushing a broom through a Circle K parking lot back home in Río Seco never occurred to me.

. . .

In the morning we rolled up our sleeping bags and packed them into the back of the Dodge Caravan that belonged to Donald's parents. We slowly made our way from Wisconsin to Illinois. Katie's family lived in Wheaton. She would be staying with them for the summer. Donald pulled into the drive in front of Katie's house. We got out of the Caravan. I hugged Katie and said goodbye. I made my way to the front passenger seat. Donald helped Katie with her things. He walked her to the door. He kissed her. I looked away. Such moments were private. They stood before the doorway. Katie opened the door and disappeared inside. Would I ever have a love like this?

. . .

Donald asked me what I wanted to do. You boys should eat before you do anything, Donald's father said from the kitchen. I sat at the dinner table with Donald, his mother and father, and Donald's younger brother Jon. Jon was a musician. He would move to California a few years later. At the table, Donald's father, a learned man, shared stories of the day's events. Talk soon turned to God. Donald's father told us the story of eternity, how God waits for us to accept Him into our hearts. We must completely surrender to Him to become one with God. God is eternal. Time as we know it doesn't exist in Heaven. Donald was horrified. Many years later Donald told me the idea of eternity terrified him. We were on the phone. He was in California. I was in Río Seco. We were much older. Ten years had passed since we'd sat at the dinner table that evening. What do you believe? Donald asked. I paused. I'm not sure what I believe, I said. I'm pretty sure it's nothing.

. . .

Now what? Donald asked. I was twenty-one. I was a stranger to the dive bars in Chicago. Let's go have a drink, I said. Donald agreed. We'll go to El Gato Negro, Donald said. He said this as if it were the most dangerous sentence in the world. In the safety of the Dodge Caravan the streets rushed beneath our tires. The rain split the windshield in two. If not my brother by blood or paper, Donald was my spiritual brother. He was a young man well-spoken in the ways of synaptic illumination. Through the windshield, a neon-lit sign of a cat in repose, a martini glass at its feet. I should warn you, Donald said. This is a tranny bar. The door closed behind us. Before I could suggest an alternative, the eyes at the bar were focused on us, if only for a moment. Most of the bar patrons were of Latin descent. When I thought of Latinos, Chicago was the last place that came to mind. Donald and I sat at the bar, the mirror behind the tap reflecting our foreignness. A thirty-something man with dark curly hair and a Guevara beard and moustache pulled a tired dishrag over the bar. Donald and I ordered. I considered my reflection in the mirror. I had a beard only slightly less full than the man behind the bar. My hands were thin and skeletal, my eyes Latinate. I summoned my biological mother's side of the bloodline, the non-Teutonic side. I remembered I was half Mexican. I still felt out of place. I lifted my butt off the barstool. I reached into my back pocket and removed my wallet. I discreetly shoved it into my front pocket. The exchange took less than three seconds. I adjusted my Levi's. I darkened my eyes to match my blood. My rum and Coke appeared as if by magic. Donald asked the bartender his name. Carlos. Eight-fifty, he said. Would I die in a knife fight tonight?

Donald gave him a ten and followed it with a five. Carlos became much friendlier. My feet felt odd in my shoes, a dead weight disconnected from my legs. I took a healthy sip of my rum. To life, my brother. To life, Donald said. We clicked our glasses together.

. . .

A glittered shadow passed behind me. A dark-haired girl with large breasts appeared at my side. She began massaging my crotch. She smelled of papaya. My name is Gia, she said. Come dance with me. I looked at Donald. He was no help. My feet moved under Gia's guidance. We were on the dance floor. My feet felt separated from my body. Gia pulled me close to her. A bright green tank top threatened to collapse under the weight of her heaving breasts. She moved my hands over them. You like them? They were soft, feminine. Yes, I said. After a three minute song that felt like ten, I invited Gia to the bar. She sat between me and Donald. I like your friend, Gia said to Donald. He's cute. Yes he is, Donald said. She smiled at me, her hands caressing my ass in a not-so-womanly manner. I was thankful I'd moved my wallet to my front pocket.

. . .

I had two or three rum and Cokes. I continued dancing with Gia in El Gato Negro, the fear of a knife in my gut all but forgotten. Gia and I were the only ones on the dance floor. An old man in an unlit corner of the bar raised his glass to us. I told Donald I was going home with Gia. Are you sure, he said. Yes, I said. Any surprises I might encounter would either end in joy or blood, but in my present condition the two choices were one and the same. I went home with her on the elevated train. I followed her perfumed rump up a fourth floor walk-up. We watched a re-run of *Quincy, M.E.* on her incredibly small television. Jack Klugman mouthed something to his lab assistant Sam, but it may as well have been in Spanish. Gia stripped me to my underwear, my white briefs illuminating the room. She slowly thumbed them down my legs, her nails red scoops. I stepped through them, kicking them aside. I took off her clothes. Her breasts were real, but she was an incomplete woman, or rather, half a man. Between her legs was a penis like any other penis. Soft when bored, hard when not. Gia was hard. What to do when one is traveling between two worlds? I recalled a passage from Kafka's diary dated August 15, 1914. In the story *Memoirs of the Kalda Railroad*, Kafka's narrator lies with the railroad inspector –

. . .

…He whispered secret promises into my ear about the career he would help me to achieve, and finally we fell together on the bunk in an embrace that often lasted ten hours unbroken…

. . .

Gia, being somewhat needy like Kafka, says do you like my breasts? To focus my attention she pulls my eyes from her contemptible penis. Yes, I say. I'm not done yet, she says. It costs so much, she says. I was about to ask how much it costs when she says Do you love me? Do you love me? In that moment I am no longer Kafka with his brutish railroad inspector. I am Molly Bloom, the true hero of Joyce's big green book. Without a moment's hesitation I say Yes I do Yes I will Yes.

Mystical Mr. Moncebaez

I hold a photograph in my hand. In the photo I'm in sixth grade, twelve years old. I stand next to a neighborhood boy. We attend the same elementary school. I'm stick thin. I'm short for my age. The boy next to me is shorter than I am. He has a smile that says *yes*. This is how old I am the first time I smoke marijuana.

. . .

Ricky was smooth, a ladies man. Even in sixth grade. He wore ironed jeans, the legs neatly creased, silk shirts with the requisite wife-beater underneath, and a gold chain with a small plain cross dangling from it. Jesus wasn't hanging from the cross in tortured Catholic agony – Ricky wanted all eyes on him. His wavy thick black hair is combed smoothly against his head. When girls speak his name, they're tracing the waves in his hair with their tongues. Girls wanted him. Boys wanted to be like him. Ricky lived a few blocks from me. We walked to school together. I asked him who ironed his clothes. I do, he said. Who taught you how to iron? I live with sisters, he said. It just happens.

. . .

Ricky wore cologne. I've never been a cologne person.

Was it an older brother's cologne? Was it a spritz from his father's bottle of Brut? Ricky had a fair complexion. His sideburns traced a path to the bottom of his earlobes. There was a dusting of fine hair on his cheekbones. By the time we were in high school, he had a full beard.

. . .

Ricky reached into his pocket one morning as I caught up with him. We were walking to school. We were both twelve. I thought you weren't coming, he said. Just late, I said. Ever smoke a joint, he asked. Yes, I said. It was a lie. I didn't want to look uncool to Ricky. He pulled a Bic lighter from his pocket. He stuck a small twisted cigarette in his mouth. He lit it and inhaled deeply. The pungent smoke smelled foreign. He passed it to me. Just breathe in, he said. Hold it in your lungs. I handled the joint gingerly, as if it were poison ivy. Ricky knew I'd never smoked marijuana, but he didn't mention it. Like all good teachers, he knew illustration was the key. We walked. We passed the joint between us until it was so short it burned the tips of my fingers. Ricky threw the roach in the dirt along the sidewalk and pocketed the lighter. The schoolyard gate loomed before us. I'll see you later, Ricky said. He left me to my own devices. My head was crowned in a ring of smoke. Walking became an unfamiliar exercise. I sat speechless in class the rest of the morning. I noticed things that had escaped me before. Teachers were strange. What rational adult would spend eight hours of their day with children who were not theirs? Language is funny. It has so many rules. Most of them don't make sense. Boys and girls look similar when in fact they are very different creatures. Colors have a specific taste. Rain is beautiful but distracting, especially when it's falling outside a schoolhouse window in the first week of May.

. . .

I'm not sure whatever became of Ricky Moncebaez. When I was about seventeen, long after I'd lost contact with him, he walked into my father's wrecking yard. He was looking for parts for his 1968 Pontiac Firebird. He still exuded cool. The silk shirts were gone. He wore Levi's and a T-shirt. His body was much thinner. Hey man, it's been a while, he said. He shook my hand. The gold chains around his neck were heavier. His wavy black hair was combed smoothly against his head. His beard was neatly trimmed. His moustache was a billboard for his full lips. With a face and hair like his a man could conquer worlds, I thought. You work here, he asked. Yes. My dad owns the place. Ricky leaned against the driver's side fender of his car. That's cool, he said. He told me what he needed for his car. We looked around the yard. We found nothing. After twenty minutes I walked Ricky back to his car. He shook my hand again. My uncle manages the Luna Lounge on Central, he said. You should drop by sometime. I work there on weekends. Thanks man, I will. I never visited Ricky at the Luna Lounge. I kept meaning to, but time somehow got away from me. The last time I drove by the bar, the sign was gone. That was many years ago. A thrift store stood in its place. The things we carry come from an infinite sadness. That sadness is the death of childhood.

Art with a capital A

My first exposure to art was around age six or seven. I may have been exposed to art at an earlier age, but I was six or seven when I first became aware of it, was able to understand art was something that existed outside of me. A cheap 24 x 20 painting of five deer bending their necks to sip water from a creek hung in our living room. The canvas was padded. The bodies of the deer appeared to be three dimensional. The surface of the painting was of woven fabric similar to the surface material of a sofa cushion. The eyes of the deer were comprised of diamonds. My six-year-old self thought they were diamonds. In reality they were cut glass with a silver backing. One of the deer, a baby, was missing an eye. Lost during a move? Since I lived in the same house from zero to seventeen, I deduced the eye must have been lost during a move my young parents had made, before I came into the picture. The painting hung from piano wire strung between two small nails in the back. All I understood or needed to know about art could be taken from this painting. It was cheap, static, and artificial. It forced a paradigm into the room. It didn't bother explaining itself. What purpose did it serve? Was it a window to the world? It could momentarily take me from the room, but after a few moments I was once again relegated to my body. I became attached to this painting as one becomes attached to a sixth finger. We become attached to everyday objects that continually occur in our environment. These objects signify that we *exist* in the world. After my father and mother divorced, mother took the painting with her when she moved into an apartment. After she started dating the Young Latino, she moved it into his house. She eventually married the Young Latino.

. . .

It was strange seeing the painting hung in a different location. It was a violation to my eyes. As one would imagine seeing the *Mona Lisa* hung anywhere other than the Louvre would be. The Young Latino had no history with the painting. Neither did his house. I resented him for this. The old nail where it used to hang from in my father's home was eventually removed with a claw hammer and the hole painted over, the second violation. My mother had taken the painting with her because it was a purchase she'd made while my parents were young newlyweds. My mother recently gave the painting to me. It hangs in my library back home in America. A few more eyes have fallen from the canvas, the deer reduced to staring at the dappled water in blindness. On the back of the painting is a small label. Royal's House of Furniture. Penciled on the label is the year 1967. I'd observed the painting so often during my childhood I could no longer see it for what it really was – a cheap painting and a misrepresentation of reality.

. . .

When we attempt to depict the real world through representation, through art, it becomes hyperreal. Reality cannot be represented by art. How can we represent what doesn't exist? In this way, art is a failure. It isn't privy to what it is representing. It cannot effectively *read* it. This doesn't mean art shouldn't be attempted. This doesn't mean art should be ridiculed. It only means any attempted representation will always fall short of reality. How can we define the undefinable? I became attached to my mother's painting of the deer, even though I understood it to be false. It defined my mother's taste in art, and it defined my taste. It was hyperreal, a window into an alternate reality. The painting understood at its basic core that it's impossible to represent reality. I loved it because it did not try to.

. . .

I was seven years old the first time I questioned the world before my eyes. My father had taken me to get a haircut. My father would get his hair cut first. Then it would be my turn. We always got our hair cut at Frank's Barbershop. None of the old men who worked at the shop were named Frank. It was a few miles from home. There was a small bell above the door that rang when the door was opened. I sat in the chair. The barber spun me around to cut the hair that hung against the nape of my neck. I saw my reflection in the mirror, which was a reflection of my reflection in another mirror. Hundreds of me disappeared to a pinpoint, the copies of my face growing smaller and smaller as the tail of reflections drew upward like a comet. I moved and they moved, but they were not me. They were only copies of what I called 'me.' But where was the real me? In the barbershop, with the circulation fan spinning over my head, the buzz of the clippers in my ear and the television on, I wasn't sure which copy was the real me anymore. My father peeked over the newspaper he was reading. He winked at me. Did he know the world was fake, a simulation? If he did, he didn't let on. Most adults don't. Recognizing the lie is the first step on the path toward adulthood. My hair continued falling to the floor in reddish-brown wisps. I moved a finger under the white apron covering my torso. I flicked my fake hair to the floor. All done said the barber as he whisked hair from my face with a talcum-powdered brush. You're a brand new man, he said as he unbuttoned the apron. What did he mean? Was he letting me in on the secret? It took a moment to realize I was still in my body as I slid off the chair. The snippets of hair lodged between my shirt and my skin reminded me I was indeed in the real world the adults so readily tried to define for me.

Grandmother and the dead Chihuahua

I hold a photograph in my hand. It's the only photo in the collection that's not of a human being. My Chihuahua Brownie is on the living room carpet. Her back is against an old beige sofa. Someone's bare foot is in the foreground. It's either my sister's foot or my stepmother's. Brownie was my companion for two years. I was six when a neighbor gave her to me. She was not my sister's dog. She was not my parents' dog. She was my dog. She had a tiny bark that sounded like a rusty door hinge. She did not like my father, but he tolerated her. I've never had a dog that didn't like me before, he said. When I came home from school Brownie would be waiting for me. When she was a puppy she tried going outside on her own. My father taught her no with a rolled newspaper. I don't want her bringing ticks in the house, he said. Paper sister 1965 had a cat and I had Brownie. Brownie didn't mind the cat. They ignored each other. My sister's cat was a white long-haired Persian named Priscilla. Priscilla always left traces of herself on the sofa, in the carpet. Brownie was a clean dog. She didn't know she was a dog. I cupped her head in my hands. It almost fit.

. . .

I jumped off the school bus one afternoon carrying papers to be placed on the refrigerator. My first grade teacher had written an A on a writing exercise. As I moved toward the house I saw Brownie. She wasn't supposed to be outside. She was on the asphalt in front of my house. She was blown open, her intestines trailing behind her. I saw things inside her I was never meant to see. I ran toward the house, tears in my eyes. She got out, my sister said, crying. This was the first time I met Death.

. . .

I was eight years old when my grandmother on my stepmother's side died. She died from complications due to a brain tumor. She died in the hospital. It was a very long, drawn-out death. She was in her early sixties. She'd been a healthy, happy woman. She was portly. Her arms were like tree stumps. Her kitchen smelled of mashed potatoes and old newspaper clippings. She was my stepmother's mother. My father often corrected me. She's your mother, not your stepmother, boy. My adoptive father and my adoptive mother did not like each other. They used to, but things had changed. My father did like other women. He liked my stepmother. He liked our next-door neighbor, Evelyn. She was a Southern woman with a shock of white hair. She used to be beautiful, my father said. He said this to me when I was very young. Evelyn carried an invisible weight on her shoulders. It was the knowledge of once having everything and now having nothing. When she looked at my father from across the fence something unspoken passed between them. When my grandmother on my stepmother's side fell ill all talk in the house ceased. My father stayed away from the bar, which meant I stayed away from the bar. We went to the hospital in the evenings to visit my grandmother. My stepmother acted weird in the front seat of the car on the way there. I was born in the same hospital my grandmother died in. I liked the hospital because I was born in it. My reverence was silly. The hospital was grey and ugly, like most hospitals. When we approached my grandmother's room the nurses at the station nodded without saying a word. There was no need to check in. We stepped into her room. The withered thing on the bed shocked me. It was not my grandmother. It was a shrunken plastic thing with nails that needed to be clipped. I could see bones underneath her skin. Mama, can I have a Coke? Yes, my stepmother said. She removed change from her coin purse and handed it to my sister. My sister walked me down the hall. We waited in a little glass alcove. We watched television. The hospital smelled of piss and rubbing alcohol and something else I couldn't identify. Watching television in a hospital was strange. There was a man and a few children in the glass room with us. They were very quiet. I wondered if their grandmother was dying, too. Can I have a Coke, I said. My sister gave me a handful of change. Get me a Dr Pepper, she said.

. . .

My grandmother, or what was left of her, was buried with a bracelet of photos around her wrist. There were eight photos on the bracelet, one for each grandchild. The photos were small ovals. One of the photos was a dime-sized photograph of me. I was her adopted grandson by marriage. I was confused. Why did she need a photo of me on her wrist? I wanted to ask my father but I didn't. I knew it was better not to ask. We sat in the front pews, near the priest. He spoke for several minutes. He said a lot of things. They didn't make sense. The words were in Latin. Then he began speaking in English. My stepmother was crying. My father held her hand. After the priest finished he made a sweeping motion with his hand. People got up. I was glad we were finally allowed to leave. My stepmother put an arm under me and pulled me against her. She usually didn't pull me close to her. When I see you, I see your mother, she'd once said. That was a long time ago. I was much younger. I'd pulled some flowers from the flowerbed she'd planted in front of our house. I wanted to make something with them but she didn't understand. I never forgot the words she said. Now she pulled me tight against her. We moved toward the casket. I didn't want to be near the casket. It looked like a pink sailboat surrounded by flowers. I didn't want to be near the plastic thing again, but I was rocked toward it by an ocean of black. Everyone wore black except my grandmother. My grandmother wore pink. We approached the casket. I saw the bracelet. I didn't want to see my grandmother. Now when I remembered her, all I would remember was the shrunken thing wearing a bracelet with my photo dangling from it. My sister's picture was on it, too. There were photos of cousins. I wanted to ask my sister about it because she was young like me, but I didn't. I knew there were certain things one didn't ask. I touched my grandmother's arm. It didn't feel like anything. The plastic thing was wearing a wig. This was the second time I met Death. The church doors opened. Finally, I thought. Sunlight touched my face. I forgot about death.

. . .

I lay quietly in bed and wondered about the photographs of the grandchildren on my grandmother's bracelet. My picture lay on her wrist. Her bracelet jingles in the silence of the casket. My youthful face clicks against old bones. I am forever trapped in the casket with her. This is the third time I met Death. I think about how I will die. Will it be in a hospital room or hotel room? Will there be a simple note? A do not resuscitate order? I think about plastic bags, bathtubs, and Jerzy Kosiński. I am going to put myself to sleep now for a bit longer than usual. Call it Eternity.

The hemline of your shirt, rising above your belly

You worked for a summer at my father's wrecking yard. We were eighteen. It was 1988. It was our last year of high school. It would be the last summer we would spend together. Your hands were strong and masculine yet somehow tender. I imagined them in the hands of a faceless girl at the prom. Did you struggle with the straps of her prom dress after the music faded? Did you drive her home, a perfect gentleman? The day you left for the Army you were still a virgin. I was sure of it. I didn't know how I knew this, but I did. It may have been in the way you moved. You were unsure of your body. I watched you when you were not looking. I thought someone who has been with a woman would not move like that.

. . .

We spent our breaks sitting on overturned quarter panels or metal milk crates. We planned the night's activities on our breaks. You learned how to drive by driving my car. Your brother was three years younger than us. He would sometimes sit in the back seat as you or I drove to a random destination. Sometimes other friends from school sat in the back as we drove nowhere. I have trouble remembering names and faces. Yours is the only one that registered as you sat next to me. On a downtown street known for its sex trade we hooted at prostitutes as we drove further into one a.m. My car did not have air conditioning. We pulled into a Circle K to buy drinks. We were too young to buy alcohol. We didn't mind. An endless group of people stumbled out of the car. It looked like a clown car. I was sad. I didn't want the night to end. You had already signed the papers. You were due to report to the Army in two weeks.

. . .

I watched you work. You didn't know I watched you. My father asked you to remove an oil pan for a customer. You drained the oil from the pan. Oil oozed between your fingers as you caught it in a drip pan. The dark oil traced the veins of your hand. I watched you remove a catalytic converter. Removing a catalytic converter is difficult. The car we worked on was held in the air by a forklift. When you raised your hands to the converter I saw the hemline of your shirt rise above your belly. The skin of your belly was whiter than your arms. Your arms were caramel from the sun. I turned away. I didn't want you to see my desire for you. When we parted that evening we shook hands. See you tomorrow, you said. Yes, I said. See you tomorrow. You spent the night at my house once. I gave you the bed. I slept on the floor. I could hear you breathing in the dark. You turned on your side, pulling the covers with you. You were so close. I had trouble sleeping. I thought of different scenarios. I couldn't turn off my brain.

. . .

I recently googled your last name. I hit the images button and there you were. There was a thumbnail of you with a female friend. She was either your wife or your girlfriend. You looked happy. You were in your early forties. You got old. I was shocked. You were pixelated under a digital microscope. Your face was soft. Your eyes were hollow. What was it? Had you suffered a bad marriage? Did your dreams never materialize? The past is best left in the past, where it belongs. Gauzy details should be kept hidden in dresser drawers. Photographs do not age if they're kept on a shelf in the dark.

. . .

You worked for a summer at my father's wrecking yard. That summer has been rendered perfectly in my mind. I have a picture of you standing in the yard, near an old car. You are eighteen. You are beautiful. I never told you my true feelings. I couldn't. I closed the thumbnail image. I had intruded on your beauty with the present. I deserved the revelation I got, but that doesn't make it easier. Everyone dies.

Dixon Ticonderoga No. 2

Twelve is a terrible age. There is the problem of the body – your body and the body of everyone else. At twelve we catalog other bodies without realizing what we are doing. We consider asses covered in denim, how corduroy accentuates curves rather than hides them. We study the round knob of a collarbone under a T-shirt. A tuft of hair tucked behind an ear. How a girl's body softens and a boy's elongates into hard, immovable type. When I was twelve I stared at the armpits of my brothers. I tried doing this without being noticed. My brother Andrew, a year younger than me, had soft down under his arms. My brother Michael, a teenager, had the aggressive black curls of a ninth grader. When I was twelve I had a girl's body. The hairless white skin under my arms looked infantile. I did not like taking showers after gym class. My body was a mollusk, a soft pink thing best seen in the dark. I traveled from shell to shell but failed to find an exterior that matched the rapid movements of my mind. I covered my body. I covered it in summer. I wore heavy jackets in winter. While other boys were parting clouds I was grounded, four-foot-two. I was very small. My feet did not stink. My legs were hairless. I swallowed my words until they matched my body. I practiced my perfection of silence.

. . .

I was not always silent. Sometimes I played the role of class clown. I opened my tiny mouth and large words came out. Timing was everything. I instinctively knew this. I was not the smartest kid in class. There was another boy who was much smarter than me. When he was up at the board, solving a math problem, I broke the silence by stuttering, making rude noises, cooing like a girl. My teacher, Mrs. Goodwin, would tell me to go outside. She raised a hooked finger, dismissing me to Siberia. There was a chair outside near the door. I was often in it. I pulled a stubby pencil from my pocket and wrote my name on the grey mortar between bricks. I was bored. Teachers would pass me as they walked briskly down the hall. A shake of the head would remind me I was a mollusk. At least I didn't have to stand.

. . .

Things changed in seventh grade. My body was constantly evolving, an eruption of fire and flesh. My face morphed so often I didn't know what I looked like. My hair, which had once been reddish-brown and straight, was now dark and curly. I couldn't control it. I tried taming it with Tres Flores. I tried taming it with water and gel. I finally asked my stepmother to shave it off. She obliged. My black locks fell in angry curls at my feet. When she was finished I looked in a mirror and inventoried the crests and valleys of my skull. My hair grew back quickly. I combed it and tamped it. I tried taming it with water and gel. I had the defiant curls of an unclaimed Latin kid. I gave up and moved on. I was very skinny. I replaced my skin with zippers, buttons and shoelaces. I covered my body. I hid in a shell on the sea floor. I rarely came up for air.

. . .

I forgot how to walk in seventh grade. My feet were still my feet, but they were suggestions more than anything. I placed one foot on the ground, lifted another in the air. I tried coordinating the two movements. Something was amiss. I watched other kids walk. Some were quite good at it – the smart boy from sixth grade homeroom, the boys who played soccer on the field. I looked to them for guidance. I watched their movements. I tried practicing what I saw, but nothing came out right. I became very conscious of walking. It should be like breathing, I thought. It should be easy.

. . .

On the first day of seventh grade my teacher, Mrs. White, told us to sit wherever we liked. I sat at the back of the class. I kept my mouth shut. I was no longer the class clown. I had grown very little over the summer. My brother Andrew and I were the same height. He was a year younger. What was wrong with me? Some boys looked six feet tall. I was a sparrow among giants. From my corner of the room I took a head count. There were other boys with curly hair. They talked to girls, passed notes. They wore corduroys. Their arms were covered in fine black down. I kept my body covered. I wore the same shoes I'd worn the previous summer. My pants were soft from riding my bike. My fingernails were dirty from the wrecking yard. My stepmother said if I were a dog I'd be the runt of the litter. I wasn't sure what to make of it. If she was insulting me, she was good at hiding it. Adults smiled while passing judgment. It was confusing.

. . .

A boy sat at the front of the class, near the teacher's desk. He was one of those, a front-row sitter. I couldn't take my eyes off him. His dark hair was smoothed against his head. Sometimes he leaned toward another boy and spoke with a voice that carried something I didn't have. He wore dark brown corduroys and a blue football jersey. He wore the latest sneakers. He had an easy way about him. He moved his hands when he talked to the other boy. I decided they were discussing football teams. The teacher, Mrs. White, called our names. I waited. His name was among the first called. Jaime Valencia, the teacher said. The boy raised his hand in the air. Here, he said. He leaned forward. He touched the hair at the nape of his neck. He had a solid, muscular back. He had fine dark hair on his upper lip. He was thirteen. I would be thirteen in a few months. Knowing he was older made him much more mysterious.

. . .

I was an excellent speller. Words came easily to me. I didn't have to think about them. If I heard a word, I knew how to spell it. The letters hardened in my mind like geodes. I moved them around until they made sense. My ears and my brain worked in tandem. I could not say the same about my brain and my fingers. The boy Jaime sometimes spoke to was named Angel. Jaime and Angel were also good at spelling. Mrs. White decided we would work together. We were given a small book with several thousand words in it. I was nervous being so close to Jaime. I chewed on my pencil. My teeth left small jagged craters in the pencil. We practiced spelling words on our lunch hour. One of us would read a word aloud. Another would spell it. We alternated. We did very well. I sat on the floor in a corner of the room. I sat next to Jaime. Sometimes our arms touched. I knew he thought nothing of it. I touched his arm as often as possible. I made it appear accidental, casual. I scanned the words in the spelling book. They were blurry. I found it hard to concentrate while sitting near Jaime. Jaime's face was soft like a girl's. He had fine dark hair on his upper lip. He had a boy's arms. He smelled like I imagined a boy should smell. He was very graceful on the soccer field. We practiced for two weeks. Finally the week came when it was time to put our exercises into practice. A spelling bee was held in the library. Those who placed in the top five would move on to the state level. I was doing well until I came to the word colloquialism. I did not make it to the state level.

. . .

I returned to my homeroom, defeated. I told Mrs. White I'd misspelled colloquialism. That's ok, she said. I can't spell it, either. Her words didn't help. I thought teachers had the answers to all possible questions. Like other adults, they too were liars. A boy named Thomas teased me about misspelling colloquialism. It was a few minutes before the lunch bell. Thomas was a tall blond boy. His face was red with acne. Guess you didn't make it, huh faggot, he said. I took Jaime's freshly-sharpened pencil from my back pocket and jammed it into the muscle of Thomas' leg. He screamed and collapsed to the floor.

. . .

I visited some old friends a few days before Christmas. I had known Victoria a long time. We went to high school together. She had a husband and two kids, a boy named Soren, aged twelve, and a girl named Ivoree, aged nine. Victoria and Miguel had done something I could never do – have children. I envied them. Having children was natural. People grow up, they get married and they have children. Victoria and Miguel lived on the edge of the city. Farmland and cotton fields lay beyond their apartment complex. I enjoyed hanging out with the kids. We watched television together. Miguel had an extensive collection of odd movies, films one wouldn't expect to find on bookshelves in the cowtown we lived in. We talked about disturbing movies. I told him about *The Piano Teacher*. He handed me a copy of *Irreversible*. Watch this, he said. The film stayed with me for days. It was a Brillo pad for my eyes.

. . .

Miguel and I were stoned. We stood outside the apartment. What are you looking for, Miguel asked. Did he really want to know, or did he only ask because he was stoned? I wasn't sure how he'd react. He had been so generous the entire evening. A boy I fell in love with when I was twelve, I said. I laughed. As soon as I said it I wanted to take it back. Miguel stood looking at me, his eyes hidden in the shadows. The December air was cold. It gathered in crystals around our mouths. I heard cows mooing in the distance. Did he love you, Miguel asked. I'm not sure, I said. So why can't you find him, he asked. You know how it is, I said. People change. Maybe he's bald. Miguel laughed. And I have _____ now. I'd be lost without him, I said.

. . .

I spend long hours at my laptop, writing. It has its price. I have bad posture. I'm a candidate for carpal tunnel surgery. I write to keep my friends alive. If I immortalize them on the page, they will exist forever. I no longer do many of the things I used to do. I don't stay up for days at a time. I stopped doing hard drugs. I still drink, but only in controlled amounts. I was bored with life. Miguel wore a beanie and muttonchops. He was at least a dozen years younger than me, born in 1981 or 1982. I didn't tell him I was bored with life. He was still young, and that's a terrible thing to say to a young person.

. . .

I sat at my desk and googled Jaime Valencia. I scanned the images. It was a few days after I'd visited Victoria and Miguel at their apartment on the edge of the city. None of the thumbnails on the screen matched my idea of who he was now. Valencia had completely disappeared. He'd become fully digitized.

. . .

My father sold the house I grew up in. He moved far away. I drove by the house six months ago. The room I'd slept in as a child had foil on the windows. There were cars in the drive. I didn't recognize any of them. The carob tree I had climbed as a child had died. Its dried bones stood against a house I no longer recognized. Without its leaves it looked naked and lonely. My father planted the carob tree the year I was born. Its trunk was the thickness of his index finger. It grew as I grew. Piñatas hung from its limbs as siblings and cousins grew older. We swung at the piñatas until they exploded, the contents of their bellies spilling onto the grass. The soil under the tree looked hard and unforgiving, unable to bear fruit. I could no longer imagine children playing under the safety of the carob tree's limbs on a Saturday afternoon. We think we know what we want, but we don't. Our hearts are empty, and our eyes lie to us.

I prefer Paris

Writers have a nasty habit of killing themselves. They enjoy committing suicide in hotels, apparently. Leave the mess for someone else to clean. It's a selfish gesture. Then again, I understand the attraction. It's nice to spend one's final days among clean towels and fresh soaps. A few souls for whom the light was left on –

. . .

Oscar Wilde, Hôtel d'Alsace, Paris, 1900
Dylan Thomas, Hotel Chelsea, New York City, 1953
Sadegh Hedayat, rented apartment, Paris, 1951
Walter Benjamin, Hotel de Francia, Portbou, 1940
Charles R. Jackson, Hotel Chelsea, New York City, 1968

. . .

The Hotel Chelsea is a popular place to kill oneself if one is a writer. It's a bit too predictable and dramatic for my taste. I don't want to die in the United States. I prefer Paris. Hotel Mistral has a nice ring to it. I'll check in with a copy of *Nausea* tucked under my arm.

. . .

The actor George Sanders checked into a hotel in Castelldefels, near Barcelona, and gobbled Nembutals like Tic Tacs. Like most creative types, he left a note. Artists are uncomfortable with silence.

. . .

Dear World, I am leaving because I am bored. I feel I have lived long enough. I am leaving you with your worries in this sweet cesspool. Good luck.

. . .

Snappy and cheerful. The Brits have a wonderful sense of humor, even when they are sad.

The arclight

I met my other half at the beginning of the new century. It was a very difficult time for America. The artificial bubble of the housing market had popped. The collapse of a questionable capitalist economy was tearing the country apart one foreclosure at a time. People were losing their homes. Middle class folks walked away from mortgages. Squatters set up camp in million dollar tract mansions. The American idea of measuring success through home ownership seemed ridiculous, as if square footing were the true measure of a man. I lived in an apartment. I owned few possessions. My books made up the bulk of my material wealth.

. . .

I met him online. It was a digital romance, yet everything was real and true. Our first dinner was at a Chinese restaurant. It wasn't at all awkward. I couldn't hear a word he said. Our table was in an unfortunate location. The din from the kitchen drowned him out. He moved his lips. I nodded. He may have said *I intend to kill your mother*, for all I know. I agreed. He called twice, then a third time. That hadn't happened before. He moved in a week later. I was in a daze. It was a very wonderful time. Meanwhile, fortunes collapsed. Beautiful homes that had once sustained green lawns had become ghost boxes. They dotted the arid landscape like brown pearls. Billionaire liars committed suicide on a weekly basis. It was a godlike form of trickle-down population control. I watched the horizon. I gleefully awaited the apocalypse. My other half and I went to several movies. We thought the end was near. I relished the cool darkness of the theater. I didn't own a house. I don't have children. The popcorn stains on my shirt were reparable. What was there to lose? I had my other half at my side. For twenty dollars we owned the inside of a movie theater for two hours. We enjoyed the final hours of old Hollywood while the world ended outside the theater doors.

Dumpster kicker

I was on my way to cultivating a serious meth habit. This was a few years after the collapse of the Twin Towers. I was thirty-three. I lived in a fourplex in a small desert town. The town looked as if it had recently suffered a nuclear blast. Midwesterners with irradiated brains had taken over. People voted Republican. Motorists drove slowly. They talked even slower. Meth heads and crack heads slept on sidewalks. They slept under the zinc shelter of bus stops. Mexicans were shot at the border. The sheriff was interviewed on the local news station about the shootings. Population control, he said. I lived in Zombietown. I was quickly becoming a Zombie.

. . .

My nephew was seventeen. He was born in 1986. He was half my age. He was the son of paper sister 1965. I was very close to him. We had done drugs together. Doing drugs with someone creates a closeness that is different from other relationships. I felt guilty about doing meth with him, but not guilty enough to stop. I figured it was better for him to get high with me than get high with a stranger.

. . .

A large brick fireplace sat under the veranda of the four-plex. The fireplace was for decoration. It wasn't intended for actual use. The bricks it was made of were real. Why not, I thought. It looked stupid and lonely. My nephew and I were high. It was a cold evening in December. Uncovered plants had withered and died. Unpicked oranges hung from skeletal limbs like shrunken heads. It was very cold outside. The desert is a place of extremes. It can be seventy-five degrees in the daytime and thirty degrees at night. One adjusts to the bipolar weather. We walked to Circle K. It was located a few blocks from my apartment. Firewood was stacked outside near the door. We took several pieces of firewood without paying for it. We ran back to my apartment, treated wood under our arms, and loaded it into the fireplace. The logs had been pretreated with an accelerant. I struck a few Diamond matches and placed them below the logs. The wood caught quickly and we were soon warm. We talked and laughed and made a general nuisance of ourselves. It was somewhere south of two in the morning. My nephew looked up. Holy shit, he said. I followed his eyes. The roof of the veranda was on fire. I grabbed the garden hose. It was wound in a neat tight coil against the wall. I was laughing so hard I couldn't turn the spigot. My nephew twisted the spigot and sprayed the roof with water. We caught it in time. The veranda sustained minimal damage.

. . .

A homosexual obsessed with Stevie Nicks lived next door to me. He was in his mid-thirties. He was short, balding and tubby. I never bothered learning his name. He worked for a janitorial service. He cleaned offices at night. He lived alone. In the middle of the afternoon the smell of nag champa drifted from his apartment. He smoked marijuana. He'd invited me over one evening and I got high with him. He put *Bella Donna* on an old turntable. He pranced around the room in a Kmart shawl. I was slumped in a secondhand chair wondering what had happened to my spine when I felt his hands tugging at my belt. I laughed and said I gotta go. I stood up and left. He didn't mention it when I saw him a few days later. I said hello. I was cordial. But I didn't like his wandering hands and his greasy, thrift store ways. Sometimes we want to be owned and sometimes we don't.

. . .

Keep it down, I said. You'll wake the neighbors. My nephew laughed. What neighbors, he said. Stevie Nicks poked his head out of his apartment door. He looked like a sequined turtle. Disaster averted, my nephew rolled up the hose and sat next to me. What's going on? Stevie asked. I laughed. Go back inside, my nephew said. My neighbor stepped outside his door. What's going on out here? When he saw my nephew his eyes lit up like cubic zirconia. Nunya, my nephew said. We laughed as he minced his way toward us. He pulled up a chair and sat next to my nephew. Want to get high, he said. Stevie fished in his robe. A moment later a fat joint materialized in his hand. He's only seventeen, I said. That's ok, honey. I'm not going to molest him. My nephew laughed. Who's your little friend? My nephew, I said. I didn't mention names. I didn't want to give Stevie anything as concrete as a name.

. . .

Sorry about the noise, I said. We passed the joint around. That's ok, dear. I don't have to work tomorrow. Uncle, can you grab us another beer? I momentarily left my nephew with Bella Donna. I didn't think it was a good idea to leave a child on the edge of seventeen with a fusty old queen, but I was stoned and I was in a forgiving mood. You want one? I asked Stevie as I opened my apartment door. Oh no, dear. I get gassy when I drink beer. My nephew's laughter splintered the darkness.

. . .

Methamphetamine is a loving woman who whispers in your ear as she twists a knife in your back. She shows you things, impossible things. My nephew and I once tried putting a motorcycle together in a hot garage using a million parts we had spread out on the floor. Somewhere around six a.m. we threw in the towel. Neither of us wanted to believe the failure at our feet. I collapsed on a sofa under the air conditioning in my sister's house. I slept until it was time to find more meth. That meant cars, streets, and driving through dangerous neighborhoods, all while maintaining the appearance of sobriety. I would sometimes let my nephew drive, but those occasions were rare. He was young and his reckless driving made me nervous. I didn't want the police involved. I usually drove while he made his presence known in other ways. One of his favorite things to do was shoot marbles at windows using a wrist rocket. You're going to get us arrested, I said. He'd laugh and load another marble. Occasionally lights would illuminate a house that only moments earlier had been a dark quiet box. I would drive faster, stoplights only a suggestion. My nephew laughed as we blew through stoplights. Brakes screeched and horns honked. I finished my beer and tossed the empty bottle in the back seat. My nephew finished his beer and whisked the empty bottle onto the asphalt. Why are you always so loud, I said. Chill out, uncle. You're worse than an old woman.

. . .

I was arrested for possession of psilocybin in May of 2004. It was a Friday night. Psilocybin is better known by its street name, mushrooms. In the State of California in 2004, possession of psilocybin meant possession of a controlled substance, in violation of Health and Safety Code section 11377(a). To wit, a felony. This happened in the County of Los Angeles. Los Angeles is not the best place to get arrested. I had twenty-eight grams of psilocybin on or near my person, in addition to the methamphetamine traveling through my body. My skin was flushed and I felt hot. I needed to shit but couldn't find a decent place to do so. It was shaping up to be a bad night.

. . .

My nephew and I drove from Río Seco to California to visit my friend Donald. Donald lived in Glendale. I was in my early thirties. Donald was a year younger. My nephew was not yet legal. We arrived at Donald's parents' house. The porch light was on. Dusk floated on the horizon in the distance. I wanted a beer. You have the shrooms? Donald asked. Yes, I said. I wanted to unwind, cast out to sea. Driving for six hours on meth is like riding in a boxcar filled with acetylene tanks. Something bad is bound to happen. I wanted to drift, sit on a lawn chair under the stars with a beer in my hand. Donald was anxious to begin the evening. I need to drop a few turtles in the pond, I said. Hurry up, he said. I said hello to his parents, introduced my nephew, excused myself, went to the bathroom, took a shit, noticed my penis had almost completely disappeared into itself, removed a small Ziploc from my pocket, and did another bump of meth. I heard echoes of chatter throughout the house. I felt very old. Our plans are stupid and often amount to nothing.

. . .

We walked to Carr Park. Donald and I were familiar with Carr Park. The night breathed heavily against our backs. A breeze caressed the back of my neck. Cars passed us on the street. A few horns honked. A hooker and a john discussed politics in front of a liquor store. Transactions were made, lives were bought and sold. I had half an ounce – fourteen grams – of psilocybin on my person. The other half was in the trunk of my car. I pulled a second Ziploc from my jeans pocket. I unzipped it. Donald and my nephew ate mushrooms in the dark under a tree. I fingered a few caps and stems. I ate them. The popcorn sugar stink needled its way into my teeth. I drank from a bottle of orange juice to mask the taste. I needed sugar. I felt weak. We found a park bench. I sat on the table top next to my nephew. My jeans were dirty. I wasn't completely sure I'd wiped my ass in Donald's parents' bathroom. A band of wire tightened around my skull. White faces floated in the darkness. They came toward me. Disembodied heads were tied to strings. What the fuck, Donald? I screamed as they came closer. Relax, man. They're just balloons. There must've been a party here earlier. I took another look. They were balloons. My nephew laughed at my stupidity. Are you feeling anything, I asked Donald. He shook his head no. I ate more psilocybin. My nephew took the Ziploc from my hands. He ate more psilocybin. Donald took the Ziploc from my nephew. He ate more psilocybin, as well. I was beginning to wonder if the kid I'd bought the mushrooms from back home had stiffed me. A three-legged black dog hobbled in the dark. I got up to investigate. It was a tricycle. I got on the tricycle. I made my way through the dark. My nephew pushed me through the cloud of balloons, a satanic congress quantifying every move I made. I laughed as the trees whispered. They were old giants. They had been there long before I was born and would likely be there long after I'd died. The veins in their leaves resembled the veins in the back of my hand. Life pulsed through us, the truth hidden just under the surface. The leaves opened their mouths in unison, a leafy chorus. You're headed down the wrong path, they said.

. . .

I was blinded by a flash of white light. Is this death? The lights pulsed and expanded into reds and blues. Malevolent orbs of light darted through the trees and surrounded us. I heard strange voices. The voices did not belong to Donald or my nephew. Tires whispered on pavement. Three cars crawled along the concrete path in the center of the park. Rude lights ignorantly blinded me. Doors opened and closed. A voice came from behind. What are you doing? Hanging out, I said. The park's closed. Fuck off. I was yanked skyward. The Big Wheel between my legs dropped to the pavement. This isn't good, I thought. God smells like cheap cologne. Someone twisted my arm behind my back. I resisted.

The prick wanted a fight. What the fuck, man? I kicked out behind me. I connected with a solid object. I was slammed onto the pavement. A moment later I found myself in the back of a squad car.

. . .

I tried committing suicide in jail. I couldn't. They took away my shoestrings. I wore jailhouse slippers. My bed was a sliver of foam. A green sheet was stretched over it. I had a bottom bunk. The sheet would not slide through the metal slats of the top bunk. The slats were tightly woven together. The County of Los Angeles had thought of everything. I was arrested on a Friday night. I was processed. Friday night bled into Saturday morning. Judges weren't available on weekends. I would see the judge on Monday. Night bled into day, day hovered over morning, and morning became night again. I shared a cell with five other males. I could not sleep. I did not look at anyone. I did not talk. I did not piss or shit. I did not shower. I kept everything to myself. I folded my head between my legs. I ate like an animal. I didn't look up from my plate. I tried determining the time of day by what was served. I could not. Were peaches a breakfast food or a lunch item? The cell was filled with bright light. The bright light was always on. A series of naked bulbs were encased in a metal cage, an impenetrable colander. I lost track of time. My body began to stink as I came down off the meth and psilocybin. A young man gravitated toward me. He was white and I was white. He was sick with drugs. I moved away from him. He stepped closer. I didn't want any problems. I had my own shit to bury. I called my father collect in Río Seco. He didn't have any money. He said what kind of bird doesn't fly? I wasn't prepared for questions. A jailbird, he said. I thought of my mother, my biological mother. My hatred bubbled to the surface. Why didn't she scrape me from the womb when she had the chance? I wanted to fill negative space. I wanted to disappear. I counted the slats of the top bunk. There were 178. 178 divided by 2 is 89. I counted them again, backwards. I sensed a slight tremor in one of my eyelids. My body wanted to release the poisons stored inside of it. I resisted. I kept counting. The metal slats were coated in grey-green plastic. We don't want you killing yourself in here, they said. The young man eventually fell asleep. I moved away from him.

. . .

The judge was Jewish. He saw my name but he did not *see my name*. God bless your people, I thought. The transmigration of souls is a felony act in the State of California, son. It comes with a $10,000 fine. Pay your tab. Next!

. . .

I was a first-time offender with no priors. The State of California offered me a 1000 P.C., which is a deferred entry of judgment. My criminal record would be expunged. My name would not have a felony attached to it. My life would continue. All I had to do was close out my tab and follow the rules. Donald scraped up $2000. His brother came up with another $1000. His aunt donated a hefty amount. I borrowed from my 401k to pay my attorney. I wouldn't be buying a house after all.

. . .

I was placed on probation for two years. I attended substance abuse classes. My attendance was required. I pissed in a cup twice a week, then once a week, then once every other week. I did this for one year. Most of the people in my substance abuse classes were kids, twenty-somethings adrift at sea and without a captain. People attended classes. They got better. They graduated. I was often the oldest person in a constantly-changing class, though not always. They called me the Mushroom Man. I laughed at my nickname. I had no anger. I earned a certificate. It looked very similar to my master's degree. I said goodbye to my classmates. I paid off my attorney. He had a nice office in Encino. I still smoked marijuana on occasion, but I stayed away from the meth.

. . .

My nephew said he had to stay clean for a while. I understood. His mother was not pleased. California was a bad dream, the jail cell a reminder of everything my brother Andrew had lost. My nephew burned a CD for me. I still have it. I cannot listen to it. If I play it in the car all the bad memories come rushing back.

. . .

We were outside my sister's house. I'd been meth-free for three days. The car's air conditioning pushed against the heat. My body felt metallic inside my clothes. My jeans stank. I hugged my nephew over the gear shift. I didn't want to go inside. I didn't want to face my sister. What will you do, I asked. I've got to get out of here, Uncle. This place is fucking nadaville. I thought of the times I'd pushed a broom through a Circle K parking lot at three in the morning, my dreams corralled by the tumbleweeds slowly closing in on me. I gave my notice. On my last night on the job I filled my gas tank and stole a bottle of Captain Morgan. I put the bottle in the passenger seat and drove home as the sun broke through the clouds. I hid the bottle in my pants as I crept past my mother. She was asleep on the couch. I got drunk in my bedroom. I didn't have to work the next day. It was a high like no other. Pink rays of sunlight announced a new day was blossoming beyond my window. What would I do for money? The thought passed as I sipped rum from a Dixie cup. I listened to my mother breathing in the living room. My records sat silent in the closet, my turntable gathered dust. Posters of bands curled away from thumbtacks, the members of Guns N' Roses attempting to escape the tiny prison of my room. I have to get out of here, I thought. This place is fucking nadaville. Wind blew against the side of the house. Dust fingered its way through the windows. I took another sip of rum and stared at the feet on the end of my dumb legs. Why was the world so ugly and unknowable?

. . .

It was four in the morning. We were coming down. In another hour the sun would break through the dark river of the world. We went into the garage and fished out two broken lawn chairs. We walked along the side of the house with the chairs folded against our hips. We made our way to the backyard. My nephew found an extension ladder. He propped it against the eaves of the roof. He climbed first. I followed. Once we were on the roof we found a spot that drifted over the slab of the back porch. I walked lightly. I didn't want to wake my sister. We pulled our chairs open and sat under the stars. My nephew sat to my left. He named the stars as I threaded them together in a spectral web. He told me his dreams, what he would do with his life. They were bold statements.

. . .

It was a Saturday night. I couldn't find my nephew. I called my nephew's mobile. It rang and rang until finally it went to voicemail. My youngest brother sold high quality marijuana. I drove to my brother's house on the far side of town. My youngest brother was my father's son and my stepmother's son. He lived with his wife. They had two daughters. My brother was not home but there was a car in the drive. A dark figure sat on a chair near the car. I recognized the car. It belonged to one of my brother's friends, a boy named Jeff. Jeff was born in 1982. He was close to my brother's age. I was a dozen years older. It was early February. The nights were still cold. I wore a Buffalo shirt and an old pair of jeans. I opened my door and stepped out of my car. Jeff said hello. I'm waiting for your brother, he said. He went to the store. They'll be back soon, he said. Jeff was handsome but he was twenty-two and I was thirty-four. We didn't have much in common. Perhaps this wasn't entirely true. He liked old cars. I did, too. We both smoked marijuana. I sat on the table top of an old park bench. Jeff moved from his chair. He sat next to me. I scanned the darkness of my brother's backyard.

. . .

My baby brother was always acquiring and selling things. He'd owned a dozen cars in his short life. A few of them sat rusting in the backyard. Jeff asked if I wanted to drive somewhere to get high. I'll drive, he said. Sure, I said. We got into his car. It was a black 1971 Monte Carlo SS. Jeff had restored it from the ground up in his father's garage. His father had helped. Jeff turned the ignition. A throaty rumble announced Jeff's presence. A stereo clicked and whirred. We drove through my brother's neighborhood until we found a cul-de-sac. Several houses on the street were under construction. The stick figure houses cast ominous silhouettes in the cold winter moonlight. The interior of Jeff's car was warm. He loaded a fresh bowl into a glass pipe. He handed it to me. Jeff knew I was queer. My brother told me he thought Jeff was queer, too, but Jeff wouldn't admit it. I understood the pain. I also understood hiding it was worse. I pulled the smoke deeply into my lungs. I passed the pipe to Jeff. I closed my eyes, drifted, and exhaled. Jeff slowly breathed through his mouth. He passed the pipe back to me. We sat in his car for ten minutes getting stoned. Jeff wore black jeans and an old bomber jacket. The steering wheel was ridiculously large and authoritative. The center console separated us. The engine coughed and rumbled like an old bulldog. The bare studs in the stick houses vibrated in their tentative foundations. Jeff's hands hung loosely at his sides. He seemed to be waiting for something. We should head back, I said. My brother is probably home by now. You're probably right, Jeff said. There was a muffled sadness in his voice. He put the car in reverse and carefully backed out of the cul-de-sac. He made a sharp left. We drove down the dark street. The houses farthest from the cul-de-sac were occupied. The blue light of television screens flickered in windows. We arrived at my brother's house. My brother's truck was parked next to my car. You lost your parking space, I said. Jeff laughed.

Wouldn't be the first thing I ever lost, he said. A pile of groceries sat on the kitchen counter. Where have you girls been, my brother said. Your brother was blowing me in a church parking lot, Jeff said. My brother laughed. I don't think so, he said. He's got higher standards than that. Jeff laughed and shook my brother's hand. Maybe so, he said.

. . .

I miss my nephew's voice. I don't see him much these days. We say hello at the occasional wedding or funeral. He has a girlfriend, an apartment, a job. He's been clean for ten years. Stevie would say children get older, and I'm getting older too. Perhaps it's for the best. As we grow older the need to sequester ourselves becomes more apparent. I tire of my own voice. I turn the mirror facedown. I shut off the lights. The curtains speak to me. I practice my perfection of silence. I enjoy sitting in the dark, the noise of a ceiling fan over my head. In the dark I can't see my face in the mirror. I can become someone else.

. . .

I began experiencing headaches. They lasted from the time I got out of bed until the evening sun colored the mountains of Río Seco pink and purple. Aspirin didn't help. I tried caffeine but it only burned small holes in my stomach. I was alone in bed. I pulled the covers over me. Something pulled them away from me. I sensed a presence directly behind me. When it wasn't directly behind me it was slightly to my right. When I moved it moved. It mimicked my exact body posture, location and position. I tried opening my mouth to scare it away with my voice, but my mouth wouldn't open. My eyes turned against me. When I closed them fireworks exploded against black velvet. When I opened them tracers streaked across my peripheral vision. The headaches were so powerful my eyes throbbed with the pressure of each heartbeat. At times they would become so irritated I wanted nothing more than to pluck them out. The presence watched me from a dark corner of the bedroom closet. It laughed at me. It grunted like a depraved child. It slowly compressed into a black ball and moved under the bed. It breathed as I did. I did not look under the bed. I knew I would die if I did. It's the meth, I told myself. It's just the meth.

. . .

I come down. I feel the earth beneath my feet. I'm not sure I recognize the view. I miss the lawn chairs on the roof. I miss the sky filled with stars whose names I can't remember. I miss my nephew sitting to my left. I cover my eyes. I fail to summon the darkness. There is only pink and purple. It's the blood surging through my fingers. Our cities are too bright. We've lost our ability to see the stars, to make our way in the dark. We have turned away from God, and He is punishing us.

Piss poor

I was a boy of eight. It was the gauzy days of the late Seventies, around the time Jim Jones permanently closed down Jonestown. My stepmother enrolled me in Boy Scouts. I lasted two weeks. I didn't like uniforms. I didn't like crowds. I didn't like taking orders. I would have made a piss poor German.

. . .

Benny Valdez and I spent many summer days at the wrecking yard. He was my friend. We were the same age. We didn't go to school together. My parents were friendly with his parents. It was a friendship by association, not school or geography. Benny spent a summer with my family in 1984. We were fourteen. His mother was having difficulty with her teenage daughter. Having Benny out of the picture allowed her to focus on her daughter. The summer of 1984 was much different from the summer of 1978. When a boy is eight, the world is an unopened letter. When a boy is fourteen, the letter has already been post-marked. Some letters are best left unsent.

. . .

Summer 1978. Bob Crane was murdered in his low-rent apartment in Scottsdale, caught up in a weird sex triangle that somehow went terribly wrong. My father often left us alone. It was necessary. Someone had to man the office while he recovered an abandoned or repossessed vehicle. You boys watch the office, he'd say. Afraid of being left alone in a bad neighborhood, Benny and I closed the gate. We hitched the chain around the post and clicked the Master Lock closed. It would only take a few moments to unlock the gate and swing it open once my father returned. With the gate locked, we stepped into the safety of the small office. Fluorescent lights hummed above our heads. I clicked the office door closed. A deadbolt protected us from the outside world. We viewed the danger through safety glass. A sticker adhered to the glass near the top of the door frame read –

. . .

THIS DOOR TO REMAIN UNLOCKED DURING BUSINESS HOURS

. . .

Outside, dark thoughts gathered around the small office building. My father's business was located in an industrial area. Automobiles were seldom seen after business hours. The fluorescent lighting gave everything in the office an unnatural tint. I enjoyed the humming. It was a reliable soundtrack. Can I have a Dr Pepper, Benny asked. I opened my father's desk drawer. He kept change in a small tin. He also kept a Colt .38 Special in his desk. The revolver was always loaded. I handed Benny the change. On a bureau next to the Coke machine sat an honesty snack box. There was a coin slot in the paperboard. I ate snacks from the box while my father was out of the office. I never paid for them. The vendor continued filling the box every two weeks. I assume my father paid for the missing snacks without saying a word.

. . .

Benny and I would roam the wrecking yard, free range ragamuffins awaiting my father's return. Dusk would be upon us. We were two boys traversing a river of dead metal. With the gate locked and the phone in the office, we were free to roam without supervision, not an adult in sight. All the cars on my father's lot had once been showroom new. It seemed impossible. The cars came alive as we walked among them, waking from a coma induced by invisible gods. What happened to the people who had owned these cars? Where were they now? How many lives had been lost? How many children abandoned by a roadside?

. . .

One of my favorite cars sat in the northeast corner of the yard, along the fence line near the office. My father was in the office with Uncle Alvin, drinking away another day of oil and metal. I sat behind the wheel of an old Sunbeam convertible, half-hidden among tall shoots of dead grass. There was a crack in the windshield on the passenger side. The soft-top had lost the fight to the elements. This is my favorite car, I said. Can I sit there, Benny asked, his finger indicating the driver's seat. I nodded yes. The Sunbeam's tires were flat. The wheels had been marked by Mocha and Cinnamon, our Dobermans. My dad says the British don't know how to make a good car, I said. Looks good to me, Benny said. I sat in the passenger seat next to my friend. We were still young enough to make the *bbbbbbbbrrrrrrr-*

rrrbbbbbbbb sound while driving. Benny's hands were firmly on the wheel. Night was falling. The dogs were restless. The shifter knob separated us. As we sat in the cracked seats of the old Sunbeam it began to rain. Fat drops rolled down the face of the dusty windshield. The rain was unexpected, like flowers growing in a junkyard. The rain came down hard. It soaked our hair, our clothes. We exited the car and ran toward the back door of the office. Mocha and Cinnamon proved to be much smarter than us. They were huddled in the blanketed safety of their plywood pens.

. . .

We sat in the safety of the office. We ate candy from the honesty box. We didn't pay for the candy. The rain came down harder. The office lights flickered. Someone in the rain pounded their fists against the glass door. Benny and I peered through the glass. A black-haired Navajo woman stood outside the door. She saw us through the glass. She began yelling at us. She tugged at the locked door handle. She was crying in the rain. The dogs barked at her through the gate. They angrily pushed their snouts toward her through the chain link. Let them go, she said. They want to be free! She motioned a hand toward the dogs. Let them go! She momentarily disappeared from view. I pushed my forehead against the glass. The woman grabbed the gate and began shaking it violently. The vibrating razor wire sliced through the rain. Mocha and Cinnamon threw themselves upon the gate with such force I thought it might come down. The woman began screaming at the dogs. You should be free, she said. You should be free! What does she want, Benny asked. I don't know, I said. I think she's drunk, I said. The dogs continued barking with shredded ferocity. I imagined their throats torn open. After a crackle of lightning the electricity went off. The asphalt of the parking lot was a black sea. The dogs continued barking in the darkness. The sound traveled from the southern corner of the lot. The woman had moved on, the dogs following her along the fence line until she disappeared.

. . .

Benny and I moved about the wrecking yard in the lazy sunlight of summer days. We were young explorers, discovering and naming continents. The only restroom on the premises was in the office. We searched through the blue and green glass in the old wooden garage that sat against the back fence of the wrecking yard. The garage smelled of oil, raw wood and gasoline, a varnish-like scent I still associate with my father. We found an old one-gallon wide-mouth glass jar. We fashioned a urinal from it. With some difficulty, we unscrewed the rusted brown lid off the jar. We placed the jar on the ground. We nestled it between fenders, quarter panels and drive shafts propped against the side of the garage. Old wheels were scattered about, thistle poking through the hubs. Glossy black widows thrived in the semi-darkness under the wheels. We unzipped and pissed in the jar. We were not shy in the least – the weird closeness of children. Crossing streams, the sound of piss hitting the glass. The simple joy of pissing in an old jar, our backs turned against the office. I don't believe it was sexual in any way. Life eventually becomes much more complicated, but the complications are unnecessary.

. . .

In my late teens I read a passage from a book by Pier Paolo Pasolini. I was seventeen or eighteen. I don't remember the name of the book. Reading the prose felt like home. Pasolini described boys pissing together in the squalor of an old shack dirtied by peasants. The scent of the shared urine brought the narrator a sense of sexual gratification, a desire he dared not name in the presence of the other boys. I remembered the old glass jar Benny and I had pissed in at the wrecking yard among quarter panels and milkweed. Hidden from view among radiators and returnable glass bottles, an adult would've had difficulty finding such an item among the accordioned metal of the wrecking yard. But Benny and I knew it was there.

. . .

Benny spent a summer with my family in 1984. We were fourteen. His mother was going through a difficult time with her daughter. She needed mental space to sort things out. Benny moved in with us, a duffel bag his only connection to the past. His feet were larger than mine, his hair kinkier. He had grown through the years, his chin speckled with soft black hair. I'd hardly grown at all, an unrealized idea. Rather than grow, I shrank. I stayed in my room. I read books. I listened to music. I preferred silence.

. . .

Summer 1984. Benny helped my father at the wrecking yard. We stripped cars. We removed parts for customers. Our hands were strong enough to turn ratchets. We were older. Like Benny, the wrecking yard changed. It was no longer the one-and-a-half acre lot of the late Seventies.

It was now a three-acre yard on the west side of town. I preferred the small salvage lot tucked in the industrial area near the greyhound racetrack. A smaller lot meant fewer cars, fewer people. Puss N' Boots was within walking distance. Joe Torelli owned Puss N' Boots. He was my father's friend. I liked him. Call me Uncle Joe, he said. I didn't really have an uncle, other than Uncle Alvin, and Uncle Alvin was crazy.

. . .

I have a few photographs from the summer of 1984. In one, Benny sits posing on a lawn chair; his arms in a he-man pose. My brother Andrew makes rabbit ears behind Benny's head with his fingers. It's either a barbeque or a birthday party. Benny wears shorts. He has the well-toned legs of a football player. In another photo I am fishing near a lake, a small boat slightly out of frame and to the left. Benny has an arm around me. I hold a fishing pole. The photo is dated May 1984. I look very small next to Benny.

. . .

Benny and I still pissed together when we were fourteen, but it was different. We turned at a slight angle toward the rusted hubs of old cars, our backs to each other. The piss jar was long gone. Fourteen is a difficult time in one's life. There are more questions than answers. I didn't much care for Benny anymore. I couldn't say why. When one is fourteen one is already preparing for death. We turn away from true friendship. We move through a world of decay. We turn our back on nature, and nature turns her back on us.

. . .

Benny Valdez is lost to me. I have only the memory of him now. The last time I saw him was a little over ten years ago. He was married. He had two children. He introduced me to his wife. She looked at me as if inspecting a head of lettuce in a grocery store.

. . .

I'm pissing in the urinal at work. I'm alone. The piss cake at the bottom of the urinal sanitizes the humanity from the restroom. Instead of pissing among the weeds at the wrecking yard, I find myself pissing in the most clinical of settings. The bathroom has one urinal and multiple stalls. There is no sense of camaraderie. I cannot summon Benny's face as I piss in the urinal. Does he remember our piss jar? Or does family life – a wife, children and a mortgage – cancel such things out? When men piss together a sense of trust develops. The public urinal has robbed us of this trust. Stalls, fluorescent lighting, automated flushers – all these things have contributed to a newfound sense of unease. When men stand apart, even in the simple act of pissing, the system collapses. We have slowly become us and them. It appears to be irreversible. If only we learned how to piss properly again, how to piss without embarrassment or fear, the world would be set right again. Wars would end. Hunger would be but a distant memory. Arguments over a dusty scrap of land would halt. Urinals and piss cakes perpetuate hatred and artifice, a separation from the tribe. They rob us of our humanity. Pasolini knew this, Grass knew this. Great men write eternal words, yet no one heeds them. Surely we must see everything is connected?

The haunted Coke machine

I hold a photograph in my hand. I am eight years old in the photo. I'm very thin. My face is smudged with dirt. I wear a T-shirt, jeans, and shoes with paper-thin soles. I am in an office. To the left of me, leaning against a honey-colored wall, is a fifty pound bag of dog food. The bag is nearly as tall as I am. The food is for Mocha and Cinnamon, our guard dogs. They are Doberman pinschers. My father named them. I associated their names with flavors. As I grew older it became apparent the names were based on colors. It seemed logical that my father knew the word cinnamon, but mocha sounded foreign in my mouth and his. *Who was this man?* My father was born in a small town in Arkansas. I later reckoned a man intelligent enough to run his own business must know several words, even words I would find surprising. I now understand he knows much more than I do. His hands know the parts of a car. His fingers hover over a plank of fresh wood. He understands how to work it, how to drive nails into it. He runs wood through a table saw. He builds things that didn't exist before. I don't have this gift. My hands know a keyboard. This is my only talent. I'm also a good reader, though sometimes even this is suspect. I lie in bed. The troubles of the day are behind me. I drift in and out. I forget who I am. The bed dissolves and the pages no longer speak to me.

. . .

Bob Crane was murdered in a city eleven miles east of the city of my birth. I was eight. I watched the news report on a Trinitron. I read grainy murder magazines with names like *True Crime* and *Master Detective*. I read DC comics. I liked the darker ones. My favorites were *The House of Mystery* and *The House of Secrets*. I drank Coke and gobbled Spanish peanuts like Benzedrine. I was very small, a black-haired kid with dark eyes. I was invisible. I found this preferable to being noticed. I sat at a bar with old drunks. I listened to their stories. I memorized them without taking notes. I looked like a normal boy.

. . .

I spent weekdays at school. I spent weeknights and weekends with my father. My father picked me up after school. He sat in his tow truck, waiting for me near the crosswalk. Day bled into night. The wrecking yard felt like home. I liked the sea of black cars. I stood on the roof of a car. I held my hand over my eyes like a sea captain. Cars stretched for miles, obliterating the earth. I spent many nights in a tow truck. My father drove through town. I sat in the passenger seat. Sometimes the police called my father. We drove to accident scenes. We towed away the mangled car. The bodies were already gone. We picked up abandoned cars at the bus station. My father had a contract with the city. Sometimes a motorist was stranded. Their car was not cooperating. They looked in the Yellow Pages. One call, that's all. My father wrote down the address. We found the motorist, usually in a phone booth or sitting inside their car. They were always happy to see us. I liked rainy nights best, when colors ran down the windshield like melted crayons.

. . .

When the day was over and the gates were closed my father said I had a good day. A few customers tried to Jew me down. It was a sentence he said often. I didn't fully understand its meaning. I was eight. A man on the street said if you're born in the United States you're a racist. I was twenty-one. I was walking on a sidewalk in Chicago. He looked at me when he said it. He tried handing me a flyer. Fuck you, I said. The man was right. It took me a few years to learn this.

. . .

An old city bus sat deep in the bowels of the wrecking yard. The Dobermans crawled under it in the heat of the day. Usually they were in their pens. Sometimes we let them roam free during business hours. My father kept pornography ransacked from abandoned cars in the bus. There were piles of clothing, dishes, family photos, transistor radios, pots and pans, LPs, eight-track tapes. Everything was neatly labeled in my father's careful hand and waiting to be claimed. My father kept valuables in a closet in the office. Titles, jewelry, silver and gold coins. Drivers' licenses and identification cards. An impossibly luxurious fur coat. On a shelf next to a safe sat a cigar box. I pulled it down and stuck my nose in it. Inside greasy plastic baggies, fingers of tight plants whose smell bled through the plastic. It was marijuana. Did my uncle smoke it? Did my father get stoned with my uncle? Would they allow me to? I had to stretch high to reach the box, all my weight on my toes. I guessed the answer was no. The smell stayed in my mind long after I placed the box back on the shelf and closed the closet door. I drank my root beer. I ate my free honesty snacks.

I watched the adults make asses of themselves. The more my father and uncle drank, the more they loved each other. Was love so easily acquired from a can or bottle? If that were the case, liquor stores were temples and 7-Elevens were drive-through chapels. I watched television on a small set in the office as my father and uncle recalled times when they were much younger and women could be plucked like grapes from the vine.

. . .

I was bored. I watched an *Ironside* rerun. Can I have money for the Coke machine? A vending machine placed by Coca-Cola stood in the office against a wall. I was generally a Coke boy though sometimes I drank Dr Pepper. There were times when I'd push the Dr Pepper button and a Barq's Root Beer would be dispensed. This wasn't as upsetting as having a Tab come out. I was convinced the Coke machine was haunted. An evil spirit inside the machine wasn't cooperating, giving me Tab when I wanted Coke. I kicked the machine violently, my Chuck Taylors communicating my anger. It felt good, but I'd still be left holding a Tab in my hand.

. . .

In 1978 a can of Coke cost thirty-five cents. My father usually limited me to one Coke a day. On nights when he was drinking at the bar he'd let me have as many Cokes as I wanted. I sat and watched the television above the bar. The old men at the bar thought nothing of it. One of my father's favorite bars was Puss N' Boots on Washington Street. It was within stumbling distance of the wrecking yard. My father and the owner Joe Torelli were friends. When I sat at the bar Joe filled a wooden bowl with peanuts and gave me as much Coke as I wanted. I'd watch my father talk to women, watch women dip their heads like hummingbirds toward their glasses, and watch lonely old men who sat at the end of the bar talk to no one. To this day sitting at a bar and watching television above a bar is my only sport. It's Tuesday afternoon and I'm sitting at the bar while respectable people are working. Does this make me an alcoholic?

. . .

You don't need money for that goddamned machine, boy. Uncle Alvin and my father were talking about home, home being Arkansas. I heard my father's voice in snippets. The only time I got a decent night's sleep is when it was raining and I slept in that little bedroom off my grandmother's kitchen, my father said. Listening to the rain hit the tin roof. Shit yes, my uncle said. I can't sleep a goddamned wink in this city and Marie don't understand why.

. . .

I was bored with the adults. Can I have money for a Coke? My father sat across from me on an old green sofa. It was greasy from years of exposure to asses that had rubbed against automobile parts. I could stretch from one end of it to the other and my feet would not touch the arms. The matted cushions were cold against my belly. My uncle, who was sitting at my father's desk, opened the top desk drawer and fidgeted with some papers. My father's .38 Special was in his hand. He aimed the firearm at the Coke machine and pulled the trigger. The gun went off with a crack that ripped the sky in two. I screamed. My father laughed. I felt weak.

Uncle Alvin said Boy what's wrong with you? I motioned my head toward the door. I'm going outside, I yelled. I opened the door, leaving the two adults inside the office. I decided to check on my bees. I floated away from the safety of fluorescent lighting and moved toward the white beehives in the dark. Mocha and Cinnamon greeted me, buffing my fingers with their snouts. I walked between cars and ran my hands along quarter panels. The bees were bearding around the hive entrances to cool off from the summer heat. I wanted to get away from the drunken men. I would not stay away long. Their stories were my stories. I'll share with you this small truth – all beekeepers are socialists.

Popov and pork chops

When I was nine, I clipped a picture from one of my father's *Hustler* bus magazines. I kept it folded in my wallet. My father said a man always carries a wallet. I took this to mean I too should carry a wallet. The picture I'd clipped from *Hustler* was of a nude young man. He had dark hair and dark eyes. When I was alone I'd take the picture from my wallet and stare at it. My eyes followed a trail of hair on his stomach to a feeling I didn't recognize. One day my father caught me looking at the picture. He was very disappointed. He took the picture from me. He said nothing. He did not give it back. I felt hot and slightly ill to my stomach. My father said get back to work, boy. My father often called me boy, as if he'd forgotten my name. Uncle Alvin also called me boy. Boy, what's wrong with you. Boy, you walk like a girl. Boy, you're just like your mother.

. . .

My father expanded his business. When I was ten he moved the wrecking yard from the tiny postage stamp of land near the greyhound track to a three acre lot he rented from a man named Ken Fleming. Mr. Fleming owned a hamburger stand on Seventh and Broadway called Pork Chops. Mr. Fleming was a short fat man who hitched his belt up over his navel. He had a constant bead of sweat on his upper lip. He slicked his hair back over his head. He often looked in the mirror in the office to make sure his hair was just so. He took a liking to me. He said Boy anytime you want a hamburger just tell your old man you're gonna ride your little bike down to my place and I'll cook you one. I wasn't sure why Mr. Fleming was interested in my nutritional needs but I thought it was a nice thing for an adult to say since adults rarely noticed anything that hovered a full foot below their line of vision. My father did not like Mr. Fleming. He rented the three acre lot from him because more land meant more cars, and more cars meant more money. Mr. Fleming arrived on the first of every month to collect a rent check. After he left my father always said things like goddamned queer or fucking queer and I understood it to mean being a fucking queer was a bad thing. I stopped cutting pictures from *Hustler* magazine. I watched my father walk toward his tow truck. I took mental notes. On slow days I would walk on the aisle runner between seats in the old bus and train myself how to walk like a boy. I was very small and did not play sports, so learning how to walk like a boy was important.

. . .

Oh, you came, said Mr. Fleming. It's nice to see you. Anything he wants, Mr. Fleming said to one of the cooks. I ordered a hamburger, french fries and a Coke. It was summer. It was very hot. I was ten. My bangs were stuck to my forehead from the bike ride. Teenagers hovered like wasps at bright red tables. Violence emanated from their bodies. They made me nervous. I sat at an empty table away from them. Orders up, the cook said. I approached the window. The boy behind the counter handed my food to me on a red tray. I sat at my table, dipping my fries in mustard. Mr. Fleming winked at me behind the screened window. How is it, he asked. It's good, I said. Thank you, I said. The teenagers looked through me. I was a sweaty kid on a ramshackle bicycle. What else would I be?

. . .

The year was 1980. My father moved the wrecking yard from the postage stamp lot on Washington Street to the lot he rented from Mr. Fleming on Broadway. He gained land but lost an office. The lot had a telephone pole with an aerial drop. It fed an old twelve by sixty single-wide trailer. My father brought the green sofa from the old office and placed it in the trailer. It was in very bad shape, and few customers sat on it for fear of dirtying their clothes. I missed the old office. It had a real bathroom with a real toilet. The trailer had a plastic sink and a plastic commode, and the shower didn't work. We're moving up in the world, my father said, laughing. More space to store more shit, Boy. I preferred the smaller office. It was easier to control one's environment when one had less space.

. . .

Mr. Fleming wore a button-down shirt. The collar of a white T-shirt was visible under the shirt. Mind the counter, he said. Mr. Fleming picked up my bike and placed it in the back of his truck. Get in, he said. I'll drive you back to your father's place. I thought it was very nice of Mr. Fleming to offer a ride back to my father's yard. The wrecking yard was at least two miles from Pork Chops. It wasn't a great distance, but in the heat of the summer people were less patient. Cars honked and belched. Red lights were only a suggestion. People were not very tolerant of boys flying through crosswalks on bikes. I slid my butt across Mr. Fleming's bench seat and pulled the door closed. The cab smelled of sunbaked rubber and old plastic. Mr. Fleming turned the ignition and worked the clutch. We hitched slightly forward before reversing. I looked at my bike through the back glass. It rested on the floorboards of the truck bed. It was safe. The sunlight glinted through the windshield. It set the cab of the truck on fire. Everything I touched was hot. The vinyl seats, the door frame, the metal door handle. The wind from the ride blew heat into my face. I thought of cupcakes, the heat coming off the door of a ticking oven. Mr. Fleming placed a hand on my leg. My legs were inside my jeans. I instinctively flinched. Mr. Fleming laughed. Don't worry, he said. He kneaded my leg through my jeans, slowly moving his hand toward my crotch. It will be our little secret, he said. I looked at my bike through the back glass. It was very far away. Traffic moved slowly through the streets. The asphalt was gummy and black. It shifted under my shoes when I walked on it. I felt lightheaded and slightly ill to my stomach. I want to go home, I said. You're almost there, Mr. Fleming said.

. . .

My stepmother was tired of my father's drinking. They would argue about it. He would leave, find a bar and drink some more. My father did not like arguments or confrontations. His distaste for such things colored my views. I did not like them, either. Get out, my mother said. My father obliged. My sister stayed at the house with my stepmother. My father took me with him. We packed a week's worth of clothes into a bag. We threw the bag in the back of the tow truck. We pulled out of the drive. Evelyn stood in her front yard watering her plants. My father gazed at her for a moment. She looked at him. She refocused her attention on her plants. So much for that, my father said.

. . .

I did not tell my father about the ride in Mr. Fleming's truck. I thought it was best if I kept quiet about it. I'm not sure why I decided this. My father hated Mr. Fleming. Could his hatred spill over onto me? I wasn't sure. I didn't want to find out. You're known by the company you keep, my father said. Mr. Fleming always smelled of cooking oil. His clothes were saturated in it. I didn't want his smell on me.

. . .

We moved into the twelve-by-sixty single-wide office trailer at the wrecking yard. My father was not pleased. I'll have to drive you to school once summer is over, he said. At least I'm away from that bitch, he said. I imagined my father driving me to school in the tow truck. It was better than walking, and preferable to the bus. The trailer had a small bedroom at one end, near the plastic bathroom. My father unfurled two sleeping bags and placed them on the floor. I had a small orange sleeping bag. I liked zipping myself into it. I hid from the world. The trailer squeaked and hissed, shuffling off the heat of the day. It moved under us, adjusting to the unexpected weight. I heard Mocha and Cinnamon moving beneath the trailer. Their backs brushed against the ribs of the floor. They were not used to us being at the wrecking yard after hours. I sometimes watched *The Rockford Files* on a small black and white television. It was one of several pieces of junk electronics that populated my childhood, a castoff labeled and forgotten in the back of the bus.

. . .

My father and my uncle were drunk on Popov. My little television sat on the center of a Formica table. It was propped on phone books. It was snowing in Los Angeles. Goddamned junk, my father said. He hit the side of the television. I'm hungry, I said. What do you want, boy, Uncle Alvin said. We have pork chops in the refrigerator, I said. My father poured another drink. The Popov was unadorned. No ice, no orange juice. Does that stove work, my uncle said. Yes, my father said. I'll heat up a pork chop for you, my uncle said. My uncle removed a package from the refrigerator. My father had cooked pork chops the previous evening. There were two left. My uncle turned on the gas and struck a Diamond match. There was a problem with the pilot lights. They never worked properly. May I have both of them, I asked. Why not, my uncle said. He placed both pork chops into a black skillet. I watched them sizzle from a distance. Alvin Eugene, you're up, my father said. My father poured my uncle another drink. They were playing a card game. I did not understand the game, but I liked the multicolored chips. I watched my father and my uncle, fascinated by their movements. Things came easily to them. They understood rules. They carried wallets and pocket knives. They carried little black combs in their back pockets. They spoke with a confidence I didn't have. They moved through the world and trampled it underfoot. They knew something I didn't, and they weren't letting on.

. . .

An orange fireball diverted my attention from the card game. We had forgotten the pork chops. The wood cabinet above the stove sang an awful paean to destruction. Shit, my father said. He grabbed a fire extinguisher nestled in a corner of the office and sprayed a white powder across the stove and cabinet. He fanned the powder across the flames until they were dead. My pork chops resembled two sad turtles under a blanket of snow. That was a close one, my father said. He laughed. My uncle laughed once he heard my father laugh. I'll drink to that, he said. My revised dinner consisted of honesty snacks and a can of Coke. I took the Coke from the refrigerator. The Coke machine was long gone, the lead of a .38 buried deep inside its guts.

. . .

My father and I lived at the wrecking yard for a little over a week. There were no more home cooked meals. The stove was off limits. We ate at fast food restaurants. I liked it best when my father drank at Puss N' Boots. I ordered a hamburger from the bar. I dipped thick cut fries into a mustard boat. Joe Torelli collected empty glasses from the bar. Good to see you, kid. Thank you, Uncle Joe. My father drank and talked to women. I ate my hamburger and fries and watched my father talk to women. I liked my new life. There were fewer rules. I could stay up as late as I wanted. My home was an office. My television sat above a bar. I didn't have to answer to anyone. It got old quick.

. . .

My stepmother asked my father to come home. I don't know what was said between them. We moved back home a week later. I missed my sister. I missed my bedroom. I missed my record collection. I glanced through the stack of records beneath my Emerson. Everything is back to normal, they said. I put them on and they sang to me. I bought more records, my sister said. They're for both of us, she said.

. . .

Mr. Fleming arrived on the first of the month to collect a rent check from my father. Mr. Fleming noticed the freshly-painted cabinets in the office. Oh, that looks good, he said. My father nodded. Here's your check, he said. Mr. Fleming took the check from my father. How about a burger, Mr. Fleming said. No thank you, I said. I'm not hungry. He's so polite, Mr. Fleming said. Yes he is, my father said. No problems, Mr. Fleming asked. No problems, my father said. See you next month, my father said. Mr. Fleming winked at me. Yes you will, he said.

In my bedroom

Kafka died of consumption, which is another way of saying he died of tuberculosis. He was forty. In the last photograph taken of Kafka, a slight smile plays across his lips. It's as if he knows something we don't. As he lay dying, he could barely talk. He was drowning in his own fluids.

. . .

Kafka had a sense of humor. How can one live with their parents for as long as he did and not have a sense of humor? He wrote upstairs in his bedroom at night. He made a perfunctory appearance at the insurance institute during the day. He did not enjoy working at the institute. He would work for six hours, then go home or go to the theater. In some small way, he was trying to please his father. Official work was only a gesture, an offering. It was during the late hours spent at his writing desk that the real work got done. Kafka and his father were two spirits passing each other in the hallway. They were only slightly aware of each other. This awareness informed all of Kafka's writing.

. . .

I found joy in making others laugh at inopportune moments. I was the class clown. Even as a child I understood the necessity of perfect timing, the importance of a well-delivered line. I was a bright boy. I was handsome, thin, and charming. The girls loved me. I had an affinity for them. They were comfortable in my arms. We played games in the back of a toolshed outside our parents' line of vision. I liked older girls, sixth grade girls. They could teach me something. I liked girls who wore baseball caps and let their hair down. But I was never happy with the final result. Something was missing. The pigtail between their legs, I imagine.

. . .

My literature professor was a grizzled old hippie who loved wool beanies and Pall Malls. Kafka was homosexual, he said. All his writing stemmed from his homosexuality, he said. I was twenty-two. I was stunned. But it made sense. I went back and reread all the stories. I read the coded text just beneath the surface. Things I didn't understand previously suddenly made sense. Other stories became more mysterious. That is the danger with Kafka. Just when you think you know him he makes a sharp turn and you end up facing a wall.

. . .

My father's garage was a thing of beauty. I spent many hours inside my father's garage when I was a boy. Tools hung from pegs on the wall. Nuts and bolts were carefully sorted and stored in Gerber jars. My father removed the labels with soap and hot water. The scent of freshly-sawn wood, old rags and WD-40 hung lazily in the air. He kept the expensive tools in a Craftsman roll-away, its drawers lined in black felt. The drawers opened easily, their silence a promise of things to come. The hand tools were arranged neatly in drawers. My father's initials were carved into each tool with an engraver. The garage was a monument to utility and common sense. Saws, rakes and shovels hung from the rafters. Rat tail files hung like stalactites between sixteen-penny nails. An old Campbell Hausfeld air compressor sat in a corner like a sleeping giant. A mirror was duct-taped to an exposed stud. I was three years old. My father picked me up. Who's that monkey in the mirror, he said.

. . .

I'm afraid of death. The fear hovers over me as I lie in bed at night. I wonder if Kafka was afraid to die. He was so young. If I had a guide to help me navigate the darkness perhaps I wouldn't be so afraid. My fear of death hasn't stopped me from ticking the days off the calendar that hangs in the kitchen. I'm not sure if the black marks are a warning or a celebration.

The Other

Mother gave me life and then she gave me away. I wish she would've walked to Rexall instead. Purchased a box of Epsom salt and ended the whole damned thing. I was spanked, the umbilical cord cut, the mucous siphoned from my nostrils. I wanted silence and a bathtub filled with blood – my own. As it is, I am here.

. . .

It's easy to find someone if one looks hard enough. The world is much smaller than it was in 1986, the year Borges died of cancer in Geneva. Did Borges regret not being able to die at Hôtel d'Alsace, where his literary hero Oscar Wilde died in room 16? Perhaps I should ask Maria Kodama. How does it feel to hold a literature of sand in one's hands? Not even Peter Raubal, Hitler's last remaining descendant, laid claim to *Mein Kampf*.

. . .

I am in Buenos Aires. My other half's father hailed from Buenos Aires. He is in the city visiting relatives. I mention I wish to go sightseeing. In reality I have found Maria Kodama's apartment. I wait near the building entrance. Mark David Chapman waited outside The Dakota on the evening of December 8, 1980. I was ten years old the night John Lennon was murdered. Everyone in the world knew his name. Very few know Maria Kodama. Now they will. I will walk where she walks. I will see what she sees. I stop her outside her apartment. I ask her to sign a few books. I speak in broken Spanish. I wear a tie. My hair is combed neatly against my head. I look harmless. She invites me in. We reciprocate in a language neither of us understands. The heavy brocade drapes obliterate the sky. I ask her why she has destroyed Borges. My hands are strong American hands. *I am become Death, the destroyer of worlds.*

Walking Spanish

Valencia. The city is an orange. I unpeel it, split it in two, and take pieces of it into my mouth. Its juices coat my lips. I leave the bar. Tourists with loud voices amble in the lobby. I look to my left, my right. The night opens before me. I cross the threshold. I think of my other half. Does he think of me? Borges was a well-dressed librarian. He was very wise. He wrote one of the most beautiful lines I've ever read –

. . .

Being with you and not being with you is the only way I have to measure time…

. . .

Marry a nice Catholic girl, my other half's mother says. Stop with this foolishness already. People rush by on the street. I fade, invisible. I hear the chatter of clucking hens. Tablecloths are unfurled. People push food into their mouths. Silverware clinks on plates. Glasses are emptied and refilled.

. . .

I've only been in two serious relationships. One has ended. The other is still very much alive. When my other half moved in with me I lived in a bachelor's apartment, a small one-bedroom in a bad part of town. A park sat across the street. Drug activity occurred. Items quickly switched hands. I observed nightly trade from my bedroom window. I didn't mind the crack heads. I lived alone. Who cares, I thought. When I met him he had a car and two suitcases. He lived with a cousin, a woman with a small child. He moved in with me. We put the two suitcases under the bed, where they gathered dust.

. . .

I did not like having his suitcases in the apartment. The suitcases meant he could leave at any time. I never told him I was uncomfortable with the suitcases. I'm not sure which is stronger, my fear of death or my fear of loneliness.

. . .

Perhaps I've been too harsh with regards to R—. He was my first partner. He worked sporadically. They were jobs one rarely thought about. They were jobs that needed to be done. He'd worked as a cashier at the local supermarket. He'd worked at a convenience store. It was attached to a gas station. He worked at the convenience store at night. Having worked at a convenience store, I knew how dangerous it was. He worked briefly as a new car salesman. The brand he sold is no longer manufactured. The company folded around the turn of the millennium. When I see one of the cars on the road, which is rare, it reminds me of him. They are cheap and poorly-made, but I have a certain fondness for them. Did our relationship collapse due to the shoddy workmanship of the cars he sold? It seemed plausible, and easier. He held small jobs off and on during the six years we were together. It was never enough. Had I been a different person and had he been a different person, it might have been different. My family got in the way. He's only using you for your money, they said. What money, I asked. I left it at that.

. . .

We were two very different people. We did not inhabit the same worlds. I needed him like a tree needs an axe. I did not understand love. I was twenty-nine. I thought if I don't try to find happiness I never will. The relationship lasted six years. Those years were a blast furnace. I kept feeding it raw materials. Nothing ever survived. There was a ten year age difference between us. When he was born in 1980 I was already a fully-formed ten-year-old with dreams and ideas. I'd been in the world long enough to want to retreat from it.

. . .

I hold a photograph in my hand. It is Christmas morning, 1980. I hold a typewriter. I reconsider the details of the photograph. It may have been my ninth Christmas. My tenth Christmas, which occurred in 1980, was spent at the home of friends who had allowed my parents to borrow their cabin for two weeks over the Christmas holiday. Paper sister 1965 and my cousin William were the only other children in the house. The cabin was buried under deep snow. It sat in the woods away from the road. It had a balcony that hovered over a ravine. The black fingers of dormant trees speared the darkness. My mother and father stayed on the ground level. My sister, my cousin and I stayed in a bedroom in the basement.

It was very cold. My sister and my cousin William were the same age. There was a strange easiness in their relationship. I did not understand it. I was a shoe with a broken string.

. . .

They included me in their conversation. I tried to follow. They spoke in a cluttered language that was difficult to understand. Everything they said meant something else. I thought about the toys under the tree. I thought about how cold the basement was. They had things sorted out. They knew much more than I did. They didn't share the things they knew with me. When he talked to her his words were turned upside down. The words were coded, and I didn't have the keys.

. . .

William talked to my sister about masturbation. I was shocked. It reminded me of the young man in the blue truck. They told stories and played games. My cousin William tried to scare me by telling ghost stories. This cabin is haunted, he said. Two people were murdered here, he said. You can hear their ghosts at night. They want to come out of the snow. My sister laughed. William said if I played with myself Santa would know and I wouldn't receive any Christmas presents. I wasn't sure I understood what he meant but I didn't want it happening to me. I still believed in Santa Claus, though there were doubts.

. . .

I turned eleven shortly after Christmas. I was entertaining myself as boys do when something happened that felt like nothing I'd ever experienced before. My older brother, who was very much a closed and self-contained person, had never bothered to explain it to me. I touched myself under the static pop of a cheap blanket. My body rebelled and created something that existed outside of me. I was simultaneously horrified and fascinated. I stopped believing in Santa Claus. My easygoing days of being the class clown came to an end. My focus became flesh-based. I too would die.

. . .

Things changed during the summer of my eleventh year. I became a very quiet boy. Electrical storms raged in my body. My voice squeaked and cracked. I forgot how to walk. You walk like a girl, my uncle said. He laughed. I was horrified. I retrained myself how to walk like a boy. When fall came I would be prepared. The fashion of the time was close-fitting jeans that hugged the body. I didn't like this style. My threadbare jeans were so worn I felt even more like a girl. I had less fabric separating me from the outside world. My stepmother always bought my clothes. I had very little say in the matter. I wanted to wear loose jeans. I asked my stepmother if I could wear something other than jeans. Like what, she asked. I thought of the Mexican boys at school. They were a tough crowd. Their pants offered nothing, no indication of the flesh beneath the fabric. Dickies, I said. Fine, she said. You'll get two pair for the school year. That's fine, I said. Can I please have some black shirts, I asked. Don't push it, she said. She caved and bought the shirts. Voilà, a uniform was born.

. . .

I turned thirteen in 1983. My body changed yet again. I didn't smell at all like a girl. I had a voice like cracked oak. When I opened my mouth a deep cavernous voice came from somewhere I didn't recognize. It sounded nothing like my old voice and not at all like a girl's voice. I retrained my voice, tweaked it. My walking issues went away. My new voice and my new body still did not reconcile with the thoughts in my head. I needed something but I wasn't sure what it was. Other boys busied themselves chasing girls on the playground. I had a girlfriend but I didn't chase her. Her name was Christina. We both had hands. We used them. I sat with her under a tree. I was a cosmonaut on the surface of the moon, picking up rocks and collecting samples to take back home. It wasn't real.

. . .

After Christina I had a girlfriend named Denise. She was half Chinese and half Mexican. She had eyes like mine. Other boys wanted to possess her. This made me feel like a real boy. She took me home one day while her mother was at work. She undressed herself in her room. Everything that said *woman* was laid out before me. I didn't know what to do. I used my fingers. She bucked under my touch. I didn't know my fingers could hold such power over another person's body. She moved away in the middle of the school year. I never saw her again. I rode my bike to her street. Her street was three blocks from my own. I stared at her house, only it wasn't her house anymore. It was just another house on another street. Her house sat across the street from Mr. Fuller's house. Mr. Fuller was an old black man who kept beehives in his backyard. I wanted to talk to him because I also had beehives. I never rang his doorbell. He died a few years later.

. . .

When I was in high school I drove by Denise's house a few times. I thought I would become a real boy if she moved back. She didn't live there and I never became a real boy. If I held my body against hers would I become a real boy? I didn't know, and the world wasn't telling.

. . .

I lived in a female world. Boys walked uneasily among girls. They tried to hide their uneasiness. I saw through it. Walking came easy to them but the walk always took them in the same direction. I was a beekeeper. I kept homing pigeons in a cage in my backyard. I walked among grasses and was silent and watched the other deer from a distance but I did not drink from the stream. I was a young buck with new, fresh antlers. The antlers felt false.

. . .

Back home the suitcases sit under the bed gathering dust. I'm no longer afraid of what they might mean. One of us will return to the United States. One of us will not. He is in Lisbon, visiting his mother. It is ten hours from Valencia. She has lived there nearly ten years. She was born in Portugal, just a few years before I was born in Río Seco. She lived in the United States, didn't like it, and returned to her homeland. I've been here in Spain, mostly reading cheap paperbacks and drinking. I walk through parts of the city close to the hotel. I do this at night. I do not dress like a tourist. My clothes are dull, dark and without tags. My face is dull, boring. The shoes I wear are fifteen years old. I do not like pain. I do not want to die in a hospital. I wish to end as I began, in salt and darkness. My walks take me from the immediate. I recognize nothing. A few youths loiter outside a café. I'm not afraid of them. The unemployment rate is very high, especially among young people. I've been approached by no one. The only people who have paid me any mind are Pedro and the kid at the bar, a temptation I've managed to avoid.

. . .

I grow tired of the night. I think of my hotel room, how still and dark it is. I'm thirsty. I look for an all-night store. In this part of the city there are only plate glass windows. Expensive items sit behind them, vacuum-packed and unobtainable. Kafka waits for me in my hotel room. I'd been rereading "The Burrow." I've read it many times. Kafka is a better version of me. We look very similar, though I'm not Jewish. I have a dark look, almond eyes. It's hard to place. I could be Israeli, Spanish, Asian, or Mexican. I walk toward the hotel. Glass and concrete are reflected in pools on the sidewalk. I walk through glass like a ghost. I move through a crevice between two buildings. An electric lantern hangs over a store. I walk into the store. Light brushes against me. The humming of electrical equipment comes from somewhere in the back. I choose a mineral water. I recognize the green glass bottle. I've always thought it too expensive, but I am unfamiliar with the other choices. Sometimes familiarity trumps experimentalism. Even Robbe-Grillet drank tap water. I pay for the water. I step back into the night. It's too noisy. Americans speak in loud, obnoxious voices. Germans cluck and huff in a language descended from Hell. Eastern Europeans wear dated track suits. My hotel is farther than I thought. The sidewalk is a dirty grey river. The street yawns before me, a painted whore with half-closed eyes. Someone is tugging at my collar. I don't turn around. I take another drink. I drop the empty bottle into a receptacle. I vomit in the semi-darkness of an alleyway. There is a cry of shock, a few whispers of disapproval. I see my other half's face reflected in a window. It isn't real. I slump to the concrete, my back against cold brick. I sit very still, my brain floating above my head. I am removed from my body. I've forgotten how to walk. There is a hand on my shoulder. Someone speaks to me in broken English. Hey buddy, you can't stay here. Too many police, it says. A dark figure hoists me up. It grabs the waistband of my pants. It pushes me forward. My collar is pulled tight against my neck. I can't breathe. I clutch my back pocket. I thumb the bump of my wallet. I walk with my hand against a solid object. The Klieg lights of the hotel beckon from across the street. I fly quiet as an owl through the front door.

. . .

I'm in my hotel room. A young man in a grey suit sits on the bed. He has a calming manner. His hair is pomaded against his scalp. A stiff white collar is attached to his shirt. He has a smell I don't recognize. He stretches over me. His coat brushes against my cheek. It's scratchy. It has the smell of old wool. He wets a washcloth in the basin. He folds it over my forehead. I try to speak. Rest, he says. His eyes are dark. I know he is dead. It does not frighten me.

. . .

In the morning I wake on the carpet. My shoes and pants are stripped from my body. My T-shirt hangs like an acid rag over my chest. I look in the mirror. The mirror says Yes.

Midwestern boy

I arrived in Cedar Rapids in greasy jeans and a six dollar haircut. I was eighteen. The first three years of college were difficult. I talked very little. I wore dark clothes. My shoes were scuffed from walking in black snow. I had few friends. I shaved my head. I did it to repel people. I read books. I studied. I wrote papers. I regurgitated what the professors said. I made good grades. It was easy.

. . .

I was temporarily placed in Greek housing. My greasy jeans and *Powerslave* T-shirt made things difficult. I kept people guessing. I didn't want them inside my head. Some days I'd wear an old Iron Maiden shirt. Other days it might be a Duran Duran shirt. My newly-bald scalp frightened people. I was placed in a non-Greek dorm before anyone could take a swing at me. My roommate was from New Delhi. He smoked cigarettes. I didn't. He opened the window when he smoked. I thought he was considerate. He told me stories of his homeland. Let's have a drink, he said. We got along fine.

. . .

I worked in the school cafeteria. I worked in the library. At first I thought I was better suited for the library job, but I soon found the cafeteria job was a better fit. It wasn't exactly a cafeteria. It was a small bar in the middle of campus. It was called The Pub. The students who worked in the cafeteria regarded me as some sort of demigod. They'd obviously never cleaned a deep fryer. I was surprised a college would have a bar on campus, especially a college as small as the one I attended. Although The Pub was located on college property, it was operated by a major hotel chain. Students used their lunch cards in much the same manner they used them in the cafeteria. The Pub served hamburgers, french fries, grilled cheese sandwiches, hot dogs, and pizza – typical fast-food items. Students could buy beer at The Pub if they were twenty-one. The Pub did not serve hard alcohol.

. . .

I was a short order cook. The woman who trained me did not like the kids who attended the college. They're spoiled, she said. I told her I thought so too. She was from Montana. She said you could go for miles in Montana without seeing another person. I said it sounded nice. I told her I wanted to be a writer. I said it was impossible. I had to work for a living. Don't worry honey, you'll make it someday. It was the nicest thing anyone had ever said to me. She was in her mid-forties. I was half her age. She was divorced. She had one daughter. The girl was in her twenties. Like you, she said. She lived in Missoula. We don't talk much, she said. What about her father, I said. My ex is a real prick, she said. I could kill that motherfucker. Her words frightened me. I wasn't sure if she was joking or if she really meant it.

. . .

I had to clean the grill once a week. The grill was cleaned after hours. The woman would sweep and wax the floors and I would scrub the grill. After I was finished I smelled like grease. I smelled like Mr. Fleming. The smell stayed on my scalp, in my hair. I had to shampoo twice to rid myself of the smell. Employees weren't supposed to drink while on duty. After the woman and I finished our work we would fill a half pitcher with Budweiser and watch the large television suspended over the booths. It was on this television that I first learned Magic Johnson was HIV-positive and a man named Jeffrey Dahmer had murdered several young men in Wisconsin. Poetry slams were sometimes held in The Pub. I attended the poetry slams to see what other writers looked like. Most of the poems were bad. One boy, a senior, told me his opinions on Joyce. He went on about how Joyce had destroyed the novel by writing *Ulysses*. I listened to him and soon realized he'd never actually read the book. I kept my mouth shut. I didn't want to embarrass him. One night I saw the same boy at a house party. He was telling other writing students his theories on Joyce. I wanted to say something but the people he was talking to didn't know how to write a sentence to save their lives so I thought why bother. I nodded and moved toward the kitchen. This is an awesome party, someone said. A girl bumped into me and spilled beer on my shoe. Yes it is, I agreed. I lied because the beer was free and I was broke. Later in the evening I scanned the spines on a bookshelf in the living room. I saw a title I liked. I picked it up. I pretended to read it. When I was sure no one was looking I slipped the book down the front of my pants. Free books and free beer – things were looking up.

. . .

I spent the evening of my twenty-first birthday getting drunk in a bar in Cedar Rapids. It was a cold night in January. The college I attended sat across the street from a dive bar called the Swizzle Stick. I'd walked to the bar many times, even in the darkness of winter. In dorm rooms kids masturbated, called parents for money, smoked marijuana, and drank heavily. A few contemplated suicide. In the bar my friend Susan and I toasted the strangeness of being twenty-one. What did it mean? Such questions were best left to the muses. Laughter bounced off the walls. A fire roared in the fireplace. Susan and I had money in our pockets. Our j-term classes were easy. We were young. The world was changing before our eyes. There was trouble in the Persian Gulf. The world was on the verge of splitting apart. I thought fuck it and ordered another round.

. . .

Susan had very white skin. The blue veins pulsing at her temples reminded me of ice on Mars. Her blonde hair was raked carelessly over her head. Boys never talked to her. They were afraid of her intelligence. She brushed them aside with a glance. We would sometimes watch *Saturday Night Live* on a small television in her dorm room. We laughed as Chris Farley crashed into a coffee table. We were dorks. We didn't care. Susan was completely open with me. She didn't hide behind a mask. I wasn't trying to get into her pants. I recently googled her. She is a doctor. She lives in California. The last time I spoke to her the Kuwaiti oil fires raged in the Gulf and great black clouds threatened to erase the sky.

. . .

I recalled a passage from Joyce. If you pissed into a commode and bubbles appeared, luck looked down kindly upon you. Bubbles edged from the center of the bowl outward. It was shaping up to be a good night. I pulled the handle and half-heartedly passed water over my hands. I opened the bathroom door. The smells of men. Spat-on sawdust, warm pungent cigarette smoke, Copenhagen, spilt beer, piss, the reek of ferment. Is this what it meant to be a man? I wanted to ask Joyce but he was nowhere in sight. I brushed off the darkness and headed toward the fire. Susan bought another pitcher. I toasted her. We drank until our money was gone. I woke up the next day with a headache. I didn't remember walking home in the snow. I was still twenty-one, but I was a day older. I ticked a day off the calendar. It's a habit I've never managed to shed.

. . .

I was attending college on a scholarship. I was poor. My situation was not uncommon. Many of the students were poor. There were wealthy students and there were poor students. The college I attended was a small private four year university. It was very expensive. If I had not been awarded a scholarship I would not have been able to go to school. Despite the scholarship I graduated owing thirty thousand dollars in student loans. One does not think of these things while one is a student. One goes to class, takes notes, and writes papers at two a.m. One gets drunk, smokes marijuana and has sex as often as possible. Student loans were only a gnat in a snowstorm.

. . .

I couldn't afford proper snow boots. To combat the cold I wore two pairs of socks on each foot. I heard the crunch of fresh snow as I walked in the quad. My feet were warm. I wore thermal underwear under my jeans. My legs were warm. Mother Nature tapped on my shoulder. I'm still here, she said.

. . .

I was in my literature professor's office. It smelled of Pall Malls and dusty paperbacks. I overheard another literature professor say she would be driving to Cedar Falls to hear a very famous writer read at the University of Northern Iowa. I enjoyed this writer's work. I asked the professor if I could accompany her to Cedar Falls. Of course, she said. It will be nice to have company, she said.

. . .

Cedar Falls is approximately sixty miles north of Cedar Rapids. We would be in her car for an hour. She was in her mid-sixties. I was twenty-one. What would we talk about? I thought about the writer. I asked which of his books she liked most. She said *Cat's Cradle*. I told her my favorite was *Welcome to the Monkey House*. Oh, that's a good one, she said. My sweater was warm but it wasn't that warm. It was an ugly orange sweater. It was two sizes too big. Someone had given it to me as a joke. I felt ridiculous wearing it. I usually wore dark clothes. Is that sweater warm enough, dear, the professor asked. She was very grandmotherly. I said I thought it was ok. I looked like a pregnant M&M.

. . .

Cedar Falls was sad and cold and grey, like an old quilt that had been forgotten in a pantry. We pulled into the parking lot near the auditorium. The writer was very famous. Tickets were necessary. Our seats were not together. She had a much better seat, though she didn't mention it. Meet me out here when it's over, dear. I said I would. I found my seat. I sat next to other students. Some of them had notebooks. They took notes. The writer talked about assault rifles. They're made to kill people, he said. That's their only purpose. They must be banned. I agreed. The world was a wicked place. Death had become impersonal. It didn't mean anything anymore.

. . .

The writer spoke for an hour. He said goodnight. People began exiting the auditorium. It was dark outside. It was very cold. I overheard pieces of conversation. Students were impressed with the writer's speech. It was easy to agree with him. I did not like guns. They were too easy, too quick. I sometimes rode on a black wave of depression. It could last for weeks. A firearm would have been too tempting. The students thinned out. I waited at the appointed spot. Tires crunched over snow. There were fewer cars in the parking lot. It grew colder. The darkness was complete. I felt stupid in my borrowed orange sweater. A group of students asked if I needed a ride. Thanks, but I'm waiting for someone, I said. Soon there was no one left to ask.

. . .

I walked down Walnut Street toward downtown. A cluster of bars sat near the campus. I took my wallet from my jeans pocket. I opened it. I had six dollars. I walked into a bar that didn't have a name. It was dark and it was warm. There were a few old men at the bar. I asked for a drink. The bartender carded me. I was a sliver over twenty-one. He handed me my ID. I ordered a cheap beer. I asked the bartender if he had anything to eat. He placed a bowl of pretzels in front of me. He was in his late twenties. There was an old television above the bar. The images on the screen blurred. The bartender said, what's wrong my friend? I told him my story. I'd come from Cedar Rapids to listen to the famous writer. I was left behind. I had no money. I tried to stop crying. I wasn't doing a very good job. The tears came quick. My scalp burned. I held a hand over my eyes. I didn't want the old men looking at me. The bartender emptied ash trays. He pulled a sour dishrag over the bar. He gathered dirty glasses and placed them onto a tray below the bar. Sit tight, he said. When the pretzels were gone he gave me another bowl. An old man said goodnight to the bartender. He pulled his coat closer to his body. The young bartender said goodnight. I tried composing myself. The images on the screen were no longer in soft focus. The bartender fanned out three twenty dollar bills near my glass like a clutch of snakes. I was shocked. Thank you, I said. My words nothing more than a mouse squeak. I asked for his home address. Don't worry about it, he said. Just get home safe. There'll come a time when someone will need your help. He told me the name of a cheap hotel. He told me where I would find the bus station. It leaves in the morning, he said. He held out his hand. I hugged him over the bar. He hugged me back. Thank you again, I said. I pushed the door open. I left the warmth and safety of the bar. The hotel was within walking distance.

The lobby smelled of stale cigarettes and old men. My room was very small. There was no television, just a dresser and a bathroom and a bed. I stripped down to my underwear and got under the covers. The moonlight was a blue pulse beyond the frost on my window. The room cost twenty-two dollars. I was warm and out of the cold and in a moment I was asleep.

. . .

In the morning I walked to the bus station. The attendant informed me the 10:15 bus had already departed. I was angry I had overslept. I asked the attendant when the next bus left for Cedar Rapids. 5:35 p.m., he said. I bought a one-way ticket. It cost nineteen dollars. I bought a Coke and a candy bar from the vending machine inside the station. I ate my breakfast on a bench. I thought of the best way to kill seven hours. I couldn't go to a bar, it was too early, and I didn't want to run into the young bartender. I walked for a bit. I made a right turn. I made another right turn. Nestled among a group of anonymous shops was a bookstore. The sign inside the window said it opened at eleven. I waited. I clicked the minutes off in my head. A woman's hand changed the closed sign to open. The same hand unlocked the door. I waited another twenty minutes. I didn't want to appear too eager. I walked to the door. I opened it and stepped inside. The woman was very friendly. She said hello. I said hello. I smiled. With my shaved head I looked like a skinhead or a religious nut. I pulled a small hardcover book I couldn't afford off a shelf. I sat in a corner on the floor. I didn't want to sit on the woman's furniture. A little bell was mounted above the door. It rang anytime someone opened it. There was rustling, then quiet, then more rustling. The phone rang. The woman answered it. I pulled my feet toward my body. I didn't want to take up any space inside the woman's shop.

. . .

The book was well-written. It took me from my present situation. The light in the room eventually changed. I felt eyes on me. I glanced up from the pages of the book. The woman looked down. She flipped the page of a catalog. She knew I wasn't going to purchase the book. I was likely a student. I had no money. My fingernails were dirty. She was no longer friendly. She looked up from her catalog. She squinted at me through her glasses. An older woman walked through the door. She asked about a particular book. I stood up. When I saw the shopkeeper's attention was completely focused on the new customer I slipped the book I'd been reading down the front of my pants. I needed something to read on the bus. I said thank you and walked out the door. In a few moments I was back at the bus station. I boarded the bus. There were very few people on the bus, a dozen at most. I sat down, grateful for the seat, the bus ticket, and the small amount of money in my wallet. Thinking about the kindness of the young bartender made me feel less hatred for the people around me. I reached into my pants. I extracted the book I'd stolen. The sun was setting behind a copse of trees. The color of winter streamed through the glass. My eyes drifted on the page. The headlights of the cars on the highway speared through the snow. The bus lurched forward. I awoke in Cedar Rapids. I left the stolen book on the bus. I didn't need the extra weight.

. . .

2010. I found myself at the door of an old friend. He was a former student of mine. He was much younger than me. I was forty and he was twenty-five. We had a lot in common. We often found ourselves in difficult situations. We made poor choices that were harmful to ourselves or others. We were reckless and selfish. We gravitated toward substance abuse. We'd both served time in jail. He was born in 1985. I'd been his fifth grade teacher. I was twenty-six at the time, his age now. I didn't do well by this kid, or any of the other kids I'd taught. I was an impostor. It was raining. I knocked on his door. I had a gift for him and his girlfriend, a small housewarming gift. No one was home. I was disappointed. Seeing his face would've reminded me I'd once been alive, I'd once been young. Behind the door was a warm house my friend lived in with his family. I'd seen him a few times throughout the years. Each time I saw him he was a little older. I couldn't see myself without the aid of a mirror so I wasn't sure if I was older. We texted each other every Christmas and New Year's Eve. He had children of his own now, but he would always be younger than me, even when he was old and I was very old. He'd once been part of my life; a life lived in bars and parking lots, a life of sleepless nights. When I heard of his struggles, his arrest, it pained me as if he were my child. I didn't leave a note, I didn't text him. I still have the gift. It's back home in the States, along with the rest of a life that no longer makes sense.

. . .

I never had teachers I could relate to. They were always very old. They were ancient texts rather than people. I felt no ill will toward any of them, though I did feel a certain hatred for the professor who had abandoned me at the University of Northern Iowa. When I was teaching I had never been so thoughtless or forgetful. I had only been a bad teacher, incapable of instructing anyone. I began teaching when I was very young. I was twenty-five. I did not know myself as I do now. I'd wanted to be an editor, or a publisher, or a college professor. She is old, I told myself. And the man in the bar had been so giving. I am much older now. I no longer have any hatred for the professor who abandoned me in a parking lot at the University of Northern Iowa. Very likely she is dead. I am capable of seeing beyond myself. Perhaps she'd truly forgotten I'd made the trip with her. Something had confused her, or she'd gotten turned around and couldn't remember where she'd told me to meet her after the event. When I saw her on campus a few days later I said nothing. I was young and hot-headed, and thought it best not to say anything. I went to my dorm room and drank. After I drank I walked to another dorm on campus and smoked marijuana with a few friends. I got high. I laughed and blacked out. I woke up in a strange bed in a strange apartment. My pants were off and my shirt was missing. Someone had written the words RED RIVER on my chest in permanent marker.

. . .

The campus was buried under black snow. I walked to my j-term class, took notes, shook my head in agreement, and walked to the girls' dorm after class. A girl I knew passed by and opened the door for me. I knocked on my girlfriend's door. She opened it. I got stoned and lay in bed with her. She was obsessed with the Soviet Union. The Soviet Union collapsed in 1991. I was twenty-one.

My Joyce professor mentioned it in passing. He looked out the window, his eyes focusing on nothing at all.

. . .

Cedar Rapids was dark and cold. It was much too late to call anyone, and who would I call? I knew a few professors, but had no access to their phone numbers. Donald would be sleeping with Katie. Susan would be sleeping alone. The only other person I knew with a car was the girl I was sleeping with. She drove an old Yugo. It was held together with Bondo and Scotch tape. She would be asleep in a dorm room cluttered with books about the collapse of the Soviet Union. If I called her she would come, but she had class in the morning. I didn't want to bother her. I waited in the bus station until someone told me I had to leave. I pushed the door open and walked downtown. This is such a hateful, ugly city, I thought. I could die here and no one would notice. I had on two pairs of socks. I often wore two pairs of socks on each foot. First one sock on one foot, and then a second sock over the first sock, and so on. I wasn't sure if other students did this. I didn't ask. Being poor did not bother me, I'd always been poor. I had my brain and my legs. My feet were separated from my brain by 67 inches. They cooperated. Money was not necessary.

. . .

I walked on First Avenue toward the college. My dorm room was warm, but it was very far away. I wore greasy old jeans and an orange sweater that did not belong to me. The stubble on my head wasn't enough to protect my scalp from the cold. My shoes were scuffed from walking in black snow. I hadn't worn a jacket. I didn't think I'd need one. Dorm to car, car to auditorium, the heat coming off the engine, light chatter as we traveled the road toward Cedar Falls, and finally the reversal of the entire process. Legally I was an adult but I was really just a child, a pinball bouncing here and there, not connecting with anything. The cold air crystallized in my nostrils. An insurance office with black windows had a side entrance off the street. Six steps led to a locked door. I looked around. I walked down the steps. I sat on the second step from the bottom. I removed my shoes. I removed the outer sock from each foot. I replaced my shoes and tied them. My fingers conspired against me in the cold. After my shoes were tied I slipped a sock over each hand. I pushed my hands deep into my pockets. The night was blue-black. I had sixteen dollars in my wallet. There wasn't a single car on the street. I walked and walked and walked. My fingers had never been so cold. A river of raw ice trickled down my cheeks. I was crying. Traffic lights blinked dumbly in the darkness. Morning would soon break through the ice, a sliver of light waking students from their beds, from other people's beds. I crossed the street and ran through the snow. I saw the lights of the campus. At last I was home.

. . .

I never read another book by the famous author. I was only mildly shocked to learn he'd died after falling down a flight of stairs many years later. I didn't care that he was suicidal. I didn't care that he was deeply depressed. The horse jumped over the fucking fence. So it goes.

. . .

A screen door closes in Cedar Rapids. It is a Friday evening. A woman walks onto her porch. She is glad the work week is over. She sits down, opens a can of beer. In a bedroom on the third floor of the house a man opens the top drawer of a nightstand. It slides smoothly and without resistance. He places the barrel of a .38 Special in his mouth. He pulls the trigger. The moon hangs above the porch in a tangle of limbs. The woman pays no attention to the distant popping coming from the third level of the house. Her husband is clumsy. He often drops things.

Boy with gun

A man in a blue truck tried to abduct me when I was ten years old. I was walking to the store to buy a pack of cigarettes. The man talked to me as a man would talk to a woman in a bar, his honey jar eyes wet with desire. He had a way with words, as all men do when their desire is laser-focused to a pinpoint.

. . .

I hold a photograph in my hand. In the photo, a young man holds a revolver in his right hand. He is handsome, clean-cut. He wears a baseball cap. He wears a green T-shirt and Levi's that are impossibly tight. He is a younger version of me. He holds a dead chicken in his left hand. He points a .22 revolver at its breast. The revolver belongs to my mother. The photo is a lie. I didn't kill the chicken. The chicken was killed by my mother. She is much stronger than me.

. . .

I was very slim when I was a young man. I had strong, muscular legs. My legs developed during my eighteenth year. I rounded up shopping carts in a grocery parking lot. An inconsequential summer job prepared me for the absurdities of adulthood. Collect the strays.

Put them in a line. Push them toward a predetermined destination.

. . .

In the photo the chicken has its ass in the air, its feet cleaved from its legs. The revolver barrel is a penis rudely pushing its way into the world. A dumb machine connected to a dumb hand. I turn the photo over. 1992 is written on the reverse. The revolver and I are both twenty-two. It was the year of Circle K parking lots, Hurricane Andrew and the Ice Boys.

. . .

My father sold the wrecking yard in 1988, the year I turned eighteen. A heart palpitation caused him to reconsider the possibility of living life beyond the age of fifty-two. If you want to live, sell the business, his doctor said. He sold the wrecking yard. I graduated from high school. I worked for a summer in a grocery parking lot. I bagged groceries. I rounded up shopping carts. I escorted women to their cars when dusk fell. I said Yes ma'am and No ma'am. I was very polite. My boss liked me. In the fall I moved fifteen hundred miles east to attend a small private college in the Midwest. I had never been away from my family. The first three years were horrible. I was depressed and miserable. I drank. I got stoned. By the fourth year I stopped ticking the days off the calendar, if only for a short time. What did it matter? Every day was the same.

. . .

I take another photograph from the cigar box. I am seven years old. A span of fifteen years separates the two photographs. I think of the dead chicken, the gun barrel, the violation of the flesh. When I was a child I raised homing pigeons. I kept the pigeons in a plywood cage in my backyard. The cage stood six-by-six. It was six feet tall. I stood inside it. My head did not touch the roof. I spread my arms wide. My hands did not touch the sides. It was constructed of two-by-fours, plywood and wire mesh. My father helped me build the cage. My childhood was a series of hexagons. Honeybees stored food and raised their young in hexagonal cells. Pigeons clucked and fluttered behind hexagonal wire. School lessons were written using a hexagon-shaped pencil. I mapped the world in my bedroom. Everything in it could be contained in seven hundred and twenty degrees.

. . .

I wanted to keep my beehives in the backyard but my stepmother wouldn't allow it. The pigeons are enough, she said. Days succumbed to nights. I slept in a bottom bunk beneath my older sister. The wooden ribs of her bed creaked as she shifted throughout the night. When I was seven I discovered the joy of slowly pulling a waistband over one's sex. When one is seven there is no danger of orgasm. My pajamas crinkled and sparked when I moved from the carpet to the bed. My sister's dresser sat to my left. A record player sat on a stand between her dresser and my bed. It was an Emerson. The sound of summer was an evaporative cooler rumbling throughout the night. I briefly lived east of the Mississippi River in my early twenties. I missed the sound of an evaporative cooler on summer nights. I had difficulty sleeping. Manhattan was simply too quiet.

. . .

Nikki Hutchinson and I raised homing pigeons together. We took swigs from Budweiser cans stolen from the refrigerator. I watched her comb her long hair in a mirror, bunched strands of dull coal collecting in her brush. We undressed each other in her bedroom while her parents were at work. I keep her memory in an aging box of photos. A backyard explored on a Saturday afternoon. A hive of bees nestled among grapevines. The clean black lines of a Daisy BB gun, its pellets a golden promise in the palm of my hand. When I am gone all this beauty will be lost.

. . .

I am a ten-year-old boy. The back of the photo is marked 7/80 in my stepmother's hand. My back is turned to the photographer. I wear very little clothing, just an undershirt and briefs. The photo is snapped as I'm removing a pair of jeans from a chest of drawers. I take another photo from the box. A smear of apricot flesh wearing very little clothing. I hold paper sister 1977 in my arms. She is a year old. I'm eight or nine. I'm shirtless. I wear briefs, she wears diapers. We would never be this free again. I place the photos back in the box, a mausoleum of dead images.

. . .

As we move closer to the digital we move closer to the fluidity of the female organism. Hard surfaces collapse. They break and wear down. To become eternal we must be willing to be broken, fed through cables and stored on silica for future use. The male mind does not like to be broken down. Graveyards are filled with analog tombstones. Only nature, infinitely-changing, can finger her way through the marble. I must succumb. I must allow myself to be split apart and reborn across epochs. I've been too male, too analog, for too long.

. . .

Summer, 1980. I am a ten-year-old boy. I look sad, lost. I stand against a slatted wooden fence. I stand underneath a lemon tree. Either the sun is in my eyes or I look through the photographer to the shadows beyond. When I was ten years old a man in a blue truck tried to abduct me. My stepmother had given me five dollars. She told me to walk to the store for a pack of Camels. The market was a Chinese store called Welcome Mart. My mother gave me a handwritten note, permission to sell. I folded it into my pocket. The man behind the counter never asked for it. You can use the change to buy whatever you want, she said. I asked for the Camels. I placed a Chick-O-Stick on the counter. I handed the man my five dollar bill. He rang me up, counted out my change. Thank you, he said. I stuff the change into my pocket. I know the man. He is very kind. His name is George. His father owns the store.

. . .

On the way home a blue Datsun pickup slowly passes me on the sidewalk. I think nothing of it. I cross the street. The truck turns into the parking lot of a dentist's office. I tear open my Chick-O-Stick with my teeth. I put an end in my mouth and bite down. An engine hums to my right. It's the man in the blue truck. He waves me over to his door. His window is rolled down. I keep a safe distance. I'm lost, he says. Do you know where this is? He holds a scrap of paper in his hand. He's young, nineteen or twenty. He is Latino. He has a crew cut. He waves the paper at me. He looks harmless. I slowly approach the truck. I close the space between myself and his window. His arm is dipping up and down. Here's the address, he says. He lowers his hand. I look into the cab of the truck, my eyes following the tiny square of paper. The young man's pants and boxers are gathered around his knees. The shock of it is a punch to the stomach. His erect penis punctures the membrane of a simple walk home. It's the first adult penis I've seen outside the pages of a pornographic magazine. The bogus address forgotten, the young man waves his penis at me. A bead of sweat trickles down his neck. It disappears into the fabric of his shirt. Tucked into the folds of the passenger seat is a revolver, much like the revolver my father has stashed in his desk at the office. I back away from the truck. His left hand flies out the window. It latches onto my collar. I twist free of his grip and run down the alley behind the dentist's office, not stopping until I reach the wooden gate leading into my backyard. I run into the house. I tell my mother about the man in the blue truck. She asks for her cigarettes. I tell her I don't want my father to know about the man in the blue truck. I don't know why I say this. My visits to the Chinese store grow increasingly rare. When I'm in seventh grade Welcome Mart closes. Doors are locked, windows boarded up. Graffiti announces the obvious. HERE LIES –

. . .

Did the young man in the blue truck know me? Did he recognize something in me? I found it difficult to believe someone would desire me. He poured his desire into the container of my being and his desire fit perfectly. I was puzzled. There was nothing good or perfect about me. The only thing I knew for certain was language, and what good was that?

. . .

I take another photograph from the box. It's one of my favorite photos. I hold a typewriter on Christmas morning. It must be 1979. It's either 1979 or 1980. I'm not sure. I'm nine or ten. The photo is unmarked. I told my father I wanted to be a writer. I wrote screenplays. My classmates were cast members. We made movies on the playground, without lighting or cameras. This is how I looked when the young man in the blue Datsun tried to abduct me. Almond eyes hidden behind dark bangs, a mouth that rarely opened. It was the perfect face for a milk carton.

. . .

My father asked what I wanted for Christmas. I told him I wanted a typewriter. There were many boxes under the tree on Christmas morning. I was only interested in one box. From its size and shape I knew a typewriter was inside the box. I opened the box as I imagined a cardiologist would open a patient's chest. The typewriter was a Sears Holiday. It came with a carrying case and an extra ribbon. On lined notepaper I tried bringing the young man back. I wrote a story called The Boy in the Blue Truck. Entire worlds were forged by the keys of my typewriter. I wanted him with me. I wanted to give him a second chance. As each key fell into place he became a possibility.

. . .

I often think of the young man in the blue truck. What if he'd caught me, if his grip hadn't failed? What if he'd opened me like a suitcase in the cab of his truck? A few months after the man in the blue truck tried to abduct me a thirteen-year-old girl came up missing in my neighborhood. She was found in a vacant lot. She'd been raped and murdered, her body stuffed into a black garbage bag. I knew it wasn't him. His eyes were too brown, his skin too soft. Years later I would google 1970s Datsun truck. The truck the young man was driving was a Datsun 620. There was one for sale on eBay. It was orange. I painted it blue in my mind.

. . .

I often think of the young man in the blue truck. He showed me things I'd never seen before. Why was I chosen? He has forgotten me, but I can never forget him. The images of that day are forever burned into my hard drive. The man in the blue truck tainted my sense of self. He hardwired me for a certain kind of pain I go to great lengths to avoid. I seek the pain out. I stuff it down inside myself. My neck is marked by the ligature of doubt, the muzzle of reason. He gave me a gift. Sex and death are one and the same, tendrils curled around the fragments of old bones. The hotel room dissolves. I am home. He whispers in my ear. It's three in the morning. My other half is asleep. I do not wake him. I pull the top drawer of my nightstand open. It slides smoothly and without resistance. I take out my father's .38 Special. I hold its heft in the darkness. My father gave me the revolver when I was in my late twenties. For protection, he said. I thumb the ramped sight. I consider the barrel in the darkness.

The barrel has an acrid taste. The young's man hair is suede against my fingers. I see his shirt, his skin. The cab of the truck is a fuse box. It is a Saturday morning. I ride my bike past brightly-colored houses. Yellow sprinklers dot summer lawns like acne.

. . .

We all have our abduction stories. Most of us forget them. Would he have liked me? Would he have loved me? Would he have bought me a Bomb Pop if I'd asked him to? I cried for what I was and for what I could've been. I imagine his hands on me, his fingers tracing the nape of my neck. A quick blow to the skull, dirt folded into the black wrinkles of a Hefty bag. He brushes the hair from my eyes, thumbs the sweat off my forehead. He kisses me one last time. He twist-ties me into a bag and tosses me into a vacant field. Blades of sunlight pierce the bag. I feel pain. It's hot inside the bag. I try to claw my way out. I have sin written on my body. I am forgiven.

Stanley Kubrick's typewriter

I hold a photo in my hand. It's a school photo, one of those pictures taken in late September when the dust has settled and students' names have been learned. It's 1981. I'm in fifth grade. My mother had combed my hair that morning. By first recess it was back in my face, hiding my eyes. My hair was long. I had bangs and sideburns, a holdover from the Seventies. My taxicab ears peek through. I wear a striped shirt. I look innocent enough. The photo is a lie, as all photographs are. The winter of my eleventh year was filled with destruction. Destruction and police cars. My brother Andrew was ten. He was born a year after me. For a few weeks in December and January we are the same age. Eventually he falls behind again. It happens every year.

. . .

The State awarded my mother visitation rights. I would see her every other weekend. Visitation began promptly at six p.m. on Friday and ended at six p.m. on Sunday. Transportation was my mother's responsibility. I spent the rest of my time with my father and his new wife. My mother's new townhouse was on the Southside of town. It contained my mother, the young Latino, and his two sons, my new brothers Michael and Andrew. Andrew and I quickly gravitated to each other. We both loved music.

. . .

The townhouse was a small two-bedroom, one bathroom patio home. It shared two common walls with the neighbors. Our neighbors to the left of us were a young couple, Mike and Joyce Hillary. Mr. Hillary was a mortician, Joyce was an office worker. Despite the way he made his living, Mr. Hillary was young, gregarious and full of life. He was a prankster. He constantly told lewd jokes. He enjoyed drinking beer on the carport with the young Latino. On the weekends Mr. Hillary would come over after dinner, his wife a few moments behind him. Mrs. Hillary had long blonde hair that fell to her buttocks. She had a large bosom. She had an easy, natural look. It's a look I haven't seen since the Seventies. She was a dead ringer for Agnetha Fältskog.

. . .

I thought I was poor. I wasn't. My mother and the young Latino were poor. They didn't have HBO. It made me feel dirty, like I was too white to be inside their house with their secondhand dishes, their old upright piano, and their small, cramped bedrooms. I was a smallpoxed foreigner on unmapped ground. The first step I took inside my mother's house reminded me of everything I had at my father's house. My sister and I had home-cooked meals, a three-bedroom house, a washer and dryer, homework. Our television was larger than the television inside my mother's house. Perhaps most embarrassing was the frivolity of cable television. HBO was a few clicks to the right on the cable box. My mother's house was bereft and forlorn. Three networks on a tired Trinitron. Everything in my mother and the young Latino's house had a cheap shine to it, like tinsel on a department store Christmas tree. I kept my mouth shut. I was polite. I did not complain. I ate three meals a day. I had a roof over my head. My mother shopped at dollar stores. I felt guilty hating her for that.

. . .

The cheapness of the situation clung to me long after my mother dropped me off at my father's house on Sunday evening. I was a toy in their eternal war to hurt each other. I was too white to feel welcome in the young Latino's house and too Mexican to feel comfortable in my father's home. After a weekend with my mother my father would say I had my ass in the air. Stop acting like a goddamned Mexican, he said.

. . .

My father and mother were advised my birth mother was Mexican and my birth father was German. They were told this before they adopted me. There was a cooling off period. It was similar to signing the papers at a car dealership. A take it back before the ink dries kind of thing. Your biological mother wasn't Mexican, boy. She was Spanish, my father said. A visit to the adoption agency when I was twenty-one confirmed what the agency had told my parents long ago. Spanish my mother was not. Was I white? Was I Mexican? Was I the horrible thing the kids on the playground insisted I was – a *half-breed?*

. . .

I was always fidgety for the first few hours. Time spent with my new brothers would eventually ease such feelings. I was a shape shifter, as fluid as the Saturdays that opened before us. I took walks in the open fields with my brothers. The world behind the townhouse was vast and unknown. Mica and creosote were crushed underfoot. Lizards were chased and caught, their tails snapping off as they jumped from our dirty hands. We fashioned tommy guns from old two-by-fours. We threw rocks at glass utility meters. We jumped in puddles when a rainstorm exploded over the desert. In the desert, my skin was brown, but then so was everyone else's.

. . .

My mother's house sat in the middle of ten townhouses that shared a common wall. Ten units, ten families. Some poor, some not. An old lady at the far end of the complex was well off. A waxed Monte Carlo sat in her carport. She had a nice lawn. Her yard was dotted with exotic trees, flowers and plants. She paid me and my brother Andrew ten dollars to mow her lawn. Five for the front and five for the back. Her backyard reminded me of English gardens I'd seen in *National Geographic*. You boys be careful out there. Don't cut down my flowers, she said.

. . .

Mike and Joyce Hillary were young and outgoing. They had simple names and open faces. Our neighbors to the right of us were Mr. and Mrs. Carlson. They did not. Mrs. Carlson, first name Marjorie. Mr. Carlson, first name Alton. Mr. Carlson was known as Big Al. Their only child, a son, was also called Alton. We called him Little Al. Little Al was seven years old. He was four years younger than me. He was a fat ball of open-mouthed laziness. Andrew and I took great joy in teasing him whenever his parents were out of earshot, which was rare. His mother was always nearby. She spoils that boy, my mother said. And she's a goddamned nudist.

. . .

Mrs. Carlson was an artist. Tubes of oil sat on the living room floor on drop cloths. An easel stood in the center of the living room. Mrs. Carlson's human figures were as well-crafted as her landscapes. Particular attention was paid to the nudes. She was an artist. She was also a technician. Curves, tones, the wet corner of an eye, the shadow under a bottom lip. The blonde cilia on a girl's summer-browned legs. Mrs. Carlson wore an old housecoat and slippers when she worked on a painting. Sometimes she painted in the nude. Little Al was oblivious to his mother's nudity. He was on the floor playing with cars or expensive-looking toys. The Carlson living room was a den of various paints, palettes and canvases. Sunlight rarely broke through the heavy brocade drapes, though spears of light occasionally threatened to set colored daubs of paint on fire. My mother said Mrs. Carlson was a hippie. And she paints in the nude. I wasn't sure what a hippie was, but the word, mouthed by my mother, seemed more like a condition than a classification. My brother and I, ever doubtful, couldn't believe someone like Mrs. Carlson, a woman who drove a car, wore mohair sweaters, shopped at the grocery store and deposited her husband's checks at the bank, would paint in the nude. My mother's unlikely claims, hissed under her breath, warranted further investigation.

. . .

God gave me a good eye and a lazy eye. I used both of them. Mrs. Carlson indeed walked around the house in the nude. I didn't understand my mother's protests. Was nudity a crime? Little Al was seven years old. The Carlson's weren't Catholic. The age of reason didn't apply. Was he conscious of his mother's nude body? As far as the law was concerned, Mrs. Carlson had every right to walk around her house bereft of clothing. My brother and I were curious. The female body was explored on Technicolor pages in magazines, but the Carlson's window offered lessons free of staples and grainy color stock.

. . .

Night slowly crawled across the desert. Geckos made their way through the darkness. Stuccoed walls were lazily festooned with spider webs. Pupils peeked through a sliver in the Carlson's living room curtains. Big Al sat on the sofa opposite the television, a bowl of popcorn on his crotch. Little Al played with his toys under an easel. Mrs. Carlson, naked as the day she entered the world, moved toward her La-Z-Boy, arms stretched over her head, the orbs of her breasts pointed toward the heavens. My groin slowly expanded in my Toughskins. Who was this woman? And how dare she parade around like this? My brother and I ducked and bobbed in the darkness, covering our mouths, not believing the gifts laid out before us.

. . .

The HBO-in-space bumper signaled something wonderful was about to happen. The opening bars, the slow burn, the music building to a crescendo. Only one other entity on television had theme music this awesome, this epic. *Dallas*. Through the glass I heard the friendly voice that would guide us through the night. *The following motion picture has been rated R.* The opening scene cemented our kneecaps to the ground. On the screen a disembodied eye hovered over a tiny car winding its way through the woods. My brother and I side by side, giggling at Mrs. Carlson's nakedness. Shut up, they'll hear us, Andrew said. Why were these people watching *The Shining* with their seven-year-old son? Mrs. Carlson reached for a tumbler on an end table. With her back to us, the nudity level was scarce. The occasional bathroom break broke up the monotony.

. . .

Little Al pushed cars along an imaginary track under an easel. On the screen, Danny Lloyd pushed cars on the Overlook Hotel's carpet, echoing Little Al's actions. A tennis ball rolls toward him. My need to take a piss overcomes my interest in the movie. I whisper my intentions to my brother. I stand in the shadows, unzip and piss in a corner of the Carlson's front yard. I write my name in passable cursive. The yard gravel crunches like snow under my feet. I crouch on the ground next to my brother. The Carlson's porch light ignites. Oh shit! My brother and I bolt toward the safety of the house, our backs tight against the wall. Our mother's 1969 Mercury Marquis sits in the darkness, a grounded trawler. A door opens but no steps come toward us, no voice calls out. There is only silence. The Carlson's porch light eventually goes black. I motion my brother toward the house. We go inside. Everyone in the house has clothes on. Shapes of bodies are only assumed, never known.

. . .

Mr. Carlson worked for the city. He was a chemist. Mrs. Carlson taught art classes at a community college. Little Alton was in daycare, too young to be a latchkey kid. School was out for winter break. The Carlson's were perfect candidates for a break-in.

. . .

We hadn't decided if we were going to steal anything. We wanted to see how Mr. and Mrs. Carlson *lived*. In what condition did they leave the house when they thought no one else was looking? My brother agreed – it was a brilliant plan.

. . .

Mr. Carlson had long greasy red hair. It fell haphazardly from his head, as if he'd forgotten it was there. A full scraggly beard hung low upon his chest. He was a menacing figure. He was six-two, possibly taller. He cast a long shadow when he stood in front of the sun. It was a Tuesday evening. Mrs. Carlson was teaching an art class. Mr. Carlson was having dinner in a café. Mr. Carlson always ate the same meal in the same café on the nights Mrs. Carlson was teaching.

. . .

We unhasped the latch and opened the gate that led to the Carlson's backyard. We walked in silence to the arcadia door. The Carlson's townhouse was an exact mirror of our own. I tried the door. It was unlocked. It pulled as if on greased ball bearings. I motioned for Andrew to follow me inside. The house was dark. The television was a dead, unblinking eye. An easel stood in the middle of the living room. I peeked under the drop cloth. A young woman lounged in a bathtub. A beautiful collection of bottles sat in a cabinet over the kitchen sink. They contained various potions that caused the body to forget itself, to say things it normally wouldn't. A few bottles held clear liquids. Others contained potions so dark they were nearly black. My father had a similar collection in a cabinet above the Amana. He marked the alcohol levels with a fine pencil, testing various children in the house.

. . .

We were in Little Al's room. Toys were strewn about carelessly. Toy boxes were so stuffed the lids wouldn't close, like sunken treasure waiting to be discovered. I picked up a white teddy bear sitting on Little Al's bed. I held its mouth to my crotch. My brother stifled a laugh. He ripped the teddy bear from my hands and thrust his zipper toward its tail. Oh yeah, baby, he said. I dropped to the floor and started pinging notes on a multicolored xylophone. My butt resting on my shoes, I belted out a polyrhythmic tune so loud it threatened to bring the roof down. My brother opened his hands toward the popcorn ceiling, a tiny conductor. I brushed the xylophone aside. Innumerable board games of every size, shape and color were hidden under Little Al's bed. I removed *Sorry!* from the darkness. The top of the box was quilted with dust bunnies. I heard the cough just as I lifted the board game from its box. I froze in silence. The cough hadn't come from my brother. It was older, wetter. Diseased.

. . .

We stood in the darkness. There was movement in the master bedroom. A light came on in the hallway. My brother and I quietly ducked out of Little Al's bedroom.

Big Al stood in the darkness at the end of the hallway. He was naked. His massive body filled the entire hallway. It absorbed all available light. He crossed the threshold of his bedroom. He charged at us, agile as a ballerina, bellowing and cursing our names. Flaming spittle landed on my back. I thought my shirt would catch fire. My hair hung in my eyes. I was running blind. My brother and I hydroplaned over the hallway and living room carpet, only hitting the high spots in the shag. I reached the front door in amphetamine panic.

. . .

Outside, daylight was fading. The desert opened her arms to the night. I touched base with the Carlson's dead grass, nearly slipped on something wet. I crossed the threshold and blasted through my mother's front door. The young Latino stood in the living room, his eyes enraged lanterns. My mother sat at the dining room table, a cigarette dangling from her mouth. A deck of cards was splayed out before her. Solitaire. It was her favorite game. Andrew flew through the door like a ghost. When he saw his father he dropped onto the carpet like a basket of wet laundry. We were doomed.

. . .

My ass connected with the young Latino's leather belt. My brother received the same treatment. After the belt we slunk down the hallway toward our bedroom. The police were batoning the door. My mother stubbed out her cigarette. The young Latino unlocked the door. Andrew and I lay crying in bed. Our brother Michael hovered over us, gloating. We heard adult voices in the living room. Footsteps in the hallway. The light flicked on. The young Latino stood in the doorway. Come on, you two. The police need to speak to you. The police officers stood waiting in the living room. Their flashlights and batons hung at their hips. A few words, then we were cuffed and hauled outside.

. . .

Mr. Carlson stood talking to the police officers. He wore a pink robe. It was Mrs. Carlson's painting robe. Daubs of paint colored the robe like an afterthought. My mother asked Mr. Carlson if all this was necessary. The assisting officer placed me and my brother in the back of the cruiser. The door closed behind us like a safe in an old movie.

. . .

Big Al looked from my mother to the police car. My mother placed a hand on his forearm. She mouthed words I couldn't hear. Big Al looked at the officers. He towered over them. The beard and the pink robe gave him a wild, shaken look. I fingered the cuffs behind my back. With some effort I was able to slip one of the cuffs over my hand. I put it back, knowing such a stunt would only cause more headaches. The police officer opened the door and told us to get out. The officer's grip was so tight it left a purple mark on my arm.

. . .

My father was going away on a business trip. I begged him to let me stay at my mother's house. He reluctantly agreed. I was shocked – I never stayed with my mother and the young Latino during the week. My stepmother was pleased. The reminder of the other woman would be out of the house. I was excused from school. Our plan was set in motion.

. . .

Andrew moved quickly. He was in fourth grade. I was a fifth grader. I was also a stranger to his school. We were much too old to be on the first grade playground. We took advantage of the elderly teachers' poor eyesight. Little Al was easy to spot. He was huddled among a loose group of first graders. I quickly scanned the field. There were no teachers in sight. Little Al's face went slack when he saw us. What do you want? Shut up and come with us, we said. It was my Daddy's fault, he said.

. . .

We grabbed Little Al. We forced him into a concrete tunnel near a stand of pines. The tunnel was a cement pipe that served no other purpose than to hide various activities on the playground. Adults understood children needed private moments to quarrel and bargain. Once we were inside the pipe I slapped Little Al on the face. My wrist went numb. It felt separated from my arm. Andrew punched Alton in the stomach. He dropped to the ground. We kicked him repeatedly, our Chuck Taylors connecting with ribs, arms, the hands zippered over his head. He begged us to stop. Say anything to your mom or dad and we'll break into your house and kill them, we said. I won't, I won't, Little Al promised.

. . .

Cover his mouth, my brother said. My fingers tightened over his lips. Mucous from his nose sprayed over my fingers. My brother reached between Little

Al's legs. He violently pinched the fabric in a twisting motion.

. . .

I felt sick to my stomach. I leaned against the side of the pipe. Little Al was bleeding. I wiped the bubble of blood from his nose with my thumb. I heard running in the distance. Several feet in soft shoes were approaching. On the far side of the field, near the drinking trough, a whistle rattled like an old woman's last breath.

. . .

I straightened Alton's clothing, pulled his shirt taut. Andrew ran a comb through his hair. I fixed his collar and pushed him toward the sunlight. I heard a teacher yelling in the distance. The first of them were upon us, the shock registering on their faces when they realized we were older kids on their section of the playground. They hesitated, their breath hitched in their throats. Alton spat on the dichondra, an asthmatic blob of spittle that felt like an unspoken agreement, a secret written on the grass beneath our shoes.

The world is a polished blue stone

I was twenty-two. I had nice skin. I fit into a normal pair of jeans. I'd returned home to Río Seco, my fancy education nothing more than a blur of bad sex and binge drinking. My bedroom was very small, a shoe closet with a borrowed bed and a paperboard nightstand. I weighed 120 pounds. I didn't need much space. If a friend came over, the only place to sit was on the bed. There was a small window directly above my bed. Dust constantly fingered its way through the window. When I lay on my bed I could smell the dust on the sheets, the pillowcase. I owned a few books. They were constantly dusty. I had two pairs of jeans and a few button-down shirts. A Plaster of Paris figurine of E.T. stood next to my nightstand. Someone had given it to me as a joke. I decorated him with beads from New Orleans. He kept me company. Everything I needed was in my bedroom. I scribbled on legal pads at night. If I took a break from writing, the legal pads sprouted dust. The 40-watt bulb in my table lamp was dull brown. My record collection suffered. My turntable was dying. The desert was trying to kill me.

. . .

I pushed a broom in a Circle K parking lot on graveyard shift. I rang up beer and condoms, talked to complete strangers, and read magazines that weren't mine. I stocked walk-in freezers with bottles of beer. The bottles were so cold I had trouble holding them in my hands. My fingers would crack and bleed from the walk-in. It wasn't always so terrible. A few friends from town, young people I met simply by working at the register, would come in and keep me company. They were high school students, only a few years younger than me. I let them have whatever they wanted. Cokes, beef jerky, whatever. It was a small town. Curfews were heeded. My friends left. I was on my own. I ate Dove candy bars. I watched ghosts in the parking lot fill their gas tanks. I cleaned the beverage dispensers and waxed floors that were smudged eight hours later. You have the best floors in town, my boss said. Perhaps that will be my legacy. I wrote a novel by the time I turned twenty-three. It was poorly written. I blame the dust.

. . .

My father owned a wrecking yard when I was a child. I was always at his side. He drove a tow truck. When he was on the road I was with him, even during late-night recoveries. Accident scenes populated my childhood. Convenience stores provided makeshift dinners. I loved the time spent with my father. He was a good man. He was a kind man. He treated customers fairly. In the end, the world doesn't care.

. . .

I shortchanged the man who adopted me, who gave me his last name. I never married. My fingers are broken from fighting. I have abused drugs. I never met a bottle I didn't like. I'm queer. I have chased obliteration. I was raised by wolves. We traveled on a perpetual highway in the blackened cab of an old tow truck. It was a 1972 Ford Holmes 440. Summer nights hummed in agreement beneath its tires. Some nights would bring another repossession of a poor family's car. A late night call from the police department. Another accident, another death. We once hauled away a small foreign car a young girl had died in. The ambulance had taken her away. Nineteen, the officer said. He shook his head. The car was a green Fiat. Above the steering wheel, hanging from buckled glass, was a clump of blonde hair. The roots were colored with blood. Sand was pulled from pails and spread on asphalt. Kitty litter worked best. I was too young to know death, but it knew me. The following school year was always the same. The same lies. Lives were simple, and too easy to be believed. How did you spend your summer? We went to Disneyland. How did you spend your summer? My dad and I towed away cars people had died in. Whispers were followed by silence. My father and I helped people. We weren't the cause of such misery.

. . .

Mine wasn't a bad childhood, it was an instructive one. Nights spent in a tow truck headed toward unclassifiable destruction. We provided a service by pulling ruined cars from horrible miscalculations. Memories fade once the chariots of destruction are hauled away to their final resting places. None of it mattered as long as I was with my father, a Coke and a beef jerky my chosen sustenance. They could keep their Disneyland, where the danger was calculated and the thrills glassine. How often does one encounter real death, barring one's own?

. . .

My father's wrecking yard was on the gloomier side of town. Whites rubbed against blacks as if by mistake. Poverty was colorblind, a charitable whore who robbed from anyone willing to fall into her arms. My father's office was nestled among automobiles that had once been showroom new. That the cars had once been new was somehow miraculous. They reminded me of the patrons on the stools of my father's favorite bar. Tired, forgotten by friends and family, lonely rusted hulks of their former selves. Grills once shiny now dull with age. Headlights broken and unseeing like tired eyes filmed over with cataracts. As day surrendered to night the cars turned malevolent. Primeval souls stirred from their innards to walk the wrecking yard in agony and anger, searching for loved ones who had long since forgotten them.

. . .

My father had many loyal customers. He treated everyone fairly. He charged reasonable prices. If a customer couldn't pay, a tab was kept. Businesses like this don't exist anymore. Businesses based on trust. There were times when my father was taken advantage of, but for the most part such occurrences were rare. A few of my father's customers come to mind. A black man named Joe Wood, who insisted on saying *motherfucker* at the end of every sentence. A man named Gregory. He constantly thanked Yahweh for everything, including his ability to buy car parts. A man with a bad rug named Stanley Kaufman, who possessed a radio announcer's voice. A suave Latino named David Ybarra who ran a messenger service. When he stopped coming around we learned he'd been accused of inappropriate sexual advances toward the women who worked in his office. An old red-faced man named Stack, who had the whitest hair I'd ever seen. I remember these men as if I'd seen them last week.

. . .

There was an old man who had a son about my age. The man and the boy lived in a cab-over camper that sat atop a late Sixties Chevrolet pickup. They had no permanent residence. The old man survived by selling turquoise jewelry he made by hand. He smelled of alcohol and piss. When he walked through the gate the boy was always a few feet behind him. The boy was about my height. He was very thin, almost ghostlike. He had dark brown hair that hung in his eyes. His fingernails were rimmed with dirt. The boy wore clothes assembled from Salvation Army donation bins. Sometimes he wore cutoffs. His kneecaps were black. There was such sadness in his eyes. He was a mirror image of me, though poorer and unloved. His father barked commands at him. He regarded him as one would a stray dog. His father's belly was huge. It poked obscenely from his undershirt. His navel pushed outward, an angry nipple. Striated veins forked across his belly like evil fingers. His big red nose was a bloodied biscuit that hung on his face like an afterthought. The boy was so small, so lost. The world was unkind. It swallowed lost people.

. . .

My father was a humanitarian. He cared about people. He let the old man set up a folding table on Saturdays in front of the office door. Customers walking through the gate would see the old man sitting behind his table, selling his handmade turquoise jewelry. The boy sat atop a wire milk crate next to his father. I asked him to walk with me as I made my rounds in the wrecking yard. The boy never came. He was afraid to leave his father's side. The old man never paid me any mind. I was as invisible to him as his own son.

. . .

Closing time was my favorite part of the day. The dogs were unleashed, the office locked. The old man and his son would box up their jewelry, close the folding table, and load everything into the battered Chevrolet pickup. The old man would grumble a few words to my father, his version of thanks. He would then squeeze his bulk between the steering wheel and the bench seat. The boy would muster all his strength to lift himself up on the passenger side. Window rolled down, the boy would stare at us as his father pulled away to another destination. Occasionally he waved goodbye, but it was the smallest of waves.

. . .

The boy approached me one Saturday evening in late July. His old man was in the Porta-John behind the office. The boy grabbed my hand and put something in it. He closed my fingers over the object. He ran toward his father's pickup, opened the door and disappeared inside. The old man eventually surfaced. He poked his head into my father's office. He closed the door and slowly made his way toward his truck. Once they pulled away, I opened my hand. In the center of my palm sat a smooth blue stone.

. . .

I've often thought about the boy. Did he learn to use his voice? I still have the stone. I keep it in a small tin box. It shares space with another object I've had since I was a boy, a 1971 Eisenhower dollar. The silver dollar was a gift from my father. Eisenhower's profile is on the obverse, an eagle landing on the moon on the reverse. I always thought it was a strange coin. It was a totem from my first year of life, the year of speechless crawling.

Misgivings

When one is adopted the world sees him as a failure. After adoption, anything he accomplishes is considered a success. I've avoided prison, bankruptcy, erectile dysfunction, and drug addiction. From here on things would be smooth sailing. Still, the adopted child must occasionally contend with the whispers, the chatter. Don't you know? He's adopted. Oh, that makes sense. He doesn't look anything like his father.

. . .

Adoption is a joke without a punch line. Great harm often comes to the adopted child. He wonders why he feels different. He wonders why he looks different. He wonders why his parents gave him away. Explanations don't help. He is miscast, a mismatched plate in a china hutch.

. . .

I'm the only child in America who was not adopted by a rich white barren couple. My parents should have been physicians or attorneys, gilded WASPS bored with their three car garage, their furniture and their cutlery. Instead, I must work for a living. This has caused me great pain. I was whisked from the delivery room before

I could lodge a formal complaint. Adopted babies don't come with receipts. You can't take this one back. I asked my father how he felt about me the day he adopted me. Of all the babies, he said, we chose you. Oh, I said. I'd like to speak to the management.

House fire

My brother is in prison. Of the many false things in the world, this one is true. He is apart from me, a brother I can no longer see. A brother I can no longer touch. He is Andrew, my paper brother.

. . .

Growing up, we rode our bikes through vacant lots. We peeped through windows that weren't ours. We walked on golf courses, collecting balls that had rolled off the green. We sold them back to golfers for a dime each. We watched our collective parents argue, curse, and throw dishes at each other. We witnessed the collapse of their marriages. He was the brother I thought of when I heard others speak the word *brother*. We did many things brothers often do together. Drug abuse was no exception.

. . .

I was twenty-two years old when my brother went to prison. He was a year younger than me. I was with my brother the first time I smoked crack. It was in the living room of a shabby apartment. His girlfriend was on the sofa. Their daughter was asleep in her tiny bedroom. My brother hit the pipe. He instructed me how to do so. His fingers were calloused from the burn of the glass. He passed the pipe. I hit it, pulling the smoke into my lungs. My head was filled with gasoline dreams. My brain steeped in ether. I passed the pipe to his girlfriend. She hit the pipe. We continued throughout the night until the crack was gone.

. . .

My brother and I broke into the laundry room of his apartment complex one night. We took a tire iron with us. We were desperate for crack. We violently smashed coin boxes that sat atop Speed Queens until they spilled their quarters onto the floor in a silver river. This was the second time I smoked crack. I loved my brother. I loved that he did not judge me. We did regretful things, stupid things, things too painful to consider in the harsh light of day. But when one is sitting in a living room high on crack at two in the morning, time doesn't matter. Shades are drawn. The television is perpetually on. And all that matters is another hit on the glass dick.

. . .

I am inside my brother's apartment. It is the night after Christmas morning. A small tree stands in the living room. The tree is dying in a corner. Strands of lights are drooping over dead limbs. The presents are gone, unwrapped and forgotten. The light of the television is reflected in the ornaments. The living room has a quiet stillness about it, as if it had snowed in the apartment. I wake in the phosphor dot serenity. I see my brother lying near the coffee table. He is asleep. People lie sleeping in the darkness of the two bedrooms. There is a humming in the darkness. It is a space heater. I have a slight headache. I say goodnight to my brother even though he is asleep and cannot hear me. I open the door quietly. I lock the door before I close it. I am outside. I stumble through the parking lot. My car sits waiting for me. It is 1992. I am twenty-two. I am high on crack cocaine. The icy moon hangs in the sky. It gives off a pale and sickly light. I close my car door. The interior is cold and black. I put the key in the ignition. The engine turns and catches. I drive into the night. It will be the last time I see my brother on the outside. I don't know this as I head toward the safety of my apartment.

. . .

True bliss is the obliteration of the ego. People have their vices, orbits they return to like a dog to its dish. I fondly recall friendships formed over dabbling sessions. A love forged in addiction that didn't stand up to the light of day. Others we get close to, a closeness that ends when someone turns away from light, love, cocaine. It's easy to turn away, is it not? We get into a car and drive toward a new destination. We adopt a new face, a new address. Addiction is only a memory in the rear view. We walked through fields of creosote and mica. We pushed a Tonka truck through the muddy yard. We listened to records on a Sansui. He was a gentle boy. He became a soft-spoken man. Somewhere in between is the brother who is now in prison. I have lost my brother, but he has lost everything. His girlfriend, his daughter, his life.

. . .

There was a fire. Four people died. My brother was taken away after the bodies were found. A list of the dead –

. . .

My brother's girlfriend
My brother's baby daughter
My brother's girlfriend's cousin
The cousin's boyfriend

. . .

I have a picture of my niece. She is in a car seat. The car seat sits on a table. She wears little pink booties on her feet. Her dark hair is twisted in a curl on her head. She looks ready to go outside, perhaps to the store with her mother. I have the photograph in my cigar box at the hotel. The photos are rubber-banded together. I keep them in the nightstand on my side of the bed. I must keep them safe. I must not forget.

. . .

I handed my brother my keys so he could open a can of beer. He was having trouble with a pull tab. I found this extremely funny. I laughed at my brother. He laughed, too. My keys were on a fob I'd purchased in New York. The fob was a tiny photo of the New York skyline. There were two keys on the fob. I kept my car key separate from my house keys. My reasoning being in case I lost my apartment keys I'd still have my car key. One of the keys on the fob opened the gate that led into the courtyard of my apartment building. The other key opened my apartment door. My apartment door had a reinforced deadbolt. I didn't live in the best neighborhood.

. . .

My apartment complex was small – thirty-six units. I felt safe. Perhaps it was the gate. A kidney-shaped pool sat in the center of the courtyard. I never swam in it. There were two levels of apartments, first floor and second floor. I lived on the first floor. When I arrived home from my brother's apartment I quickly realized my apartment keys were not in my pocket. I was locked out of the courtyard gate. I was locked out of my apartment. I grew angry at my own stupidity. I remembered my brother's battle with the beer can. Whatever fun we'd had was now lost as I sat on the lawn in front of my apartment building. I waited. I watched strangers move in the shadows across the street. The cold and the darkness snuffed out my high. I didn't have change for a payphone. This was in the days before cell phones.

. . .

The bodies were found close together. My brother's girlfriend's cousin was in the guest bedroom, lying next to her boyfriend on a second-hand mattress. My brother's girlfriend was found in the master bedroom. The baby was in her crib. For some reason I'll never understand, the baby's crib had a piece of plywood over it. On the center of the plywood was a tire rim. It was one of my brother's fancy wheels, a heavy silver starfish. It was curb-damaged, and my brother and his girlfriend thought this was a better use for it. There were whispers, tales told by people who were not there. My brother's mother said his girlfriend was a bad mother, a liar and a user. She's a selfish girl. If only she had let me watch the baby, she said. But *if only* can drive a person mad. I didn't find my brother's girlfriend to be a bad mother. She loved her daughter, I could see that. And I knew she loved my brother.

. . .

I lost my keys in the fire. I lost my keys, my brother and my niece. My niece was a baby girl with brown hair and dark eyes. She was beautiful in the way little girls usually are. My brother was taken away after the bodies were found. I didn't know about the fire. I didn't know about the bodies. I waited on the lawn outside my apartment. I waited for another resident to come home from God knows where. While I waited on the lawn, my brother lay sleeping in his apartment. In the apartment lay my brother's girlfriend, my brother's baby daughter, my brother's girlfriend's cousin, and the cousin's boyfriend. All, with the exception of my brother, soon to be dead – an unvented space heater sucking the life from them as they slept in two bedrooms off the hall. My brother survives. He is passed out in the living room, far away from the space heater. The propane radiant heater catches a cabinet door on fire. The cabinet door is the door to the laundry closet. The closet sits in the middle of the hallway. The guest bedroom and the master bedroom terminate at the end of the hall. It is an apartment like many apartments, like thousands of apartments. It has no special qualities.

. . .

Either my brother or my brother's girlfriend placed the space heater in the center of the hall for maximum coverage. The heater is a gift from my brother's mother. It is old, without labels or directions. It doesn't have a built-in sensor that shuts off the unit if an object such as a cabinet door sits too close to it. When the cabinet door to the laundry closet catches fire a dozing smoke alarm screams my brother awake. I sit on the lawn outside my apartment building. I wait for another resident to come home from the bar, a lover's house, a graveyard shift. My brother's girlfriend, his baby daughter, the girlfriend's cousin and the cousin's boyfriend are dead. I know none of this. I only know my headache is gone and I am too lazy to get back into my car and drive to my brother's apartment to retrieve my keys from his coffee table. It is cold outside and my ass is wet through my jeans. There is frost on the lawn. It is the night after the day after Christmas.

. . .

Above the entrance of my apartment building, strung along the gate and fingered through the bars, are Christmas lights. They twinkle in red, blue, and green. I am awakened by a resident I vaguely recognize, someone from the second floor. I tell him I'm locked out. He lets me in. He says I can sleep on his couch until morning. I take him up on his offer. A tiny Christmas tree shines in a corner of his apartment. I'll turn it off, he says. The tree goes dark with the click of a switch. I am twenty-two. My brother Andrew is twenty-two. We are caught in the dark space between December and January, the few weeks when we are both the same age. I pass out on the man's couch, fully clothed, my ass still wet from the lawn. I dream I have a headache. I dream the headache goes away. I wake in the morning to the smell of coffee. I am in unfamiliar territory. I push my hand into my jeans pocket. I remember my keys are missing. There is a knock at the door. My neighbor says a few words. I know who it is before I can wipe the sleep from my eyes.

. . .

I am taken by squad car to the police station. I am questioned by the police. I answer their questions. I am released. Before I leave, the detective asks if I lost something in the fire. Is it a trick question? I'm not sure how to answer. My brother? My niece? Did you lose your keys, son? Yes, my keys. I haven't seen the inside of my apartment in forever. He slides the keys across the table. They are heavier, tainted. I am released. I take a bus home to an empty apartment. I strip off my jeans, my T-shirt. I take a shower. When I step out of the shower I still feel dirty. I cannot get the smell of smoke out of my lungs. I know the smell is imaginary. I throw my New York City key fob away. My keys are loose in my pocket. Ten years would pass before I dared smoke crack again. I would learn nothing, and the lessons would be much harder.

. . .

Involuntary manslaughter is a Class 2 felony offense. My brother was given seven to twenty-one years. I was twenty-two. That was twenty years ago. My brother is still in prison. I have guilt. I could have turned the space heater off. I have pain. My brother is no longer with me. I am filled with wonder. I survived. If I had slept too close to the space heater my headache would've been so much more. The heater was designed to be used outside, on camping trips, under a canopy of pine trees shouldered together against the darkness. I opened the door and walked into the night. I said goodbye to my brother as I did so. He did not hear me. I do not deserve a name.

. . .

I have lived in many different places since the fire. I've never felt at home in any of them. I still have the keys from so long ago. I keep my current keys on a simple ring, but the two keys from my apartment when I was twenty-two stay loose in my pocket. They are constant companions, totemic reminders of the loss I suffered, the loss my brother suffered. The gate key carries a simple warning. DO NOT DUPLICATE. Who would duplicate such a horrible night? The apartment door key reads CITY LOCK & SAFE. My keys have been replaced many times, yet these two remain. I have lived in apartment buildings tucked safely behind locked gates. The gates are a lie. One is never safe. I have been inside many homes. None of them belonged to me. Home is a Christmas tree in the corner, frost on the lawn, and doors securely closed. I have none of that now.

Kafka and I

One of my favorite photographs of Kafka can be found in the book *Jeremy Adler's Franz Kafka*. The photo is on page 114. It was taken on the beach in Marielyst, Denmark in 1914. Kafka is sitting next to his friend, the doctor and writer Ernst Weiss. Both men are in swimming trunks. Kafka is sitting on the sand, shirtless. He leans slightly toward the camera. On his face is an expression of absolute joy. His ears poke childishly from his head, his grin not the smile one would expect on the face of the man who was in the midst of writing *The Trial*. He is thirty or thirty-one. His body is hairless, the body of an adolescent. Weiss has the body of a man, thick, hairy, accustomed to the disappointments of the world. Kafka is very much a child, though in reality he was wrestling the demons of boredom and corralling them into what would become his second novel. *The Trial* was written in various places, including the 'little house at 22 Golden Lane' (Adler), which Kafka and his sister Ottla thought would be most conducive to his writing. Kafka found a measure of peace walking down the steps that led away from Prague Castle toward Golden Lane. But never the joy he felt on that day at the beach in 1914.

. . .

Like a dog whose face begins to resemble the face of his master, I look shockingly like Kafka. The dark hair. The big, boyish ears. The seeing but unseeing eyes. My face is Kafka's face. My body is Kafka's body. But there is a subtle difference. I do not have the weight of five thousand years of Jewish persecution on my shoulders. I am the persecutor, the foreign tongue in Kafka's mouth.

. . .

Kafka is always at my side. He is with me in the car. When I am at the office, another day spent in a grey cubicle, Kafka informs my decisions, my humor. Where shall we go for lunch? How about that little sandwich shop on Third Street, he replies. Kafka is a fastidious dresser. One might even say a dandy, though his dress is much too austere to be the clothes of a dandy. In his appearance as in his writing, everything has its place. He wears pomade in his hair, a dressing that has sadly gone away. Men don't fret over their hair as they once did one hundred years ago. Kafka gets out of the car, looks around. People on the street pay us no mind. They walk quickly to their fast food deaths. These silent underlings do everything one supposes them to be doing, Kafka says. Before I can ask Kafka to expound, we walk into the sandwich shop on Third Street. An obese woman barks a question in our direction. Kafka winces. I touch him lightly on the forearm. So many sandwiches, Kafka says. They beckon you like whores.

Elizabeth and Grand

I arrived in Manhattan in greasy jeans and a six dollar haircut. I was twenty-one. I wore clothes I'd been wearing since high school. My body hadn't changed. I was one hundred and twenty pounds, a sliver of an idea. The year was 1991. My clothes were the clothes of a salvage lot boy. People on the sidewalk didn't notice. They pushed through their days with an importance I didn't understand. Briefcases held entire worlds. Handbags were clutched like bejeweled secrets. New York had not yet been sanitized by Giuliani; it was still dirty enough to feel dangerous. I lived in New York during the spring semester of my junior year of college. The college I attended in Iowa offered an off-campus study program. I could live in Los Angeles, Chicago, or New York for a semester. I chose New York.

. . .

It was late January. My plane landed at JFK. It was cold, but not as cold as Iowa. It was a wetter cold. It sank through one's body. I walked down sidewalks I'd only dreamed of, the Manhattan of a hundred films. I was among the anonymous and the faceless. A thousand dreams turned behind the eyes of each face I looked into. How did she get here? What did he do for a living? I walked among them. I too was anonymous.

. . .

Three students from my college had chosen to live in New York for a semester. We were all boys. Other than William the Blind, they were the only people I knew in New York. In 1991, William the Blind was a young writer with two novels and a book of short stories under his belt. I hadn't met him yet. I was nervous.

. . .

The college advised us to be on our best behavior. We were representatives of the college, after all. I only knew the three other boys in passing. It was a small college. One boy was a theater major. One boy was a business major. The third boy, my roommate, was a musician. I was majoring in English. We had simple American names. The college placed us on the fourteenth floor of a pre-war hotel. It was called the _____ _____ Hotel. It was dirty but familiar, like an old friend coming off a three-day meth binge. We were juniors, all twenty-one. We were in the greatest city in the world. She opened her legs to us. We went inside. We drank, and drank some more. I took in her odor. She beckoned me, undressed me, and stripped me naked. She showed me many things. I cannot name them all.

. . .

Our favorite bar didn't have a name. The business major was from Omaha. I think these guys are homos, he said. I looked at the clientele. They were old perfumed dolls wrapped in cellophane. I recognized the history of secret lives. I think you're right, I said. Brian shrugged. Doesn't matter, he said.

. . .

The boy I got along with the easiest was the theater major. Shockingly, he wasn't queer. He had a girlfriend. She was a theater major, too. The theater major was interested in set design. Why, I asked. I like the idea of creating new worlds, he said. We're not that different, I said. No, he said. One night I went with Kevin, the theater major, to the unnamed bar. A man approached him as we sat talking on our barstools. I'm with him, Kevin said, pointing a finger in my direction. The man looked me up and down, made a hissing noise and walked away. It was as if I didn't exist. He must like Asians, Kevin said. A rice queen, I said. Kevin laughed. We ordered a pitcher of Miller Genuine Draft. People came and went. Most of them were old men. We were the youngest people in the bar. Somewhere north of our third pitcher I told Kevin he was beautiful. Thank you, he said. I kissed him on the lips. You're drunk, he said. Have another beer, he said. He laughed as he poured warm beer into my glass. It was the extent of our romance.

. . .

I walked the streets of Manhattan at night. I walked them alone. The college had warned us not to. The sidewalks didn't know the letters in my name. I liked the idea of not having a history. I could be anything I wanted to be. I chose to be a piece of garbage. I had a size twenty-nine waist and a clean white dick. I would fuck anything. I would only be young once, I thought. I found myself on the corner of Elizabeth Street and Grand Street. There were Asian characters on the marquees and Asian characters in the shadows. I wished Kevin, my beautiful Chinese friend, were with me. I heard a voice come from a wedge between two buildings. Hey boy, you need some company? Yes, I said. How polite, I thought. This is a great town. An old black woman emerged from the shadows. She wore a calico rabbit fur coat. It fell to her ankles in a rainbow. The material looked cheap and prickly. We're both poor, I thought. She grabbed my hand. Her hand was calloused and grimy. Mine was soft and unfamiliar with the dark shadows of the world. I felt very worldly, walking with a lady of the shadows. An elderly man tapping a cane on the sidewalk looked at us. He quickly looked elsewhere. The woman pushed open the glass door of an apartment building. The lobby smelled of mothballs and sickly layers of old paint. She guided me to a stairwell. She got on her knees, her coat sweeping the floor beneath us. With a snap of her wrist she unbuttoned my jeans. She opened the fly of my briefs. In a moment my penis was in her mouth. Her mouth was warm yet detached. I looked down. My penis had a condom on it. I felt the warm rush of history. I came into the condom. She stripped it off, spat, and threw it on the floor. I pushed myself back inside my jeans. She opened the door. The night hit us full-on. It was much colder than it had been only a few moments earlier. I gotta eat, she said. How much money you got? I pulled my wallet from my front pocket. My father told me to keep it there. Harder to steal, he said. I had a twenty and two ones. Twenty dollars, I said. Is that all you got, she said. I searched the pockets of my jeans. I removed stray change and a few subway tokens. I opened my hands to show her I was telling the truth. Give it to me, she said. I gave her everything. She fingered the night's quarry. After a moment she handed the subway tokens back to me. You gonna need those, honey. We walked together a few more steps. She touched the small of my back, then turned and disappeared into the shadows. I searched my pockets. I was hungry and now I had nothing.

. . .

I'd wanted to be a musician, not a writer. I shared this with the musician. So why aren't you a musician, he asked. I can't read music, I said. He laughed. I didn't like the musician. I thought I did, but I didn't. He came from a wealthy family. His parents were divorced. His father lived in Chicago. His mother lived in Santa Fe. He was an only child. He had a real name but everyone called him by his nickname. I'll call him Chad. He laughed like a strangled finch. He was a drummer. I don't want to play something dumb like the drums, I said. I want to play keyboards. A short thin sound passed between his lips. The words pissed him off. I knew they would.

. . .

The college placed us on the fourteenth floor of an old hotel near W 75th Street and Amsterdam Avenue. I could see the Beacon Theatre from my window. Kevin roomed with Brian, and I roomed with Chad. I wanted to room with Kevin. We weren't given a choice. I tried to like Chad. He made it difficult. He was very particular about his face, his clothes. He kept his drums in a corner near the door. They're very expensive, he said. His father had shipped them from Iowa to New York. They took up a lot of room. I had to be very careful when I opened the door. I was a writer. All I needed was a notebook and a pen. The room didn't have a desk. When I wrote I lay on my stomach on my bed. It didn't affect my writing. In New York we had four professors who worked closely with us. There was a music professor, an art professor, an English professor and a theater professor. The music professor was a man in his late sixties named Murray. He lived in Manhattan during the week. He spent the weekends in Marblehead, Massachusetts. I suspected he was queer.

. . .

The art professor was named Kathy. She lived in the city full-time. She had a studio on W 39th Street between 8th and 9th Avenues. She was in her late forties. She had short-cropped hair and a long, severe face. She wore heavy black glasses. They sat on the bridge of her nose or dangled from a beaded necklace that appeared to be handmade. The English professor was a woman in her late fifties named Ana. She had written articles for the *Village Voice* and other periodicals of some note. Before the New York semester I'd written to Ana and asked her if it would be possible to meet with William the Blind. I told her of *The Rainbow Stories*, how his words had changed the way I thought about writing. She said she would see what she could do. I expect it shouldn't be difficult, she said. I studied his words. The words rearranged my thought patterns. I waited to hear back from her. I had my doubts. I drank, got stoned, went to class, and slept with my girlfriend. November bled into December. I continued writing. The sentences I wrote got longer and longer. I didn't like them. They sounded false. I scratched dark lines through them. I was awake most nights. I hacked at my words until only the bones remained. Snow fell outside my dorm room window. I wanted my words to fall as lightly as the snow.

. . .

My girlfriend read books about the collapse of the Soviet Union. She didn't have much time for me. If she was busy I'd walk back across campus to my dorm room. I'd get stoned and strip down to my underwear. I was a junior. I lived alone. My dorm room was on the eighth floor of The Tower. It was known by most kids as the dork's dorm. One had to have a 3.0 or higher to live in it. I wondered what happened behind the closed doors of the other dorm rooms. Were people getting stoned, drinking, having sex? Calling their mothers to ask for money? Sometimes when I was bored I'd get stoned and play a game I'd read about in *Hustler* magazine. I tied an end of my belt to my doorknob. I looped the other end around my neck. I pulled the belt tight and leaned forward until I nearly passed out. I pushed the pads of my feet against the door. My body was a compressed spring. I drifted in the darkness. The dim flash of orange on the underside of my eyelids illuminated the room. I felt the warm rush of history. The floor was concrete. It was easy to clean.

. . .

My advisor called me into his office shortly before fall semester ended. The writer has agreed to meet with you, he said. Congratulations. Please remember to use your time wisely. I promised him I would. I left his small office. I imagined the young writer living in New York. I returned to my dorm room. I looked at his photograph on the dust jacket of *You Bright and Risen Angels*. He looked mild and bookish. It was a lie, I thought. He had witnessed the horrors of the world. He recounted them with clinical precision. Misery is manifold. The wretchedness of the earth is uniform. I memorized the words. I, too, lived in darkness.

. . .

William the Blind had published three books. The books had caused a bit of a stir in the literary world. I owned all three in hardcover. *The Rainbow Stories* had changed the way I perceived the world. Someone in the world shared my afflictions. I would work with William and report what I had learned to my professors. Was it possible to learn how to write? I didn't think so. But I thought it possible to relearn how to *see*.

. . .

Ana was in her late fifties. She and her husband had an apartment on the Upper West Side. I looked closely at her face. I could tell she had been beautiful when she was young. She and her husband did not have children. Two small dogs sat on the sofa near her. I sat across from Ana in a wingback chair. The dogs flattened their ears against their heads. They pointed their noses toward me and regarded me with suspicion. Ana's apartment was filled with books and paintings. I couldn't tell if the paintings were right side up or upside down.

. . .

Ana was massive. Her thighs were two great logs cooling in a fire. Not even the elements could alter them. William will meet with you soon, she said. Yes, I said. In a few days, I said. Her husband popped his head around a partition that separated the kitchen from the living room. He was a balding man with a slight build. He wore a cardigan and tie. I was sure he was retired. Would you like a glass of wine, he asked. Yes, I said. I didn't know anything about wine, though I'd once gotten deathly-drunk on a bottle of Night Train in high school. The only thing I was sure of was my ignorance. You'll need a typewriter to write, Ana said. I have an old IBM Selectric. You may borrow it, if you like. Thank you, I said. I'll have it delivered to your hotel, she said. The dogs looked at me from their perch near Ana's legs. You're garbage, they said.

. . .

The musician possessed a certain beauty that came from privilege, but his outlook soured anything remotely beautiful about him. He could play music but he didn't understand the meaning of compassion. His parents' divorce had little effect on him. He'd been sour a long time. What's wrong with you? I asked. I don't know what you're talking about, he said. He unbuttoned his shirt. He stripped off his undershirt. He had the body of a malnourished boy. He held a bottle to his chest. The smell of cologne filled the air, changed its shape. I didn't wear cologne or jewelry. I didn't wear a watch. I did nothing to ornament my body. A writer should be faceless and forgettable. I rolled onto my stomach. I wrote notes in my composition book. He pulled on a clean T-shirt. I'm going out, he said. Good, I said. He closed and locked the door. Thoreau wrote how vain it is to sit down to write when you have not stood up to live. I believed Thoreau was telling me I needed to fuck more whores, but I wasn't sure. I kicked off my shoes and drifted, the sounds of Manhattan squawking fourteen floors below me.

. . .

Ana's IBM Selectric was delivered to the hotel by courier. When it arrived I went out and purchased a cheap writing desk from a thrift shop. It was made of wood, simple and unadorned. I carried it through the lobby and into the elevator. The clerk nodded and continued reading a paper. I returned to the lobby and asked the clerk if he had a spare chair I could borrow. He had a thick Indian accent. I'll see what I can find, he said. Ana's Selectric was reddish-orange. It had rounded edges. It was very heavy. I moved my writing desk under the window and placed the Selectric in the center of it. I plugged it in and turned it on. The typewriter had a satisfying hum. I liked the chunky sound it made when I ran my fingers over the home row. The desk clerk rang a few hours later. I found a chair, he said. Thank you, I said. I would now record everything Manhattan had to teach me on clean white sheets.

. . .

I came home drunk after spending an evening with Kevin. We went to a club to meet people. Everyone assumed we were together. Neither of us found a stranger to go home with. I didn't think Kevin would sleep with anyone. He was very committed to his girlfriend. I decided the next time I went out I would go alone. I wanted to witness the flesh parade the city had to offer. Kevin was at my side. I sheared off the top of my skull, scooped out my brain and soaked it in rum. We left the club near closing time and disappeared into the bowels of the subway. I'd forgotten how to walk. My feet were in my shoes but they weren't cooperating. Up and down, I told myself, up and down. We exited the subway and walked a few blocks. The smudged glass doors of our hotel stood before us. Kevin rang the buzzer. The night clerk let us in. Kevin pushed the door open. I hooked a finger in one of his belt loops and followed him into the elevator.

. . .

Kevin helped me to my door. After I unlocked it he walked down the hall toward his room. I pushed the door open but something was blocking the doorway. I pushed harder. Hey, asshole! Chad yelled. Those are my fucking drums! I was disappointed to see Chad home so early. Sorry, I said. I shut the door with a click. Manhattan was safely contained on the other side of the door. Chad reminded me how expensive his drums were. I'm sorry, I said. You're drunk, he said. I sat on the chair the desk clerk had loaned me. I don't touch your stupid typewriter, asshole. I looked at Chad and covered my ears with my hands. He raised a middle finger. You need to get laid, I said. Fuck off, he said. I lined my fingers up on home row. Each time I pressed a button I heard a solid chunk chunk chunk but nothing came out right. I hit the keys with a violence that manifested itself as nonsense on the paper. I bent over the desk and opened the window. The cold wind of Manhattan settled on the blankets. I grabbed the cord of the Selectric and gave it a quick yank. I picked it up with both hands and tossed it out the window. Jesus Christ! Chad yelled. A loud crash sounded in the street below. Someone shouted *fuck you!* I opened the door. Chad and I raced toward the elevator at the end of the hall. I can't believe you did that, he said. It was very late. The night clerk looked up as we passed his desk. I buzzed the door open. I pushed the heavy glass toward the night. A few people strolled along the sidewalk like ghosts. Ana's typewriter sat in the middle of the street, mangled and unrecognizable. Chad and I picked the pieces off the street and dropped them in a gutter behind a salt-stained car. I'm fucked, I said. Chad laughed. We should get back inside, he said. It was the first time the little finch had laughed in weeks.

. . .

I was at the Village Vanguard with Kevin, Chad, Brian, and our music professor Murray. A band I didn't recognize was playing music I didn't know. It was apparently popular with old white men. Murray ordered a drink. We watched him for subtle cues. Order a drink, he said. You're all twenty-one. Once Murray's approval had been secured we ordered drinks. I ordered a rum and Coke. Chad ordered an Old Fashioned, a drink he'd obviously heard his father order. Kevin ordered a Long Island Iced Tea. Brian ordered a rum and Coke, which surprised me. He usually drank beer.

. . .

Halfway into the second set Murray asked how my writing was coming. Not good, I said. I threw Ana's typewriter out the window the other night. Fourteen floors down, I said. I illustrated my point by dragging my index finger from an imaginary hotel window to the imaginary street below. Booooooooeeeewwwww, I said. Pwwwwccchhhhh. Someone kicked me under the table. Murray laughed. You're joking? I wish I were, I said. Murray didn't appear surprised. I laughed and took another drink. I was young and strong. Murray was old and weak. What could he do to me? Murray quietly cleared his throat. The band played for another half hour. When they finished we got up and said goodnight. Murray quickly turned and headed out the door. It was cold outside. The warmth of the club had nearly lulled me to sleep. Outside, the rain reminded me I was alive and very much alone in a big city that didn't know my name. Taxis chortled and honked, their wheels in cahoots with the wet asphalt. Did that really happen? Kevin asked. I nodded my head yes. Yes, I said, it did. My stomach felt heavy. I knew I'd made a mistake.

. . .

Two days after my confession Murray came to see me at my hotel room on the fourteenth floor. He was dressed in dark green slacks and a brown cardigan. He reminded me of a religious studies professor I'd taken a class with in Cedar Rapids. Gather up your things, he said quietly. I placed my clothes and my books in my ugly brown suitcase. I threw my composition book on top of everything. I closed the suitcase and snapped the latches in place. I'll need your room key, Murray said. I dug into my jeans pocket. I followed Murray into the elevator. Nothing was said between us. He looked down. I looked down. I considered the worn floor of the elevator. It had no knowledge to impart. Murray stopped at the front desk. The clerk understood I was checking out. He nodded. Murray thanked him. Let's grab something to eat, Murray said. He held the hotel door open for me. A cab was waiting. I got in. Murray got in behind me. At the café I placed my suitcase against the wall of the booth. It was suddenly very small. Murray sat across from me. He placed his order. I ordered a large breakfast. I wasn't sure when I'd eat again. The waitress brought our drinks. Once she was out of earshot Murray said you've been expelled from the program. I'm sorry. You can't stay in your old room. And it's best if you don't associate with the other students. I stared at my iced tea. Should I return to Cedar Rapids? I asked. I think you need to return home. I don't have enough money for a plane ticket, I said. Perhaps you should contact your parents, Murray said. We've rented you a hotel room for three nights. You should have things sorted out by then. I'm sorry, son. I brushed away a tear with the back of my hand. My face felt hot. You could've killed someone, Murray said. You're damned lucky.

. . .

I took a bus to William and Janice's apartment on East 66th Street and York Avenue. William was preparing to go on a trip to a faraway land, a land of ice and mystery. He showed me a handmade book he called *The Happy Girls*. The cover was made of metal. What should I do? I asked. William the Blind was only eleven years older than me, but those eleven years had been very instructive. They kicked me out of the program. I've been expelled from school. I don't have any money, I said. I was on the verge of crying. I did not want to cry in front of William the Blind. William was very patient and very polite. He had the patience of a much older man. *The Happy Girls* was illuminated by red bulbs. I must have looked like a lost child scanning the aisles of a grocery store for its mother. Batteries, William said.

. . .

William thought for a moment. You're young. You have a nice body. You could dance for money. Dancing always leads to other things, you know. You could do that, William said. William's girlfriend Janice had made beef jerky for his trip. He bit off an end and handed it to me. It tasted good. I never thought of that, I said. I didn't want to admit to William the Blind that the idea of prostitution scared me. It was fine if other people sold their bodies, but I didn't want to resort to selling my own. There was death, disease, and queer bashing to consider. It was too much to turn over in my mind. I was not brave like William the Blind. I never would be. I said yes, I would do that. I lied. Good luck on your trip, I said. I left the student apartment William and Janice shared near the Memorial Sloan Kettering Cancer Center on East 66th Street and York Avenue. I wouldn't see him again for another twelve years. When I saw him again we would both be in Los Angeles, far away from New York. I would be old and he would be older. The years would pass between us as years pass between brothers. The names remain the same and nothing seems to change.

. . .

Magda lived on the twelfth floor of the _____ _____ Hotel. The first time I saw her I was feeding a roll of quarters into a payphone in the lobby. I was talking to a friend in Río Seco. I turned and there was Magdalena. She was slowly walking through the lobby. She was in her late sixties. She was dressed in red and gold. She wore a flamboyant hat. She moved very deliberately. It pained me to watch her walk. I was dressed in my usual garb, old Levi's and a black T-shirt. Magda slowly lifted a hand and waved. I waved back. I saw her again at the mailboxes a few days later. She wore a different hat. I was expecting a letter from my mother. Someone said hello. I turned. It was Magda, though I didn't know her name at the time. I said hello. She stepped closer and grabbed my penis through my jeans. You're such a sweet boy, she said. Come see me sometime. I'm in 1216. She turned and shuffled toward the elevators. Was she a succubus? A demon roaming the halls of the hotel? I wasn't sure. I was too naive to understand such things.

. . .

I found myself at her door. I was holding my ugly brown suitcase. Magda was poor but she had two small television sets. One was in the bedroom. The other sat on the counter in the kitchen. They were always on. They spoke to me in Spanish. I liked this. I didn't have to think. Her front door opened into a kitchen and a living room. The bathroom was in one corner. The bedroom was nothing more than a bed separated by thrift store partitions. A heavy green fabric was draped across the partitions. Her window looked out onto a different view of the city than the one Chad and I had shared. I couldn't see the Beacon Theatre from her window. I leaned out as far as possible. No, no, mijo. You'll fall! Like many New Yorkers, her entire life was contained in five hundred square feet. My bedroom back home in Río Seco was smaller than a whore's shoe closet. I was used to small spaces.

. . .

I quickly determined Magdalena was not a woman, though she always dressed as one. I didn't own the words to describe her. She kept both televisions on simultaneously. They were on Spanish channels, though not the same channel. Broadcasters echoed and mimicked each other. Commercials battled for my attention. Garish shows clanged against each other like Fiestaware.

I was convinced Magda was trying to rewire my brain. She cooked things I didn't like. The dishes were too hot. I didn't recognize the names of them. I bent over the commode one evening and watched everything I'd eaten exit my mouth in a violent red swirl. I was too weak to shower. Magda bathed me. Why get dressed if you're not going out? Magda asked. If I wanted money all I had to do was walk or lie around the apartment in my briefs and nothing else. I would sit across from her in the kitchen with my ass on a flimsy chair, my legs draped across the sofa. Her apartment was an exact replica of the one I'd shared with Chad. It was small and chipped and dull. The muscles of my legs twitched like a rabbit held against its will. I stretched out on the sofa with my hands behind my head and the heels of my feet against the opposite armrest. I became so accustomed to wearing briefs and nothing else I once stepped outside the door and entered the hallway only to realize I had no clothes on. I jogged back down the hall and knocked on Magda's door, a pink naked idiot.

. . .

Magdalena was from Ecuador. I was born Nicolás Lara, she said. I come here when I was very little, just a girl. My mother was very disappointed when I was born. I already have three boys, she said. I want a girl! Growing up I knew I had a boy's body but I was really a girl. I told my mother. Never tell anyone, she said. Life will be very hard for you. I come to New York. It was much different back then. Not so expensive. I went to school to learn English. I taught myself how to walk like a boy, but it was no use. I was not a boy. I learned English. I cleaned houses. I made money but I was very sad. One night I went to a club with a friend and saw mariposas, men dressed as women. I finally found others like me. I missed my home, mi familia, but I knew it could never be like this. I would never be free. Magda held a pocket square to her eye. I listened to her story. I searched for Nicolás Lara under the clothes, the makeup. I could not find him.

. . .

One evening I lay on the sofa watching *Sábado Gigante*. I drifted off, woke up, drifted again, dreamt I was wearing a uniform. I pushed a broom in a parking lot. Was it my father's wrecking yard? A pad of asphalt sat in front of his office, but I didn't recognize the surroundings. I felt a vague presence hovering over me. The broom made swishing sounds as I pushed a small pile of gravel along the black surface. Someone whispered my name. I opened my eyes to find Magda leaning over me. She was bathed in the phosphor-blue light of the television. She had the twisted face of a demon. She slowly rematerialized into human form. She was dressed in a pink nightgown. I looked for breasts. I couldn't see any. She clicked her nails against my skin and slowly pulled my briefs to my ankles. I lay motionless. I tried to speak. I couldn't. Magda pulled a kitchen chair close to the sofa. She sat on it. Play with yourself, she said. I closed my eyes. I moved my hands over my body. I pictured Kevin's face. The flickering light of the television tinted my skin milk-blue. I heard a rustling in the darkness. Magdalena murmured words I didn't understand. After I finished she cleaned me with a dry washcloth. She held the washcloth to her nose. Her face looked younger, her hair darker. I want to take a shower, I said. Go ahead, mijo. I crossed the floor with my bare feet. The floor was very cold. Outside Magdalena's open window Manhattan squonked and hissed. I wondered how many apartments entertained unnamed horrors behind closed doors.

. . .

Can I have some money? Of course, mijo. Get my purse. She always called me by something other than my name – honey, mijo, baby. I was not a baby. I was twenty-one. I never corrected her. She fed me. She let me live with her. She rarely touched me. What did I care if she got off watching me walk around in my underwear? If I had to jerk off for her, so be it. I was hungry and the city waited outside the door. We all make accommodations. Mother once told me men are never satisfied. She was right. Plates in the Earth moved against each other. Mountains slowly turned to sand. The seafloor drifted from blue to darkness, and things between Magda and me quickly changed.

. . .

I became a prostitute. I offered myself to her three nights after I moved in. Candles were lit. An old Spanish movie played on the television in the bedroom. It was her idea of romance. Her eyes were obsidian. I lay on the bed. Her hands drifted over my body. I pulled off my briefs. She stopped me. Let me do it, she said. I felt her nails against my skin. Her gnarled fingers played my body like a grand piano. They summoned notes I didn't recognize. Your skin is so white, she said. I shut my eyes. Her mouth closed over me. I felt weak. I couldn't move. I thought only of good things. I was grateful to be out of the cold and away from everything I knew. I thought of the money she gave me. Sometimes we are vampires and sometimes we fall prey to them.

. . .

The days stretched out like an old snake warming itself in the sun. There was always a Spanish program on the televisions. Candles flickered in the shadows. Magdalena blessed the dark corners of the apartment with pungent oils. She spoke to black formless shadows. They whispered back. She applied makeup in the morning but never went anywhere. I grew bored. I read my books, the only books in the apartment in English, but I quickly grew tired of them. Magda had an old pair of hair clippers in the medicine cabinet. I stripped off my briefs one morning as she watched television and boiled a pot of tea on the stove. I plugged the clippers into an outlet above the bathroom sink. I turned them on without a guard in place. I started from the front of my scalp and moved the clippers over my skull. The oily buzzing of the clippers was reassuring. My hair fell into the sink, the wastebasket, on the floor. When I was done I scooped up my hair and put it in the trash. My scalp was white. I rubbed my hands against it. Hair drifted into the sink. I turned on the water and stepped into the shower. When I stood under the water black pieces of me swirled down the drain. I felt lighter. The water ricocheted off my skull. I turned the water off and dried my scalp with an old soft towel that had been washed a hundred times. I dried my body and walked nude into the little kitchen where Magda sat watching her program. My skin was pink from the hot shower. It tightened and pulled against itself. Magda rarely turned the heat on. Too expensive, she said. I stood naked before Magda, bald and pink. She stifled a little cry. She crossed herself. You're not a boy anymore, she said. She hugged me in the cold air of the apartment. I felt trapped. If I don't leave soon, I thought, I may never leave.

. . .

I got a job as a short order cook at a small diner near Amsterdam Avenue and West 80th Street. The old man who hired me was friendly but terse. You done this kind of work before, kid? Yes sir, I said. Can you start tomorrow? Yes sir. Call me Lloyd, he said. You'll start at minimum wage. You live close by? 75th Street and Amsterdam, I said. Good. Make sure you're here on time. Come with me. I followed him into a small office. A sign on the door said EMPLOYEES ONLY. He took down Magdalena's phone number, which was really the phone number of one of the three payphones in the lobby. He handed me a black apron. This one's yours. I'll see you tomorrow, yes? Yes sir, I said. Call me Lloyd, he said. I shook his hand and told him thank you. Be sure you're here at six a.m., he said.

. . .

I would be free of Magda's apartment with its Spanish programs and butterscotch walls. I would be free of her restless hands, if only for a few hours. I walked toward the hotel. Magda had talked to the night clerk. He lives with me now, she said. I never saw my friends Kevin or Brian. I imagined them somewhere in the city taking tours with professors and writing down important things in notebooks. I thought of the musician, my stupidity at tossing the typewriter out the window. I stretched onto the bed and cried with my back against the sound of the dueling televisions. I sensed Magdalena was standing behind me. What's wrong, mijo? I thought of my mother and father, my siblings. I thought of my friends in Cedar Rapids. I was very far away from everything I knew. I got a job today, I said. The cold air of the apartment brushed against my back. Oh, that's good, she said. That's very good. She rolled me onto my back. Despite her age, she was very strong. Her hands tugged at the waistband of my jeans. I ran my hand over the surface of a wall. Nothing in the world belonged to me, not even myself.

. . .

I worked long enough to collect one paycheck. The money was very insignificant. I smelled of grease each afternoon as I made my way home. The smell stayed in my hair. Shampooing my scalp didn't help. I hated my job. I hated Magda's bony fingers. I hated Manhattan.

. . .

I told Magda I wanted to go home. She was upset. She sat at the little kitchen table and shook like a dog. She held a pocket square in her hand. She dabbed her eyes. Her eyeliner was smeared against the broken surface of her cheeks. Do what you must, dear. If you want to go home, you should go home. I understand. Broke and broken, I called the elevator. When the doors opened I approached the payphone in the lobby downstairs. I dialed my father's number. It was late March. I'd been living with Magdalena for a month. I'd told my father I lived with an older woman. What he didn't know was the older woman was a man from Ecuador who dressed as a woman. My stepmother answered the phone. She sounded five thousand miles away. I asked to speak to my father. Río Seco was three hours behind New York. It was early evening on the West Coast. I want to come home, Dad. My father was silent. I imagined him sitting in his La-Z-Boy, watching one of his programs. You tired of living in that big city, son? Yes, I said. I did not hesitate. Well, come on home. I'll put money in your account. Call us with your flight number. We'll pick you up. I replaced the receiver in its cradle. I got back in the elevator and made my way up to 1216. I unlocked the door. Magdalena sat on a chair watching the television in the kitchen. She would not look at me.

. . .

My entire life fit inside an ugly brown Samsonite. I packed my clothes and the few books I'd brought from home. I threw my notebook in my suitcase. Nothing I've seen is worth saving, I said. Don't say that, Magda said. You may think that now, but it's not true. The things you learned here will mean something to you one day. Trust me, mijo. She gave me oranges for the trip. She gave me a handful of candies wrapped in crepe paper. The gold foil of the candies shone through the paper. I didn't like the candies. I didn't like Magda's old ways. But she had kept me off the street. When I was cold, she kept me warm. I tried not thinking of the other things. There was always a price to pay. I opened the crepe paper and stuck a few candies in my pocket for the flight home. On the plane I leaned against the Plexiglas and imagined my father picking me up at the airport in his old Ford truck. I pulled the shade down to blot out the light. I wanted to forget Manhattan, forget Iowa. I awoke when the plane hit a patch of turbulence. An old man sitting next to me tried making conversation, but I ignored him. I pushed my hand into my pocket and removed one of Magdalena's candies. The butterscotch candy was cheap and brightly-colored, much like Magda.

. . .

A writer is never up front and center, a writer is always in the shadows. A writer observes. He does not participate. A writer must take notes in his head. People don't trust people who carry notebooks. A writer never passes judgment on people who populate his fiction. A writer loves words but also knows when to do away with them. I thought I understood these things when I was young. I did not. I only understood one volume setting – loud. I was a fool. I shouted yet I had nothing to say. I was a compass yet I had no sense of direction. A real writer has no soul, William the Blind said. A writer's job is to observe and reflect, to be a mirror and a chameleon. William tried telling me this. I was young. I did not listen. It would take years to learn what he meant. I tripped. I fell. I shunned friends and family. I spent days in my bedroom at my keyboard. I typed until my back ached. I spoke to black formless shadows. They whispered back. I emerged from the darkness. The sun was very bright. At last, I thought. I am a recording angel.

. . .

I've only returned to New York twice since I lived there so long ago in 1991. The streets have the same names. The buildings are the same, but there is a subtle difference. The danger is gone. The sidewalks are clean. I see my face reflected in shop windows. Old grates and metalwork have been burnished by people who were not born there. I miss the dirt. I walked by my old hotel, the hotel where I lived, where Magda lived. It is no longer called the _____ _____ Hotel. It is no longer a hotel. It now houses condos, or apartments, or flats. It doesn't matter. I could not afford to live here now. Neither could my teacher, William the Blind. The true artist and the middle class have been trampled underfoot by a million polished soles. The shop windows look through me. They do not see me. I thought of Magdalena, how kind she'd been to me. I'd treated her poorly. I'd been ungrateful. I was young. I was sure she was dead. I got drunk in the Village and raised a glass to her. An old queen tried hitting on me. I pushed through him and stumbled toward the door. I pissed in an alley near W 10th Street and Waverly Place. Fuck you, New York. Fuck the brocaded nouveau riche with their rhinestoned assholes. I never knew you.

. . .

Magdalena died a few years after I left. She died in 1993, when I was twenty-three. River Phoenix also died in 1993. It was such a shock because we were the same age. 1993 was a bad year. Two plus three is five. Not a good number.

. . .

I never wrote to Magda, though I said I would. Once I returned to Río Seco she rarely crossed my mind. She had shared her bed, her tiny apartment, her life with me. We talked in her kitchen among cutlery and old china. She lit a candle in front of her mother's image every day. She taught me to have faith in myself. You are your own person, she said. No one can take your beauty from you.

You must live life while you are young, she said. When you're old all you have left are shadows.

. . .

I have very few things left from my time in New York. There is an old composition book. A few faded photographs. A New York Public Library card issued to me by the borough of Manhattan. A bill from Dr. Irene Shapiro, a physician on Central Park West who treated an unidentified illness I wrestled with for a week. There is Kevin's face, lingering in my mind. In late March the grey concrete of the sidewalks flowed into the gutters, the alleyways, the passages between thoughts. All these things fit neatly inside a velvet-lined funerary box. It measures six inches wide by ten inches long. I put it away and seldom open it. It is in a closet somewhere in Río Seco, in a home that no longer feels like home. I tick days off the calendar. Each strikethrough equals one day closer to death. I am alive, and my time here is very brief. I packed my suitcase and took the A train to John F. Kennedy. Before I left Magdalena held me one last time, her entire body shaking beneath her clothes. She pushed a tight roll of money into my jeans pocket. Live each day like you've got a full refrigerator, mijo. The bastards won't know the difference.

Notes on my brother's eyes

When I was a young boy the world was ruled by identical twin girls. Their names were Jessica and Jessica. I don't know why they were twins. I don't know why they shared the same name. Was it meant to cause confusion? To generate awe as our hearts rushed with patriotism? The girls ruled with an iron hand. They appeared on television each morning. In the afternoon loudspeakers mounted on telephone poles carried their friendly yet firm voices into the neighborhood –

. . .

Mind your neighbors, they're minding you
Would you still do it if you weren't alone?
Mirrors are inverted lies
Everything is ridiculous, when one thinks of Death

. . .

I spent hours running around trees in the front yard. My stepmother said she thought I was possessed. I was running from the girls, Jessica and Jessica. I didn't want their voices in my head. And then one day she came. A new girl arrived in the neighborhood. She had long hair and dark eyes. She lived two doors down. She opened the door and stepped into her new front yard. She pulled oranges from a tree in a corner of the yard. After she arrived the two Jessicas went away. They never came back. I thought I was running away from something. I was too young to realize I was running toward it.

. . .

I hold a photograph in my hand. In the photo a girl and I stand next to a pigeon cage. The girl was named Nikki Hutchinson. She had long dark hair. Comb it, she said. We were alone. I used my green comb. I slowly pulled it through her hair until it was smooth and perfect. She shared a bedroom with her younger sister. I looked around the room. I'd never been alone with a girl in her room. My sister's room didn't count. Nikki was eleven. Three years older than me. She wore loose jeans. Sometimes when she moved in them I could tell she was a girl. She put my hand between her breasts. They were small. I could feel her heart beating in her chest. We both liked pigeons. My father is building a cage, I said. We should raise them together. We should, she said. We can train them how to deliver letters. We'll write tiny love letters to each other, she said. We'll tie them to their legs.

. . .

My father bought a dozen homing pigeon message capsules from a hobby shop in Río Seco. I'd asked him to. You need to focus, boy. It's either the bees or the pigeons, he said. You pay too much attention to one and you'll neglect both. I promise I'll take care of them, I said. I wrote a message on a tiny scrap of paper and placed it inside a plastic capsule. I secured the capsule to the leg of Nikki's favorite pigeon, a white homing pigeon named Lucky. I opened my arms and released Lucky to the heavens.

. . .

When I was a boy I stood on the playground away from the other children. I observed schoolyard politics, cataloged how people dressed, and made a mental note of the troublesome kids who always got into skirmishes. Rods and cones detected light; signals in my brain moved my body to dark areas of the playground. I observed and cataloged the world. I dressed in browns and blacks. I faded into the environment. I was an invisible boy. My brain was a notepad, my fingertips restless antennae.

. . .

I was seven the first time I saw a vagina. Tracy was a girl in my homeroom class. She often reeked of piss. We went home on the same bus. She exited the bus before I did. I was always one of the last kids off the bus. Tracy lived at the Lo Lo Mai trailer court. She lived in a pink Airfloat. I tried imagining her entire family living in the small tin box that sat three spaces from the road. The yard in front of her trailer was colored rock. The rocks were pink. I deduced Tracy's mother, who I'd never seen, liked the color pink. Tracy wore pink dresses. She usually wore the same dress day after day. Like my jeans, her dresses were possessed. We were on the field one morning before the first bell. She scaled the jungle gym to join a few boys at the top. I looked up toward the sun. Tracy was not wearing underwear. Her vagina was a split peach. My bangs did not shield my eyes. I was in shock. So this is the world, I thought, unmoored from its axis.

. . .

We're moving to California. Why? I asked. My dad got a better job there, Nikki said. Please take care of my pigeons, she said. They won't stay, I said. I was angry. I hid in my pigeon cage for several hours. It was summer. The days were getting longer. I hunkered down in the darkness of the cage. My stepmother called my name. There was anger in her voice. I did not come out until I stopped crying. It was dark when I finally made my way toward the back door. It was one of the few times my father spanked me. Goddamnit boy, don't ever do that again.

. . .

I visited my brother in prison. I was twenty-two. We were both young. They gave me fourteen to twenty-one, brother. I didn't know what to say, so I said nothing. You stopped writing, my brother said. I had nothing left to say, I said. You know how it is. I didn't think you wanted to hear the same old bullshit, I said. My brother sat behind tempered glass. He looked at me. His eyes, which had once been so kind, were dead. I couldn't read them. That old bullshit is the only thing that keeps me alive, he said. Ok, I said. I promise I'll write you letters. At least once a week, I said. That's good, he said. How's mom, he asked. She's the same, I said. She never changes.

. . .

Nikki promised she would write me once she was in California. I gave her my address. I waited for her letter. It never came. I asked my stepmother why Nikki hadn't sent a letter, even though she said she would. Girls say things they don't mean, she said. That's the way of the world.

. . .

I stopped tying notes to pigeons. There will be no more dispatches. I write letters, I forget to mail them. They sit unopened on refrigerators. They gather dust on night-stands. I'm tired of writing letters. A letter is not my brother. A letter is not Nikki Hutchinson. I cannot hold it against me. I cannot feel its heart beat against mine. I've written my final letter. I will write no more.

Brothers and mirrors

It was August. Valencia was cold and dark. Not what I expected. The hotel air conditioning wasn't working properly. My stomach gave me trouble. I got up twice during the night feeling as though I needed to vomit. The second time I awoke, around three in the morning, I did vomit. I'd eaten paella without meat the previous evening. After vomiting, the back of my throat continued to burn. I brushed my teeth. I swallowed cold water. I tried drifting back to sleep. I had too many things on my mind. I was afraid of death. I was afraid of eternal nothingness. The room was dark. Strange noises came from beyond the threshold. I thought of waking my other half. I decided against it. In the morning I vomited a third time, though there was very little of anything left in my stomach. A greenish-yellow liquid floated in the commode. I flushed my fear. I looked in the mirror. Somewhere under all the grey flesh was the young man I used to be. The days were getting shorter, the nights restless. The stars in the sky didn't mean what they used to. I slept very little. I looked at the handheld device on my nightstand. I watched my other half sleep. I did not sleep well.

. . .

I visited a cemetery in Callosa d'en Sarrià. I thought visiting the dead would relieve my uneasy spirit. After the fireworks of a life, it all ends quietly among grass and stone. I'd lived a long time, over forty years. Longer than Kafka. I'd learned very little about the human heart and its capacity for darkness. I learned even less about myself. I took a cab back to my hotel. I unlocked my door. I locked it behind me. My other half was out. I was alone.

. . .

I powered up my handheld device. I was trying to finish my book. It wasn't going well. As I was writing a glitch occurred. The notes I had written disappeared. My stomach dropped. All my work was gone. The screen hiccupped and corrected itself. The notes mysteriously rematerialized. I sat at the writing desk. I quickly scanned my notes. They were jarring, as if rearranged. As I was reading them I sensed a presence directly behind me. When it wasn't directly behind me it was slightly to my right. When I moved it moved. It mimicked my exact body posture, location and position. I raised my feet off the floor. I sat on my haunches on the hotel chair. I jumped from the chair to the bed. I did not want my feet touching the floor. I remembered the visitation had occurred once before. It had happened while I was coming down off methamphetamine. Surely my brain was misreading environmental cues? I gathered the comforter around me. I tried hiding my body. The presence watched me from a dark corner of the hotel closet. It laughed at me. It grunted like a depraved child. It slowly compressed into a black ball and moved under the bed. It breathed as I did. I did not look under the bed. I knew I would die if I did. I shut down my handheld device. I turned on the lamps on either side of the bed. I couldn't shake the horrible darkness that enveloped me. My eyes played tricks with me. Nothing was real. I remembered the rules of programming language. All information is inherently unstable.

. . .

The world was supposed to have ended by now. I was in a car. Mother was driving. Our destination was a fabric store in Los Angeles. It was a hot summer afternoon. Mother, whom I had known only a few months, shared something with me I had suspected all along. I had an identical twin, a brother. We were Catholic, she said. My father said you were cursed because you killed your brother. Your umbilical cord was wrapped around his neck. He died shortly after you were born. You were born first. I should have told you sooner. I'm sorry. On another occasion she'd told me my twin brother was born first, my umbilical cord wrapped around his neck. You came from the womb clutching his heel, she said. He died two minutes after birth. I grew frustrated listening to Mother. Her stories were as various and multi-faceted as the cuts in a diamond. I wanted to know more about my phantom brother. The more I asked the more her answers became either I don't know, I'm not sure or maybe. She told the story, and then she dropped it. I didn't press the issue. I am uncertain which version of the story is correct. My birth certificate and my brother's death certificate list us both as being born at the same time. I wasn't sure who was who anymore.

. . .

Cars rushed by. Each driver was headed toward an unknown destination. Drivers never looked at other drivers, they only stared ahead. Mother continued speaking.

I found it impossible to infer any meaning from her words. I followed her as she moved through the aisles of the fabric store. Her nimble hands assessed bolts of cloth with an expertise that was increasingly rare in a digitized world. A ribbon of red fabric in a sample bin resembled an umbilical cord. I thought of my dead brother. I turned from the fabric in disgust.

. . .

I've been haunted by my dead twin my entire life. My brother Andrew and I formed a connection through our love of music. We were paper brothers. I went away to school. He got lost in a perpetual loop of addiction. I believe my mother's divorce from his father had a lot to do with his need to find solace in something inhuman. When he was sent to prison, the only brother I had ever known was effectively sentenced to death. He will be released in a few years, but what world would he be released to? It would certainly not be a world worth living in. I'd always had a fascination with mirrors. If you scratched the black backing away with a fingernail it was only glass. You disappeared. It now made sense. I opened my hand, looked at it. I closed my fingers over my palm. My dead brother's hand was my hand. We fought for space in the amniotic darkness. There was a sudden opening. The lights were blinding. My stomach was pulled toward an unnamed center. I was severed from Mother, swabbed with a tincture of iodine and catalogued. My only connection to my brother dried to a nub and fell off.

. . .

The hotel room is empty. I open the closet door. A mirror on the inside of the door splits me in two. We are two exact copies. A few shirts hang in the darkness. I look into the mirror. I don't recognize the reflection. I always felt I looked better in the dark. I am a nothing man, going nowhere. I speak, yet my lips don't move. I see, yet my eyes are sewn shut. My brother whispers in my ear. If you don't like the reflection don't look in the mirror. I don't care.

Hotels and mirrors

Like a visitor from another planet in an old sci-fi movie, he spoke perfect English. I was nursing a rum and Coke. A kid in his early twenties emerged from the shadows. He sat next to me. It was the same kid I'd noticed a few days earlier. He was a hustler. His dark hair was piled on his head like a coronation. I imagined my fingers getting lost in it. Are you here on vacation with your wife, he asked. I knew where this was going. He was a trick with dirty fingernails. No, I said. I laughed. He was a bad actor. How old are you, I asked. Twenty-two, he said. Would you like a drink? Sure, he said. I'll have what you're having. Pedro, a rum and Coke for my friend.

. . .

Pedro glanced at us, then looked back up at the television screen above the bar. A moment later, the kid had a drink in front of him. Are you from here? I asked. Yes, he said. To your beautiful city, I said. We clicked our glasses together.

. . .

Young men are rude, pushing their penises through the ice of the world. Old men spend their days fearing death. I fall somewhere between the two.

Boxes and closets

I remember very little of 1978. I was eight years old. There was the Jonestown thing. My aunt, who lived in California, visited us. She died the following year in a car accident. My stepmother was catatonic for an entire week. I was secretly happy. Stepmother never expected much of me. I vacuumed the living room and the hallway. I took out the trash every morning. I cleaned my bedroom, which I shared with my older sister. I washed the dishes every night. My jeans were paper-thin. My soles were slick. They made squishy sounds on the linoleum. My stepmother hated me, but she also loved me. I was a physical reminder of the other woman. She taught me many things. How to hold a vacuum. How to sweep the floor. How to fold sheets properly before placing them in the pantry. All men are liars, she said. I still take out the trash. I still wash the dishes. I never vacuum. My other half does that.

. . .

If the world was sound and true I'd live in an apartment in Los Angeles. It would have wood floors, not carpet. The faucet wouldn't leak in the kitchen. But we can't always choose these things. I guess I did alright. I didn't end up in the nuthouse. I've never been to prison. You're too book-smart, my stepmother said. I was twelve or thirteen. Perhaps she's right. An education doesn't amount to much in the end. Degrees stored in boxes, gathering dust like an accusation. Sometimes the weight of the world rests in a single solitary box.

I prefer Paris

I have become despite myself the most famous beekeeper in the world. These are the words of Jean Paucton, seventy-seven years old, who keeps beehives on the rooftop of Opéra Garnier, the Paris Opera house. My lifelong hobby isn't so arcane anymore. Should I leave the hotel? Should I leave Valencia? And return to what? I own less than nothing, and America has become the nightmare I wish to forget. I dream of a small house, a cluster of citrus trees in bloom, and the buzz of a few beehives in a far corner of the backyard. But these are only boyhood dreams. They are the hardest to kick.

Checking out

Writers have a nasty habit of killing themselves. The question is, home or hotel? In the mood for one final roll call? A few writers who had the decency to commit suicide in the privacy of their own home –

. . .

Ernest Hemingway, Idaho, 1961
Sylvia Plath, London, 1963
Anne Sexton, Weston, Massachusetts, 1974
Richard Brautigan, Bolinas, California, 1984
Jerzy Kosinski, New York City, 1991
Hunter S. Thompson, Woody Creek, Colorado, 2005
David Foster Wallace, Claremont, California, 2008

. . .

The name on this list that upsets me most is David Foster Wallace. I was at work the day the news broke. Like William the Blind, Wallace had always been in the background, reminding me the world is false. He ended it in the backyard. The dogs were safely inside the house. I was stupefied, lost, and angry. I went downstairs to the break room. I wanted to be among others, to dispatch with the loss. The only person in the break room was a gentleman in his mid-fifties. He'd never heard of Wallace.

He misunderstood me, thinking I was related to the deceased. I'm sorry for your loss, he said. He appeared genuinely concerned. Thank you, I said.

. . .

I headed back up the stairs to my cubicle. My computer screen held no answers, only names and dates. I had read *Infinite Jest* in 1996. I was twenty-six years old. It took me six months. It was an absolute joy. I'd purchased the hardcover first edition published by Little, Brown. It must have weighed three pounds. It spoke to me. The photo of Wallace on the back flap of the dust jacket, the misspelling of William the Blind's last name on the back cover, the endless notes and errata – it was all of a piece. How to live, how to die? *In a drunken state.*

Milk of amnesia

How much is a life worth if it doesn't end? He has dark hair and dark eyes. His skin has an acrid taste. He has the thick lips of a peasant. His hands divulge none of his secrets. He may work in an office. He may work for a construction crew digging fence post holes. His beauty comes easily. To be twenty-two is to be completely alive. Delete that pic, he says. I don't want my girlfriend seeing it. I reach for my mobile, choose the right options. I delete the evidence. There. It's like you never existed. Do you have any money, he asks. I lie. I may need the last of it for a drink. No, I say. You never told me your name, I say. Jaime Valencia, he says. I think I mishear him. I ask him to repeat it. Jaime Valencia, he says. My destiny. At last.

. . .

He wears khakis, a black T-shirt and engineer boots. I hold his left foot between my legs. I work the boot back and forth. I drop the boot to the floor. I pick up his right foot, hold it between my legs, and drop the other boot to the floor. He pulls his shirt over his head. For a moment his head disappears and there is only a headless torso. His skin is caramel. Rum comes to mind. The pants come off, as I knew they would.

. . .

He thumbs off his boxers. I pull him close. His lower back arches forward, following my lead. We are all women at times. In the womb, God makes choices. For a few weeks we can go either way, a universe of possibilities. A name typed on a certificate. It is a name that has no connection to you. It is only ink drying on a page.

. . .

He lies on his back, his fingers threaded behind his head. His sex rests loosely between his legs. My wallet is on the nightstand. He picks it up, opens it. I try to take it from him. A flash of silver slices the room in two. I reach for his forearm but he's too fast. My stomach is a blast furnace. I put my hand to my navel. The warmth pulses between my fingers. I fall to the floor. Dust bunnies conspire among electric cords. I watch him step away from the bed, open the door. It comes easily, like nodding off on the couch.

Placed by The Gideons

From January through December winter touches winter as two lovers rub their backs together in the dark. The death I have so often imagined never comes. I lie in a dark room. On the nightstand is a box of photographs that once seemed important. The documents of a life often go untouched. Legal pads filled with random thoughts, details of vacations never taken, letters never sent. Faded receipts remind me of where I've been and who I was. Could an entire life be rebuilt from such minutiae? Joyce thought so. I throw away small pieces as I can. The gathering weight conspires against my better intentions. Leave not a trace. I ignore the voice in my head. I place a fifty dollar bill inside the Bible. I place a photo inside the Bible. I place the Bible in the nightstand. I close the drawer.

. . .

George Eastman understood the importance of comedic timing. To my friends – my work is done. Why wait? I thought of leaving a simple note. *I can't get these images out of my head.* I decided against it. And so this ends as it begins, with a photograph. Thank you, Mr. Eastman. You've given our memories substance, our dreams color.

. . .

Some mornings I wake with a song in my head. I've never heard the song before. It is beautiful, and there is a certain skill involved. I don't read music. I never learned how. This is called history. My history is simple enough. It is the history of all those who have come before me, and those who will come after. It is a history that is often much too heavy to bear. The weight builds, the structure collapses. The final refusal to carry this history is called *Death*. Eventually, we all refuse.

. . .

I am but a single flower in a field of poppies. I stand next to my brothers and sisters, my comrades, and I am no different. For a time, I loved and was loved. Life begins and ends in much the same way, without fanfare or flash. We begin and end in a hospital room, a doctor hovering over us, a man who does not know our name and does not care to. Fast forward to a simple churchyard, a rainy morning, a few nameless gathered. When the mower comes I too will be cut down. The skies will darken, the earth will harden, and fresh snow will blanket the ground. I will be forgotten under a field of glistening crystals. Spring will come, bees will buzz to and fro, and butterflies will flutter about. The whole process begins again. New poppies stretch from the dark moist soil, their heads raised toward the sun. For a brief moment they shine brightly. They bow and dip their heads in gossip. A chosen few stand higher than the others. They only make it easier for the caretaker to see them amongst the jostling throng. I hear the singing of the soil, the trilling of the blades. The caretaker is close. I stand very still. I practice my perfection of silence.

Acknowledgements

A book is never written alone. I would like to thank Donald Berry, Brittany Benz, Dennis Cooper, Victoria Cordova, Rodney Cox, Jr., Jason Crye, Anita Dalton, Briar Doty, Steven Estrada, Carri and Mark Huerta, Monica de la Garza, Kevin Killian, Thomas Moore, Conor Oberst, Michael Salerno, Kevin Slaughter, Chip Smith and Nine-Banded Books, Patrick Stickles and Titus Andronicus, Miguel Swanty, Michael Torrez, and William T. Vollmann.

Thank you to my teachers Charles Aukema and Philip Mandel.

. . .

Old friends / faded photographs

The friendships made in childhood are more real than the friendships made as an adult. Or so it would seem. In remembrance of Monica Becerra, Arthur Benavidez, Rachel Benavidez, Cindy Chavez, James Childers ,Tom Frizzell, Mark Huerta, Nikki Hutchinson, Stephanie Jones, Denise Lanvin, Angel Lopez, Alicia Mayroyal, MP McBride, Yvette Mendoza, David Murguia, Eddy Piascik, James Piascik, Orlando Rascon, Nikki and Lisa Reyes, Charles Robertson, Chris Shivers, Roberto Ubierta, Benito Valdez, Joe Vaquera, Carlos Velarde, and Charles Wright.

About the Author

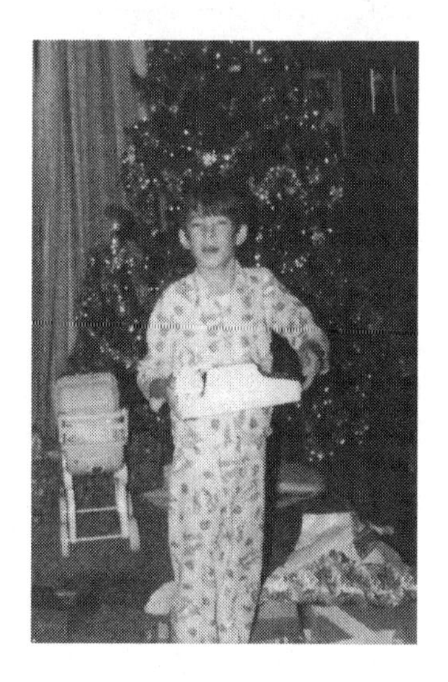

JAMES NULICK was born in 1970. He holds a BA in English from Coe College and an MA in Library Science from the University of Arizona. He is the author of *Distemper* (2006). He lives in Seattle, Washington.

NineBandedBooks.com